Praise for

THE PARIS DEADLINE

FINALIST FOR *KIRKUS REVIEWS'* 10 BEST CRIME
NOVELS OF 2012

"Anyone fascinated by automates will enjoy Max Byrd's new
thriller . . . it reminds us of a time when complex and delicate
automates spoke vividly of the human power of invention."

—*New York Times Book Review*

"Wow! This is storytelling at its very best. Max Byrd uses the whole
deck of cards—character, place, history, humor, and intrigue—to
weave his magical story. You want a good ride? *The Paris Deadline*
is your ticket!"

—Michael Connelly, author of *The Brass Verdict*
and *The Scarecrow*

"Max Byrd's *The Paris Deadline* is the best 'code and cipher' novel
I've ever read, a wonderful historical thriller, combining terrific
characters with wit, erudition, more cool facts than your average
encyclopedia, and a blistering narrative drive that makes the
pages fly. Do not deny yourself the pleasure of reading this book!"

—John Lescroart, author of *The Thirteenth Juror*
and *Betrayal*

"Some of the things I love most about the book—the wit and
erudition, the scholarship, the interesting things about the
underground war and automates—are not the things other people
will like. They'll be caught up in the mystery of the duck and the

love story between the appealing Toby and Elsie, and the fact that it's set in Paris. Of course, I love that too!"

—Diane Johnson, author of *Le Divorce*
and *The Shadow Knows*

"Byrd's standalone blends humor and suspense well. . . . Fans of *The Maltese Falcon* open to a funny riff on its plot will be delighted."

—*Publishers Weekly*

THE PARIS DEADLINE

Also by Max Byrd

MAX BYRD

THE PARIS DEADLINE

A NOVEL

TURNER
PUBLISHING COMPANY

Turner Publishing Company
424 Church Street • Suite 2240 Nashville, Tennessee 37219
445 Park Avenue • 9th Floor New York, New York 10022

www.turnerpublishing.com

The Paris Deadline

Cover design: Gina Binkley
Book design: Glen Edelstein

Cover image: Paris, France: Gargoyles of the Notre-Dame cathedral. 1960s.
Photograph by Janine Niepce (1921-2007). © Janine Niepce / Roger-Viollet / The
Image Works

Library of Congress Cataloging-in-Publication Data

Byrd, Max.
The Paris Deadline / By Max Byrd.
   pages cm
ISBN 978-1-62045-380-3 (pbk.)
I. Title.
PS3552.Y675P37 2013
813'.54--dc23

                              2013024443
                              2012014190
Printed in the United States of America

13 14 15 16 17 18—0 9 8 7 6 5 4 3 2 1

For my granddaughters,
Haley, Abigail, and Noelle

The Gyroscope, familiar to millions as a children's toy, was invented, it is thought, in Paris in 1852 by a French physicist named J.B.L. Foucault, though this is disputed by some authorities. As a device, it possesses the remarkable ability to define a direction in space with a great degree of accuracy, so much so that in 1910 the first workable gyrocompass was installed on the German warship "Duisberg," for the purpose of keeping it precisely on course.

—*Encyclopedia Britannica, 12th edition*

"I suppose I would have to agree," said Dr. Robert Goddard, the mild-mannered inventor of the liquid-fuelled ballistic missile, "that this has made the world a more dangerous place."

—*New York Times, March 17, 1926*

Any sufficiently advanced technology is indistinguishable from magic.

—*Arthur C. Clark*

THE PARIS DEADLINE

PART ONE

Vaucanson's Duck

One

THE EIGHTH WINTER AFTER THE WAR, I was living in a one-room garret, a fourth-floor walk-up not much wider than a coat hanger, on the disreputable rue du Dragon.

And no, to get the question out of the way at once, I didn't know Hemingway, though it was Paris and the year was 1926 and every other expatriate American in the city seemed to trip over his feet or lend him money as a daily occurrence. (Years later I did stand behind him in the mail line at American Express and listen to him denounce Woodrow Wilson in very loud and Hemingwayesque French, which had the slow, clear, menacing cadence of a bull's hoof pawing the ground.)

The only literary person I actually did know, besides Gertrude Stein's landlord, was the journalist who sat on the other side of the desk we shared at the *Chicago Tribune* offices on the rue Lamartine.

He was a slender, amiable young man named Waverley Root. He was twenty-six that year, the same as the century, five years younger than I was, not quite old enough to have been in the army. Root was a remarkable person who wrote English like a puckish angel and spoke French as if he had a mouthful of cheese, and a decade or so later he was to find his true calling as a celebrated food critic for the *New York Herald*. The last time I saw him he wore nothing but yellow shirts and had gotten so fat he appeared to have inflated himself in one push of a button, like a rubber raft on a ship.

But in those days celebrity was far over the horizon, and Waverley Root was simply another vagabond reporter who had washed up on the cobblestoned shores of the Right Bank in search of a job. He had gone to Tufts. I had gone to Harvard. He had worked for the *New York World*. I had worked for the *Boston Globe*. He drank anisette and I drank Scotch, and this small divergence in personal character accounted for the fact that on the chilly, rainy Monday morning of December 7, he was leaning against my chair, nursing a French hangover (as he nicely put it), rigid, classical, and comprehensive.

"Toby," he said, "I will never drink alcohol again."

"I know it."

"An owl slept in my mouth last night. My teeth turned green. My poor eyes look like two bags of blood."

"They look like two bags of ink." I typed "30"—newspaperese for "The End"—on a sheet of yellow paper and swiveled to hand it through a hole in the wall—literally.

The Paris edition of the *Tribune* occupied the top three floors of a rambling nineteenth-century structure that had not been designed with modern journalism in mind. Apart from the Managing Editor's sanctum behind a frosted glass door, our editorial offices consisted of one long city room, which held a collection of sprung leather chairs, a long oval table covered with typewriters and ashtrays, and a string of smaller rewrite desks like ours, crammed off to the sides and in the corners. All practically deserted, of course, at this time of the morning. Bedlam arrived later, with the regular reporters, at the civilized hour of noon.

The composing rooms were downstairs (we lowered copy by force of gravity, through a chute in the middle of the floor) and the printing presses were in the basement. Our copyeditors had been banished to an interior room mysteriously inaccessible to us except by going down two flights of stairs and up again three, hence the hole in the wall. More than one visitor, seeing a disembodied hand waving vaguely through a slot in the plaster, had been put in mind of the House of Usher.

"And there is no health in me," Root said and sat down heavily on his side of the desk.

"It's nine thirty-one," I said. "She told us to be there at ten."

Our urchinish French copy boy plopped a thick stack of rubber composing mats on my blotter, murmured "Mon cher Papa," as he did every morning, and sidled away, smoking a torpedo-sized Gitane, to the dark little basement cubby he inhabited down among the rolls of newsprint. He called me "Old Dad," because even at thirty-one, my hair was mostly silver-gray, almost white, like a policeman's helmet. Many people, especially women, assumed sympathetically that something had turned it that way in the war, and if they were young and attractive, I had been known not to correct them. In fact, it had simply happened overnight when I was nineteen, and for some obscure reason, possibly modesty, probably vanity, I had never tried to dye it.

"Goddam 'The Gumps,'" Root said and picked up one of the composing mats.

I sighed and took it back. "The Gumps" had nothing to do with his hangover. They were the Paris edition's most popular comic strip (followed closely by "The Katzenjammer Kids" and "Gasoline Alley"). On Colonel McCormick's personal instructions, the comic strip mats were mailed to us from Chicago twice a month, filed in a cupboard behind the City Editor's desk, and delivered to me every Monday to be arranged in chronological order and chuted down to the printing room.

"She asked for both of us," I reminded him. "Tous les deux. Root and Keats, Keats and Root."

Root closed his eyes in anisette-induced meditation.

I sighed again like the Lady of Shalot and got to my feet. "Suite twenty-five, Hôtel Ritz, if you change your mind."

"Suites to the suite," Root said, with eyes still closed. And as I reached the door he added, sotto voce, "Lambs to the slaughter."

Outside on the rue Lamartine it was raining softly in the slow, sad Parisian winter way and the street was almost deserted: a few soggy shoppers, a gendarme in his cape, a pair of disheartened workmen on ladders stringing waterlogged loops of Christmas tinsel between the lampposts. Another crew was silently studying an enormous and inexplicable pit in the pavement, part of the endless cycle of street repair and excavations in post-war Paris.

I took thirty seconds to gulp a thimbleful of black coffee from the stall in front of our door, and another thirty seconds to frown at the cold gray sky and disapprove of our climate. Then I made my way around the pit and started out, an obedient lamb, for the Ritz.

The *Chicago Tribune* and its Paris subsidiary were owned at that time by Colonel Robert Rutherford McCormick, who had won the Medal of Honor at Cantigny (a battle I'd also attended, in a minor role), and who ran his newspaper along much the same military principles of fear and feudalism that he had evidently employed in the Army.

Fortunately for us, he managed the paper at a distance, coming to Paris only once or twice a year for what he jocularly called "little friendly look-sees," but which had the grim, white-gloved, pursed lips air of a regimental inspection. Like other monarchs he was invariably referred to by his title—in three years at the *Tribune* I had never heard him called anything except "the Colonel"—and like other monarchs as well, he was seriously burdened by family.

In his case, the burden was the Queen Mother, Mrs. Katherine Van Etta Medill McCormick, a grande dame about a hundred and fifty years old, daughter of the famous Civil War reporter Joseph Medill, eccentric even for a newspaper family, and much too fond (in the opinion of the *Tribune* staff) of visiting Paris. She called the Colonel "Bertie," which he hated, and had previously called him, against all evidence, "Katrina," until at the age of nine he rebelled.

Mrs. McCormick liked Root, as everybody did, and the Colonel liked me, because he thought I was a project in need of completing. When Mrs. McCormick had errands to be done in Paris, she summoned us both and reported the results, good or bad, directly back to Bertie.

I stopped at the corner of the rue de Provence and watched a girl herding five or six goats down the street, still not an unusual sight in Paris in the twenties. An old man leaned out of a third-floor window and shouted to her, and while I crossed to the rue Rossini I could hear the goats' hoofs clattering as they went up the stairs to be milked.

I was a long way from Boston, I thought, or even Cantigny, and turned my gaze to the smallish blonde woman on the opposite sidewalk.

She was studying a tray of croissants in a bakery window, she had no herd of goats, and she was well worth looking at. She wore a nicely tailored green waterproof coat, which was beaded with rain and showed off her waist and her calves and her sensible brown brogues. Her hat was a blue trilby of a style I had never seen before and which, if I were not five thousand miles from home, I would have called foreign. And she had a brilliant red feather in the hatband, like a Christmas tree bulb.

In the buttery reflection of the shop window it was hard to see her face. She seemed to be counting coins in her palm. And despite the relative emptiness of the street, she also seemed completely unaware that she was being followed.

The follower in question was half a block down the sidewalk, a squat, broad-shouldered, gypsy-featured man about my age. He wore a dirty gray quilted jacket and a scowl, and carried a leather-covered billy in one hand, like a swagger stick, and moment by moment he was inching closer to her.

Up to no good. Obviously a pickpocket, I thought, and I took a step off the curb with the idea of making some sort of warning gesture to my fellow foreigner. The swarthy man transferred his scowl to me and then, to my utter astonishment, bared his teeth in a wolfish snarl.

At which precise moment the skies over Paris broke apart in a stupendous clap of thunder and a squall of freezing hard rain swept across the cobblestones with the rattling sound of coal going down a slide.

I don't mind rain. I grew up in New Mexico, where rain is so important that the Navajos have dozens of different names for it, the way Eskimos have for snow. But thunder and lightning are another story, another story for a soldier—ask Colonel McCormick about it. As the first boom rolled overhead I closed my eyes and clenched my fists as I always do, and counted silently till the last vibration had died away.

When I opened my eyes again both Red Feather and Dirty Jacket had vanished like a dream.

TWO

"AND I INSIST THAT YOU GET THEM BACK," Mrs. McCormick said, staring at me imperiously but myopically through her jeweled lorgnette. "At once. Toot sweet!" she added for the benefit of the two frock-coated Ritz Hôtel dignitaries who stood in the center of the carpet, joined at the elbow.

They bowed in synchronized acknowledgement and resumed their impression of stuffed frogs. Mrs. McCormick sniffed; twirled her lorgnette once by the stem like a drum majorette; turned majestically toward the Louis XV gold-filigreed table by the window.

"And I want you to dispose of *that*."

Many Parisians regard the first floor (second floor American) as the floor of most prestige in a residence, because it's away from the servants and the street. For reasons of entitlement and vanity, therefore, Mrs. McCormick always asked for and got the same four-room suite on the first floor of the Ritz, looking out on the traffic in the place Vendôme and well above the busy sidewalk just below. It had the added advantage of facing east, so that even on this damp and gloomy morning, enough sunlight crept into the room to illuminate the memorably unimpressive object now sitting on the Louis XV table.

"That *thing*, Mr. Keats." She swept her hand back and forth like a little broom, as if to whisk it away.

The thing in question was, of all things in the world, a life-sized metal duck. It had a faded brown body and a faintly green head, like a mallard, and it was nesting, so to speak, in a white pasteboard box stuffed with cut paper. The morning light around it looked like a puddle of foil.

"The ones I ordered were much larger and very well made," said Mrs. McCormick, "and there were two of them."

Lightning flashed across the window, raindrops spattered on the glass, and as I closed my eyes again and counted till the thunder came, I almost imagined she was speaking of the odd pair I had seen on the rue Rossini ten minutes earlier.

But of course she was not. She was speaking of the curious antiques she had purchased ("for a goodly price, Mr. Keats") on Saturday afternoon all the way across the Seine on the rue Bonaparte.

"Two absolutely marvelous 'automats,'" she assured us, pronouncing the last word with so flat a midwestern accent that for a moment I imagined that she had strolled out into Paris and bought a pair of coin-operated cafeterias like Horn & Hardart's in New York. "They were South American parrots with green ceramic legs and hooked beaks, and they flapped their wings and spread their tails when you wound them up with a key."

"Ah," said one of the Ritz brothers, "automates."

"What I said." Mrs. McCormick wheeled the lorgnette in my direction like a double-barreled cannon. "I hate this damn country, you know. I fell out of bed here once."

The Ritz men were conferring in sibilant French whispers.

I advanced boldly on the duck which, under the faded paint, appeared to be made out of some kind of plated copper. It had a sad little fantail of five or six dried out feathers. The copper was tarnished, its webbed feet were covered with wrinkled orange leather, and the whole thing looked, as far as you could say it about an object made of metal, moth-eaten.

"Easy there, boy," I said, bending forward.

An automate or "automaton" was a mechanical creature that simulated the motions of a living being. Fifty years ago, in the 1870s, they were supposed to be wildly popular in France, and you could still run across them from time to time in arcades and carnivals. In a street fair over by the Bourse I had once seen a windup automate magician on display, about ten inches high, who bowed left and right when you fed him a coin, then swiveled to a little felt-covered table, tipped his hat, and made a thumb-sized cotton rabbit appear. But science had marched on, and automates were hard to find now in the age of Maxim machine guns, wireless radios, and motion pictures.

I poked at the duck's beak. Its long, solemn face stirred something odd and offbeat in my memory.

A name, a place in Switzerland—somebody's duck? Who?

There was no obvious key or lever to make it move or quack or do anything at all except sit in the wet gray light of the place Vendôme and stare at the street. A melancholy duck. I rather liked it.

Behind me Mrs. McCormick was explaining that the wretched shop on the rue Bonaparte had sent over this morning, not her two splendid South American automatic parrots, for which she had given seventy-five dollars in cash, but this miserable, inactive, mechanical canard.

That seemed a little harsh, I thought, and stroked the poor fellow's moldy back.

"You will want to return it," Mrs. McCormick announced, "posthaste, in a taxi."

A maid was quickly summoned to take the duck away and rewrap it, and the hôtel emissaries disappeared to fire an indignant letter across the bow of the rue Bonaparte, while Mrs. McCormick retired to bathe her temples in eau de cologne.

When the maid reappeared with my package I tucked it under my arm, gave her an unauthorized five francs from Mrs. McCormick's taxi money, and oiled my way, as Bertie Wooster said of his manservant Jeeves, across the bespangled lobby of the Ritz and out into the place Vendôme.

It was raining harder by then, backing up the gutters, giving the cobblestones a wicked, slippery sheen. I waited five or six minutes for an unoccupied cab to spit itself out from the scrum of cars and taxis slowly revolving past the hôtel awning; mentally calculated how long I could live in the South of France on what Mrs. McCormick spent on ceramic parrots (the Colonel paid his Paris reporters a starting salary of fifteen dollars a week). There was a bus stop on the other side of the hôtel, I thought impatiently, on the rue Saint-Honoré. And though I normally wouldn't go down a narrow Parisian alley—or any kind of alley, for that matter—I needed to get back to the paper for the afternoon rush. There was a shortcut I knew around the corner from the hôtel entrance. I waited another two minutes, pulled up my collar, and stepped out into the rain.

I had just reached the narrowest, darkest part of the alley when a sudden cloudburst swept out of the sky from the east, and the walls on either side appeared to collapse inward around me, like the walls of a cave, and then exploded into thousands of dancing gray diamonds of rain.

I pressed my back against a door, under an eave. As a new peal of thunder began, I closed my eyes and hunched my shoulders, and something much heavier than raindrops hit me with a colossal bang and I staggered sideways. Another blow caught me in the neck. Hands dug at my coat. Thunder clapped again, a huge, rolling artillery boom that carried me eight years backward in time and, gasping from shock and pain, I went down to one knee and slowly tumbled over, just as I had before, into a roaring, buffeting, many-fisted darkness.

When I came to, I was sitting up against the alley wall and three or four pale white faces were floating in front of me, blinking on and off like fireflies.

Somebody started to pull on my shoulders. I shook him off. Amazingly, I still had Mrs. McCormick's package under my left arm, in an iron grip like a football. Somebody else said in French that I must have slipped and fallen in the cloudburst and knocked my head on the cobblestones. Then Waverley Root's kindly, hung-over features wobbled into focus. He changed his mind, I thought stupidly. And as he knelt on the pavement beside me I heard his familiar ironic voice begin to scold, "Well, Toby, nice weather for—"

"Vaucanson's Duck!" I said, remembering.

Three

But alas, that was just about all I remembered. The name Vaucanson—was it Blaise or François, or maybe Pierre? With my throbbing head and ringing ears I couldn't concentrate enough to be sure. An old toymaker, I thought. A faintly scandalous person. A joke by Voltaire . . .

By the time I had eased myself into the cab that Root and the Ritz doorman had whistled over, even that much was slipping away, and the wet brown package under my arm had resumed its role as simply one more item in Mrs. McCormick's gallery of imperial eccentricities, to be delivered, as she said, posthaste.

"If somebody actually hit you," Root said doubtfully, leaning his big round face into the taxi window like an arriving planet, "I guess you should report it."

I shook my head, regretted it. The prospect of a damp afternoon filling out quintuplicate forms in a French gendarmerie was worse than any headache. My coat was torn, my cheek was bruised, but I was otherwise unbloodied.

"I probably imagined it," I told him. "It was raining pretty hard. There was thunder."

"Ah. Thunder. An alley." He studied me for a moment longer, then repeated the address to the driver and thumped the roof of the cab with his hand. When I looked back he was heading into a bar.

Then and now, the rue Bonaparte lies all the way over on the other side of the Seine, on the Left Bank. Its southern and more fashionable part serves as the western border of the place Saint-Suplice, where the big church sports its ancient twin towers like a pair of gigantic municipal inkwells and the wealthy, retired Left Bankers sit in their shadow in the Café de la Mairie and feed the pigeons.

Its northern part is livelier, a dilapidated little medieval corridor that runs from the Saint-Germain church up to the river and the quai Malaquais. Sometimes very late in the evening its stagnant smells and overhanging timbered gables make me think of medieval Paris, where wolves would skulk into the city under the city gallows at Montfaucon and wander down to drink from the cool, clear waters of the Seine. But in fact, by day at least, it is largely a street of more or less respectable antiquarian shops, picture framers, and bookbinders, with a few students from the nearby Beaux Arts School drifting up its tributaries and lending it a slightly bohemian air.

At quarter to twelve, just as the rain was tapering off to a drizzle, my cab pulled up in front of the church, where more pits and excavations in the nearby pavement brought traffic to a standstill. The driver shrugged. I shrugged. I paid him the rest of Mrs. McCormick's money and stepped out. I peered longingly for a moment at the Café Les Deux-Magots, where dry, clear-headed patrons were bent over an early lunch. Then I waited for an elephant-hipped omnibus to lumber by, and I splashed off down the rue Bonaparte, over a necklace of puddles, to the nearest awning.

The degree of specialization in Parisian shops, I had learned a long time ago, is something no American, brought up on the easy-going concept of a "general" store or a five-and-dime, can readily understand. On my block of the rue du Dragon there was a shop about twelve feet wide, counting the door, which sold nothing but pet goldfish. Next to it an Alsatian butcher sold no beef, only horse meat. (Am I making this up? No. The goldfish shop was called "La Vie Silencieuse.")

Here on the rue Bonaparte specialization was also alive and well. The tiny shop in front of me had evidently decided to confine itself to nothing but antique armchairs. The shop window next to it had a jumbled display of what seemed to be old ceramic bowls, but which turned out to be, on closer inspection, eighteenth-century chamber pots. One of them was ornamented on the bottom with a faintly discolored portrait of Benjamin Franklin in his famous round fur hat.

I paused, shifted my package to my other arm, and tried to imagine what offense had brought the great Pennsylvanian so low. Tant pis, I decided, and walked half a block down the street to number 24.

Here, by contrast, the single display window was absolutely empty—no chamber pots, no goldfish. The sign on the lintel said "Objets Divers de la Magie et des Automates," followed by the name of the proprietor, "Patrice Bassot, Ancien Professeur d'Histoire à la Sorbonne." The big pasteboard card hanging from the door handle said emphatically, in both French and English, "Closed."

Rain from the awning was dripping in cold little worms down my collar. My head ached. I had worked on a newspaper long enough not to believe anything I saw in print. I turned the handle and stepped inside.

Four

"AND?" SAID WAVERLEY ROOT, leaning back in his chair and locking his hands behind his head. "And?"

"And nothing. Nobody home," I said. "It was empty. Just a few wooden birds on a shelf and a cabinet full of painted eggs."

"Hmmph." Root swiveled to look at the window. "'Some days in Paris,'" he muttered, "'it failed to rain.'" Which, I assumed, was the first sentence of yet another of his unwritten, unpublished short stories.

"Actually, there was a boy in the back," I said, "about sixteen or seventeen, packing up boxes. He told me the store had been sold to a taxidermist."

Root swiveled back around and frowned at our duck—my duck, I supposed—now reposing in a sort of moldy contentment in the middle of our shared desk. "And the automatic parrots?"

"No idea. The boy never heard of them. I left a note in the door and a message at the Ritz."

"She won't be happy."

"She's going to the Riviera in a week."

Root grunted and counted out six aspirins from a tin box. He gave me two and swallowed the rest himself.

"I hope that damn thing can type," said B. J. Kospoth, stopping beside my desk. He handed me a stack of manila folders.

"Just hunt and peck," I said.

Kospoth doesn't approve of me. He says I lack ambition and live in a shell like a hermit and I ought to get over the goddam war. Now he gave a mirthless laugh, favored Root with his usual dyspeptic nod, and went on down the room, toward the outside corridor, where an apparatus the French mistook for an elevator separated us from the offices of "Atlantic and Pacific Photos."

It was half past two, and the day staff of the *Trib* was about as hard at work as it was likely to get. Kospoth, whose initials are unexplained to this day, was our Day Editor, Art Critic, and Photography Chairman, a taciturn mustachioed fifty-year-old veteran of two or three now defunct Midwestern papers. Since we had no staff photographers of any kind—Root occasionally took photographs with his own equipment—Kospoth's Photography Chairmanship consisted chiefly of crossing the hall once a day and selecting a few stock pictures from Atlantic and Pacific, who were also owned by Colonel McCormick and so had to give them to us for free.

On the other side of the city room two men about my own age were going over the "local" copy—as a newspaper for Americans abroad, much of our space was devoted to steamship arrivals, departures, and noteworthy scandals of visiting compatriots (B. J. liked to average at least one divorce or jewel theft a week). The day reporters trekked every morning to the dozen or so major hôtels and took down names and hometowns of American guests, as supplied by hôtel clerks or inscribed in the Visitors Book the *Trib* kept in a little Information Office over on the rue Scribe. When I had first started at the *Trib* we also sent a man to the steamship companies for their passenger lists, but now the companies just mailed us the names of notable personages we might want to interview.

"I never heard of Vaucanson," Root said from the other side of the desk.

I let that pass. Bill Shirer, our resident human encyclopedia, hadn't heard of him either, though Shirer, a bright kid one year out of college, with a taste for slang, had promised he would dig it up for me, "absitoively, posilutely."

Meanwhile, Root and I were quietly working our way through Kospoth's manila folders, which contained, as usual, batches of editorials clipped from the mother paper back in Chicago. From the very start, evidently, the Colonel had distrusted the effect of Parisian immorality on the political views of his staff. Even during the war, when the paper was published exclusively for the army in Europe, he had insisted that all editorials had to come from Chicago. Now every two weeks he still personally mailed us a selection. Those he marked "A" in bright red pencil had to be run as soon as possible, before the Democrats took the Republic down the road to ruin. Those he marked "B" were potentially heretical, but might be run if we were short of space. Those that had somehow slipped into the paper without his approval were marked "NO-NO-NO."

"I think it's hollow." Root picked up the duck. "Or at least its gizzards are loose."

I had noticed the same thing. The duck's belly had a sliding panel that opened to reveal a pattern of holes about the diameter of a pipe cleaner. If you turned it slowly from one side to the other you could hear tiny metallic pins clinking about.

"Give it an aspirin," I said as a joke.

Root cocked his head at me. Then he slowly produced his tin box again. He held out his palm and pushed the duck's head forward with one finger, and we both watched in astonishment as the neck and skull bent and curved down in a perfectly life-like motion and the two halves of the beak fell open just above the aspirin.

"If it starts to quack and crap, you're out of here," said Kospoth, passing by our desk in the other direction with a packet of photos under his arm. More a prophet than he would ever know.

Over his shoulder he added, "And you had two messages, Keats, by the way, while you were out. Man from the Army Archives again. And somebody who wouldn't leave her name."

"What did you tell the Army?"

"I said you were a gently oozing spring of information about toy ducks, but you wouldn't tell him a damn thing about the war. Now please, little boys, put that in a sock and get to work."

Kospoth was far from being a tyrannical boss, but there was a certain note of reasonable exasperation in his voice. Across the room two day reporters sniggered. The French copy boy lit a fresh blue Gitane and leered, and Herol Egan, our Sports Editor, who had just walked in from a three-hour lunch, grinned and tossed a paper wad in our direction. Root lowered his head to the editorials. I slipped the duck into the hollow space below my typewriter and we did, conspicuously, get to work.

We were, as I told you, rewrite men. Sometimes, when things were busy, Root and I served as actual reporters, going out on actual news stories, though this was not at any time a strength of the *Tribune*. Most days we pasted in the editorials and put together the news stories for the first four pages—in those days the Paris edition was normally eight to ten pages long, much of it sports scores and stock market numbers. For home news, to save money the Colonel limited our incoming cables to fifty words a night. The result was that often we were presented with a stingy four-word summary from Chicago ("Pres speaks Protestant Conv") and expected to spin out a full six-inch story from that. Root was a gifted and uninhibited spinner, especially good at political vacuousness, and his more exuberant inventions were occasionally picked up and reprinted by the wire services, to the mild confusion of those who had actually witnessed an event. ("President Coolidge told a rapt audience of two thousand clerics at the National Protestant convention yesterday that 'a man who does not pray is not a praying man.'") When things were slow he chafed and muttered and played with his scissors.

By five o'clock I had selected a harmless pair of editorials for the next day, put the Gumps where they belonged, and made two supplementary trips across the hall to Atlantic and Pacific, where the eye-squeezing burnt almond fumes of the photographers' chemicals bothered me almost as much as thunder.

As I came back from my second trip I noticed that the city room had settled into full deadline speed. Egan was typing furiously, one cigarette in his mouth, one in his ashtray. Two men were piecing together the disastrous stock market quotes, like the ruins of Carthage. Others were sitting down at the big table to type or scuttling in and out of Kospoth's office, shouting.

I handed my photos to the copy boy and went to the window beside our desk. It had long ago gotten dark—Paris in December, not for sun worshippers—and an oddly sad person with silver-white hair gazed incuriously back at me from the glass, like a laminated ghost of myself. I pressed my forehead to the cold window and looked at the street. The rain had given way to blowing sheets of snow down on the rue Lamartine. In the penumbra of the nearest streetlamp tumbling snowflakes caught the light and seemed to burst into flame.

I shifted a step to the right and peered at the people hurrying home. I have a bad habit of staring at faces in the street. Sometimes that's all I can see: pale, gaunt, mesmerizing faces everywhere, ghost-like—people I used to know, leave it at that. *What the hell is he looking at?* I had once heard Shirer ask Root, and Root had taken him aside and whispered. But the kid was too young, Root himself was too young. This time, however, down at the corner where the rue Lamartine met the rue de Maubeuge, the face I saw was not one of my eccentric visitations. The workmen of that morning had strung their Christmas tinsel quite low, and as it spun and flashed in the wind I had a very clear view of the dark-haired gypsy-featured man in the quilted jacket.

I leaned forward, one hand on the window handle.

Then I looked over at my desk and the little coppery reflection in the space below the typewriter.

Jacques de Vaucanson, I thought.

Five

TELEPHONES IN THE TWENTIES had no dials, nor had it occurred to shirt manufacturers then to make their shirts with different sleeve lengths, so men with short arms used cloth-covered elastic bands of varying degrees of nattiness to hold their cuffs back. I turned around to see Kospoth fumbling with his left armband and the long coiled wires of a telephone snagged on it, making him look for a moment like the Laocoon of the city room. He handed me the earpiece, growled something about calls at work, and disappeared into his office.

I put the piece to my ear, jiggled the bar, and listened to a woman's faraway voice pronounce my name impatiently. Then the line went dead.

Modern French philosophy is preoccupied with the Problem of Communication, a direct consequence, I think, of their telephone system. I jiggled a few more times and gave up. Root handed me my coat.

"We're going to Balzar's for dinner," he said. "The kid too." He nodded toward Shirer, who was standing by the long table trying to light a pipe. "Choucroute alsacienne, with herring to start."

"We don't have to take the Métro," Shirer said earnestly. "I know you don't take the Métro."

It was a subject of some conversation around the paper that I didn't take the Métro and usually ate dinner alone or just with Root. Damn snobby Harvard recluse, was Kospoth's much-repeated verdict.

"Not tonight, sorry," I said. "Still have an editorial to finish." Root grunted suspiciously, and I watched them clump out into the corridor and start down the stairs with Herol Egan, chattering and laughing.

For the next five minutes I prowled aimlessly around the city room, straightening files that didn't need to be straightened. Then I took a deep breath and went out to the rue Lamartine. My gypsy-featured ghost was gone. The snow had stopped. The night had settled into a Parisian deep freeze.

Ten blocks away, directly opposite the Comédie Française, I pushed open the door of a bookshop called the "Librarie La Pautre" and strolled in a lordly manner, like a paying customer, down the center aisle. At the reference section I lifted the big one-volume Larousse Encyclopedia from the shelf and balanced it on the corner of a table. If that thing starts to quack and crap, Kospoth had said . . . Out of the mouths of babes. I flipped the pages until I found the Vs. I was the only customer in the store, and the clerk over by the cash register leaned forward on his elbows and frowned hard at me. I ran my finger down one column and read.

"'Without Vaucanson's shitting duck, there would be nothing left to remind us of the glory of France.'—Voltaire, 1757."

I laughed out loud and the clerk glared. I turned the page.

Jacques de Vaucanson merited exactly seven sentences in the encyclopedia, not counting Voltaire's sardonic tribute. He had been born in Grenoble in 1709 and died in Paris in 1782 and in between apparently enjoyed two remarkable careers.

First, as an eighteenth-century P. T. Barnum he had created a number of life-sized automatons that were exhibited all over Europe and made him a famous man. And second, in 1741, having somehow become the personal friend of Louis XV, he was appointed Royal Inspector to the Silk Manufactures of Lyon, where he invented silk weaving machines of such efficiency and genius that they displaced thousands of workers from their jobs. These same workers thereupon rioted and chased him back to Paris, where he lived till his death. His best-known automatons were a flute player that actually played the flute, a tambourine player who actually played the tambourine, and a mechanical duck that ate food with its beak, digested it, and actually . . . excreted it. (Am I making this up? No. There was Voltaire's epigram; there, on page 678, was reproduced an eighteenth-century drawing of the celebrated duck on exhibit in Germany.)

Stranger still, Vaucanson's Duck, once the toast of Europe, after a wildly successful tour of France, Germany, and Italy, had mysteriously disappeared, perhaps stolen by rival inventors. Imitations, non-excreting, had often been made. But no trace of the original duck had been seen since the early nineteenth century.

Finally, with the introduction of rubber to Europe in 1745, the seventh and last magisterial sentence of the encyclopedia explained, Vaucanson had reportedly embarked on a secret and blasphemous and no doubt entirely fictitious project for the king, nothing less than to create . . .

"Monsieur."

The clerk switched the display window lights off and made a show of loudly opening and closing the cash register.

The Larousse Encyclopedia was probably the most expensive book in the store. It cost two hundred and twenty francs and even at twenty-five francs to the dollar it was out of my budget (the Colonel paid us twice a month, by cash, not check). I took one more look at the little eighteenth-century drawing and reluctantly replaced the book. On my way out the clerk nodded with the chilly condescension of one scholar to another. I emerged on the sidewalk, turned up my collar and pulled down my hat, and started to walk.

I don't take the Métro because you have to go down long flights of stairs into a tunnel and the electric lights in the trains often flicker off for a second or two between stations. Besides, if there was ever a good city for walking . . .

I let the sentence drift away unfinished and watched the cars race at each other like jousting bulls, horns blaring, headlights flashing. My father, who distrusted all mechanical transportation, had once told me that around the turn of the century, when there were only two automobiles in the entire state of New Mexico, naturally they had run into each other.

At the Louvre I took the long way around, despite the wind and cold, and went over the river at the Carrousel Bridge. On the Left Bank side, as usual, a very old, very frail man sat doing a jigsaw puzzle on a square of cardboard. Too proud to beg. Doing what he could. I knew how he felt. I dropped a coin in his hat and went to a little café on a side street for a steak and frites.

And with the coffee and brandy I tried to remember what else I might know about Jacques de Vaucanson. Nothing. The silk workers riots were news to me. Louis XV, I dimly recalled, had suffered from a royal assortment of ailments, diseases, phobias and had no doubt consulted—I was not proud of this pun—every quack in the kingdom. It was quite possible, I thought with a grin, that Mrs. McCormick had bought herself an imitation shitting duck.

I tried to imagine telling her that, but despite Root's aspirin and the medicinal wine, the dull pain in my head from the morning fall had started to come back stronger than ever. I stared out the café window and watched my thoughts scatter like marbles.

"Well, of course, you had a visitor," said the concierge at my building, Madame Serboff. She poked her head over the Dutch-door counter that separated her from the rest of the world, looked left and right at the empty street, and wrinkled her nose like Mrs. Tiggle Winkle. "You finally had a visitor, and of course you were out."

"From the newspaper?"

"It was a woman," she said with inexpressible disapproval and regret. "Young. She went away."

"Is she coming back?"

The French think pessimism is a sign of intelligence. Madame Serboff shook her head conclusively and handed me my key. "She won't be back."

My flat was four floors up a rickety spiral staircase. At every landing there was a water spigot and basin and a recessed closet with a pissoir and a slops jar, just like at my grandfather's old farm in Massachusetts. Bathtubs were all the way downstairs again in the basement, next to a row of tiny locked rooms Madame Serboff rented out for storage. From the window on my landing, next to my door, I had a panorama of moonlit tile rooftops, church towers, red chimneys, and off in the distance, also to remind us of the glory of France, there was the great golden dome of Napoleon's tomb.

I would take another fistful of aspirin for my aching head tonight, I thought, and go over in the morning to the American Library to look up more about Vaucanson.

I put my key in the lock and opened the door and the girl in the trilby hat sprang out of my one and only chair and threw a shoe right past my ear.

"Dammit, Mr. Toby Keats! Why don't you answer your horrible phone?" she said, and promptly burst into tears.

Six

"I NEVER CRY," SHE SAID, and blew her nose and burst into tears again.

I bent and picked up the shoe.

"Never," she said, wiping her nose with her handkerchief. "I telephoned you five times at your office and when I finally got you, all you could say was 'Allo?' over and over like a stupid Frenchman."

"The Problem of Communication," I said.

"And then you hung up."

I put the shoe on the corner of my desk. Back in the chair by the window the girl had removed her trilby hat and used it to cover the purse in her lap. She had quite pale blonde hair, I could see now, bobbed close like a Viking's helmet. Her face was bright and round, and despite the red eyes and tears, she had a general air of being ready to jump up and start catapulting shoes all over again. If you were my grandfather, you might have said that there was a good deal of the West Highland terrier about her. She was still wearing her waterproof coat, but the wet Paris snow had soaked her head and shoulders so thoroughly her collar had turned dark and her mascara was beginning to run. Before she could shake herself dry on the carpet I went over to the bed and sat down.

She looked at me warily and slid the chair a few inches to the left.

"My name is Elsie Short."

I nodded noncommittally. Her accent was unmistakably American, though I couldn't place it.

"I came up the back stairs when your landlady wasn't looking."

"Burglars usually just toss a bone to distract her."

"I'm not a burglar!"

Elsie Short sat up straight and lifted her chin defiantly. Then she evidently thought about the burglar idea, sniffed again, and let her gaze travel about the little room until it stopped at the desk and the ancient clothes wardrobe next to it. The doors of the wardrobe were still wide open. The papers and notebooks on the desk had been raked to one side and quite obviously tossed like a salad.

"Well." She stuffed her handkerchief into her purse and snapped it shut. "Anyway, I apologize for throwing your shoe at you."

"That's okay. I wasn't wearing it."

"But I want my duck back."

"Ah."

She moved her eyes around the tiny room again, from the desk to the Matisse lithograph of a nude on the wall, to the two bookcases overflowing with second-hand books from the stalls along the Seine. There were even more books on the floor and on the windowsill, looking out at Napoleon's tomb. Root had visited once and said my room had books the way other places had ants.

"It's a Christmas gift for my nephew," Elsie Short said, bringing her eyes back to me. "He lives in Rye, New York. He's an invalid. He spends all day in bed. It's of no interest to anybody else, I should think. A trinket. Worthless, really. But he likes ducks."

I didn't say anything.

"I know you have it," she said, sniffing. "A maid at the Ritz Hôtel told me you took it away in a taxi."

"And you're sure this duck is yours?"

"Of course I am! This is Monday. On Saturday I went to that little man's shop on the rue Bonaparte and bought it for a hundred and fifty francs, except I didn't have that much cash on me and Monsieur Bassot, who is by the way a very lecherous person, wouldn't let me take it without full payment, or . . . never mind. I said he was lecherous. I gave him fifty francs and came back that night with the rest, but he was closed and wouldn't answer the door. And then this morning he told me his boy had sent it to an American woman at the Ritz by mistake." She dug into her purse and came up with a yellow sheet of paper, which she spread out on the corner of my desk. "That's my receipt."

I picked up the paper and tried to decipher somebody's water-soaked French scrawl.

"It isn't here," Elsie Short went on, "the duck isn't. I know because I admit I looked."

"It's safe in the inky bosom of the *Trib*."

"You mean your office?"

I nodded and handed her back the paper.

"You talk funny," she said. "And I don't think you believe a solitary word I've said."

There were not many female reporters in Paris—two or three chain-smoking ice-cube chewing basilisks over at the *New York Herald,* a nice woman named Flanner who wrote witty articles for the *New Yorker* magazine, an elderly matron who served as the *Tribune's* fashion editor, but wisely stayed as far away as possible from the male clubhouse atmosphere of the city room. I had forgotten how direct, straightforward, and untrustworthy the American Girl could be.

"Nope. Not a solitary word."

Elsie Short's face was not difficult to read. A flush began at her collarbone and moved slowly up her neck. She opened her mouth, closed it again, and glowered.

"Let us," I said foolishly, "go and have a cup of coffee and I'll tell you why."

Seven

IN RETROSPECT, I SHOULD HAVE STOPPED right there. Politely shaken her hand and said goodbye. Then gone back into my cozy room a free man, murmuring the words of that lifelong bachelor Thomas Gray, "Where ignorance is bliss . . ." Or possibly Goldsmith, "When lovely woman stoops to folly . . ."

Should have done. Of course, in retrospect, I should have also gone to Yale instead of Harvard, learned Spanish instead of French, and volunteered for the New Mexican Navy or the Dirigible and Hot Air Balloon Corps instead of the Third Army Engineers.

There were at least five cafés at the bottom of the rue du Dragon, including the noisy and expensive Café de Flore, where hardy Parisians sat outside on the terrace all winter long, warmed by charcoal braziers placed on tripods among the tables.

But my taste doesn't run to the expatriate crowd at the Flore, and we went into a snug, lace-curtained café next door, "Le Camargue," empty except for us, the Greek owner by the zinc bar, and a lanky brown and white cat named Byron. Elsie Short gave the cat a suspicious look right out of the terrier universe and ordered a hot chocolate. I ordered a plate of cheese and a half bottle of Fleurie and from long habit pulled the curtain to one side so I could see outside. It was snowing lightly again. The pavement glinted under a white skin of ice that would still be there in the morning.

"Well," said Elsie Short stiffly when the wine and chocolate had come. "Why don't you believe a solitary word I say, Mr. Toby Keats?"

I poured myself a glass of the Fleurie. "In the first place," I said, "the duck in question is much too old and beaten up to be a Christmas gift, even for an invalid nephew. In the second place, given the French telephone system, nobody would go to the trouble of calling me five times and breaking into my room, not for a toy like that, when you could buy a brand-new toy for next to nothing at the Samaratine. Is the nephew real, by the way?"

"He's fictional," she said glumly. She shoveled, God bless her, two heaping spoonsful of sugar into the already sweetened chocolate. "I was going to call him Conrad if you asked."

"Conrad Short?"

"Short is my real name. I work for the Thomas Edison Company, if you must know. I'm here in Paris on business."

"You're an inventor?" I had a hard time keeping the surprise out of my voice. Even in the third decade of the twentieth century, when progress had broken all the moulds, I had never heard of a female inventor, certainly not one who looked like young Elsie Short.

She wrinkled her nose, and I thought she might growl. Instead, she stuck out her lower lip and appeared to come to a decision.

"I work for the Talking Doll Division of Mr. Edison's company," she said rather formally, and produced from the purse a square white business card with her name on it, followed by "Thomas A. Edison Company, West Orange, New Jersey," and a little drawing of a lightbulb.

"All right."

"I'm what you might call a kind of scout, or roving agent."

"All right again."

"You've probably never heard of Mr. Edison's Doll Company," Elsie Short said, cocking her head as if to gauge the full extent of my ignorance.

"I'm an only child," I said, "no sisters, no nieces, no dolls."

"Well, not many people remember it now. But almost as soon as he invented the phonograph—you have heard of the phonograph?—Mr. Edison began to try to make it smaller, miniature, in fact. He likes to make his inventions on the smallest scale he can. In 1878 he actually exhibited a doll right here in Paris that had a little phonograph built right into its body."

She dove into the purse again and came out with a glossy 2x3 photograph of a repellently ugly pigtailed doll. It had pursed lips and enormous fat cheeks and was wearing a billowing white garment that somebody in West Orange, New Jersey might think was an Alpine milkmaid's dress. Out of the top of her head, like a smokestack, rose a freakish horn-shaped funnel.

Elsie Short made a sympathetic face.

"I know. That's the speaker for the phonograph. The doll was almost two feet tall. You put in a wax recording cylinder and wound her up in the back and out of the funnel she recited 'Mary Had a Little Lamb' or 'Jack and Jill.' Mr. Edison eventually made the phonograph a little smaller, but the speaker still came out of the top of her head. He set up a factory and manufactured several thousand of them, but they never sold well, and the factory went out of business in 1890."

She replaced the photograph in the purse. "As you may imagine," she said, "Mr. Edison is not a man who gives up easily. He's seventy-eight years old and he's still full of projects. About a year ago he decided to start a new doll factory, with an improved phonograph. But he also wanted a much prettier doll, and the truth is, the American doll industry doesn't amount to much.

Most dolls sold at home are actually made here in France or in Germany. My job is to find five or six perfect models to hold the new and improved phonograph, and buy the rights to them."

She shook her blonde helmet of hair and selected a small, bright, vulnerable smile from her repertoire. "I've only been in Europe two weeks, and when I saw the duck in that store window I thought he would be a terrific novelty item—he could quack and waddle and recite a nursery rhyme through his beak."

"Who was Jacques de Vaucanson?"

The smile wobbled a little, but held firm. "Jacques de Vaucanson," she said, "was an eighteenth-century inventor of automates. And so yes, you've found out my secret. Vaucanson built a famous duck that could flap its wings and walk. Mr. Edison is a great admirer of his."

"This isn't Vaucanson's Duck?"

She laughed out loud. "Not a chance, I'm afraid. He looks like Vaucanson's Duck. A little bit. Or so I think. There are only one or two old engravings to go by. But the real duck was destroyed in a fire at the end of the eighteenth century, all of Vaucanson's automatons were. Several people, however, made imitations from the original model. What I bought, I'm sure, is an imitation made about 1880 by Robert Houdin, the famous Paris magician. He loved old automates and used to build copies as a hobby. I recognized it right away—Mr. Edison would, too—but Bassot had no idea, even though he said he's a specialist in automatons. And then when the duck didn't arrive at my hôtel and it turned out you had it and you wouldn't answer your telephone—"

Here she broke off because the Greek owner of the restaurant had come over to refill my glass. Meanwhile the cat, Byron, in a friendly gesture, had jumped on the empty chair beside Elsie. She was not a cat person. She scooped it up like a halfback and handed it to the Greek.

I leaned back in my chair and watched while she readjusted the waterproof coat and brushed away invisible cat hair from her collar. By my unpracticed estimation, she was twenty-five or twenty-six years old, very young to be a personal agent of Thomas Alva Edison. Already, in the space of not quite twenty minutes, she had wept, smiled, lied (at least once), frowned (or glowered), and delivered a brief, informative lecture on mechanical dolls. French philosophy has not yet gotten around to the Problem of Woman, probably because it knows an insoluble thing when it sees it.

"I thought you were much older, at first," she said, "when I saw your hair. Were you in the war? Is that why it's so gray?"

I usually avoid the subject of the war with a joke. "It probably turned gray," I said, "this very afternoon, when somebody knocked me on my head in the rain. For a moment I even thought they were trying to steal our mutual duck."

On the other side of the table Elsie Short's healthy young face turned to chalk. She bolted straight up from her chair.

"I need some air," she said.

Eight

IN THOSE YEARS PARISIAN GENDARMES still wore black silk-lined capes in the winter. The slang term for policemen then was hirondelles—swallows—because as they went down the dark streets on their bicycles, the capes rose and flapped behind them like tails and they looked like swooping birds. To me they looked like bats.

Two of them were standing by a lamppost when we came out of the café. They turned with a swish of their capes and watched us curiously.

Elsie ignored them. She began to walk so fast that I had to stretch my legs to keep up with her. At the boulevard Saint-Germain she looked left and right, then spotted a taxi rank half a block past the church and started toward it.

"Well, I talk too much," she said as we weaved through the terrace tables of the Flore. She thrust her hands in her raincoat pockets and slowed her pace, but not much. "I never listen, it's my biggest fault. I should go back to my hôtel. Who tried to hit you on the head? Did they steal the duck? No, you said it's at your office."

This was, I could imagine Root telling me, a suspiciously large amount of nervous energy to spend on a wind-up toy. By this time we had reached the terrace of the Deux Magots and the big hedges in boxes that the café used in the winter as a windscreen. One of the waiters lifted his tray like a drawbridge to let us pass, and we came to a temporary halt at the corner in front of the Saint-Germain church.

Elsie Short peered up at the stiff white Romanesque tower, with its tall black steeple glistening in the night sky, lit by an Edisonian spotlight. One of the two or three most beautiful structures in Paris, I always thought, but Elsie merely furrowed her brow and tapped her sensible brown shoe on the sidewalk.

"This is the rue Bonaparte," she said with surprise when we crossed over.

"The lower part of it," I agreed, and thought of telling her that until a hundred years ago it was called the rue des Petits Augustins, and before that it wasn't a street but a canal to the Seine, part of an enormous garden that belonged to Queen Margot of Navarre.

But my Paris history lectures don't appeal to everybody, and Elsie had already wheeled left and started down the street. Snow was drifting between buildings in gauzy patches now. Here and there it caught a burst of wind and swirled off the pavement in a white spinning cone that looked like a mummy coming unwound. Two steps ahead of me Elsie pointed at a street sign that said rue Jacob.

"Bassot's store was three or four blocks past this," she muttered, "I had no idea it was so close. If he's there I can prove I bought the duck."

I glanced at my watch. The French are economical with lights. The boulevard Saint-Germain was busy and fairly bright, but the rue Bonaparte was dark and shadowy, and as far as I could tell there were just two feeble street lamps between us and the distant

Seine. I don't like the dark. My head hurt and I wanted to go home and resume being a recluse. Like a chump, I trailed after the comet Elsie.

We reached the antique shops that sold nothing but armchairs and chamber pots. Next door, Bassot's window was black and empty except for the hand-lettered sign that said, "CLOSED." In the back a thin bar of light was just visible on the floor. Elsie knocked and rattled the door.

Down the block, perhaps thirty yards away, two more gendarmes appeared in silhouette and a man staggered drunkenly out of a doorway. While we watched, the taller of the two policemen turned a half-step sideways and spread his black cape. The drunk stepped behind it and bent his head, and after a moment what Root would term an unmistakable hydraulic process began.

"Well, I never," said Elsie Short.

It was called the privilège de la cape, a Paris custom, the partial, momentary concealment behind a gendarme's outspread cloak of a gentleman on the street with a pressing need. Parisian homosexuals made something of a game of it, I was told, approaching the best-looking young gendarme they could find. I couldn't think of a good way to explain it. The drunk finished his business, Elsie shook her head, and the drunk and gendarme trio walked away toward the river. Another gust of wind filled the narrow corridor of the rue Bonaparte with a full sail of snow. When it subsided we had the street to ourselves.

"Let's go in," said Elsie Short.

"It's closed," I reminded her.

Elsie knocked twice more. "He's there, I'm sure of it," Elsie said. "I didn't like Bassot at all, you know. He wears a filthy red beret and stands too close. You can explain about my duck in French. He has very bad English." She knocked again and the light in the back went out.

Elsie looked at me triumphantly. Then she rattled the door handle one more time and pushed. The door swung slowly open.

She stepped inside, lost at once in the shadows. I stayed where I was on the sidewalk.

"You're not afraid of the dark, are you?" She poked her head out again.

I looked down the street toward the invisible river, up the street toward the glow of the boulevard Saint-Germain. I jammed my hands in my coat pockets and, after five or six heartbeats, followed her in.

The front room of the shop was as empty as the window. We passed through it in slow motion, holding our arms in front of us like two people pantomiming a swim. I was sweating now, despite the cold stream of air from the open door behind me. Elsie's blue trilby hat picked up a beam of light from the street and bobbed in the darkness like a buoy.

A rustling noise somewhere to the right made her stop and quickly back up two steps, and I smelled her wet hair and hat and felt her shoulders turn and brush against mine.

"A rat," she whispered. I made no answer. I don't talk in the dark. I make no noise in the dark. "Mr. Bassot?" she called in a normal voice. "Monsieur?"

Straight ahead of us an electric light blazed on and off and we heard a back door slam.

There was a time when I could see everything there was to be seen in the darkness, in a single quick pulse of light like that. In an instant I was around Elsie Short, pulling on a lamp cord inside a door.

It was a storeroom of some kind, no bigger than my garret, filled ceiling to floor with a jumble of packing crates and chairs and pasteboard boxes.

Elsie said something I didn't hear. Two of the boxes were open. I saw a tiny leg and foot in a clown's costume hooked over one of the edges. A wooden tiger. A Chinese doll. On its side, a brass birdcage with two large porcelain parrots on a perch. 'Automat' parrots, I thought, exhaling loudly, thinking of Mrs. McCormick.

I straightened and started to turn back to Elsie when my eye fell on a shape behind the packing crates, against a whitewashed wall. The dim yellowish French lightbulb that served the storeroom as illumination was still swinging gently back and forth on its cord, like a pendulum. At each pass it shone, just for a moment, on a red beret, a patch of dirty brown hair, a neck bent at an unnatural angle.

Behind me I heard Elsie gasp and felt her hand clasp my arm.

I backed up slowly, keeping a watchful eye on the unmoving head and shoulders of what I presumed was Patrice Bassot, Very Late Professor at the Sorbonne.

In the war most people got used to corpses. You slept beside them, ate beside them, carried them through the trenches on your shoulders like sacks of sand. Not me. I never did.

I backed up another step, and my heels bumped against something, and I spun and faced the front of the shop. Elsie's hand fumbled for mine. She was trembling like a child. A car passed down the dark street, feeling its way like a beetle toward the Seine. A pale sigh of exhaust fumes floated in through the open door.

In the cold, swaying darkness of the rue Bonaparte there was a strange absence of sound and breath that I can only call a European silence.

PART TWO

Birds of a Feather

Nine

It was Thursday, December 10, three full days after Elsie Short had first appeared in my garret on the rue du Dragon, when B. J. Kospoth walked over to my desk, leaned forward, and balanced himself carefully, simian-like, on his eight bare knuckles.

"Claims he has a letter for you," he said, and jerked his head in the direction of a short, fair-haired man about my own age, standing just to his left and clutching a leather briefcase to his chest. The stranger had the flattest face I had ever seen. When he turned to cough, diffidently into his fist, it was like squinting sideways at a sheet of paper.

"Not my idea to bother you, Mr. Keats," he apologized, handing me the letter, "though I did call several times. Mr. Kospoth may not have given you the message. I'm Henry Cross."

The letter was in a small, crisp, expensive vellum envelope, buff-colored, with my name in bold pen strokes on the front. For a moment I thought it might be from Elsie Short, but when I turned it over the return address, printed in grim, muscular Roman type, was "1519 Astor Street, Chicago." There was no stamp or postmark.

"He had it sent over in the embassy courier bag," Cross said, "that's why there's no stamp."

I opened the envelope and pulled out a single stiff note card, which read, in its entirety, "TALK TO THIS MAN, DAMMIT— MCCORMICK."

I looked up at Henry Cross. "I'm from the Army Archives," he said. "I'm actually Major Cross, but I didn't want to upset Mister Kospoth by throwing rank around." He threw, if not his rank, at least a glance around the noisy city room, where half the places at the big oval table were now taken.

It was well past three o'clock in the afternoon. The financial writers were hunched over a galley, arguing about J.P. Morgan. The travel editor, whose name I could never remember, had joined Kospoth by the windows for a heated conference that apparently required reading aloud from their notebooks simultaneously. Herol Egan was at his typewriter, fingers curled like Paderewski above the keys, his eyes fixed on a pencil stuck in the ceiling.

"Perhaps there's a quieter place?" Cross suggested in his mild way.

I looked at the note card again. Over the course of four years I had received maybe six or seven handwritten letters from the Colonel. They were unmistakable in their brevity, their very bad penmanship, which made the letters look like little spiders mashed violently into the paper, and their unanswerability. I would talk to the man.

"I have to go out," I told him, "on an errand. If you don't mind walking with me."

He gave another glance around the room and allowed that walking would be fine.

Outside on the rue Lamartine Major Cross produced first his diffident cough, then from the leather briefcase a military-style manila folder tipped at the corners with red elastic bands.

It was one of those bright, sunny, almost-warm winter afternoons that made you forget that Paris enjoyed approximately the same climate as London and Munich. The sky was scrubbed blue. There was no sign whatsoever of the snow that had powdered the old city like an eighteenth-century wig on Monday. Down the street, on the opposite side of the rue Lamartine, came a troop of French schoolchildren dressed in their uniforms of black aprons and white collars. They all wore wooden-soled shoes, as high-topped as boots, and made an ear-splitting clatter as they ran along the sidewalk.

"You're a hard man to get hold of, Mr. Keats," said Major Cross. "I'm told the War Department sent somebody last year and you wouldn't see him. In July they sent two men."

"I believe I was traveling in July."

He flipped a page in the folder as he walked. "Actually," he said, "you were right here in Paris and you called our people 'mongrel beef-witted lords' and said if they came back again you would make them the 'loathsomest scabs in all Greece.' Shakespeare, I think, *Troilus and Cressida.*"

He closed the folder and gave me a small, tight smile. I shrugged.

"Your editor said you keep pretty much to yourself. He called you a hermit when you're not at work."

I shrugged again. By this time we had reached the rue de Trévise and were stopped on the curb, waiting for some empty trucks to rattle past on their way back from les Halles.

"Even so, Colonel McCormick was very anxious we should have your interview," he said. "The Army wants to publish an official history of the war and they plan to bring out Volume One by next summer—June 24, in fact. That's the ten-year anniversary of Pershing's first landing in France. "

I pushed off the curb and we crossed together. The Major fell automatically into step with me.

"And the Colonel's role in this?"

"He's underwriting the publication costs," Cross said, "of Volume One, anyway—for patriotic reasons, he says, but of course he gets his name on the title page and he gets to say a good deal about the contents. He seems to feel a chapter on your people is absolutely indispensable."

"My people," I said.

"The Tunnelers Corps, the underground bombers. The Moles." One more snap of the bands on his folder. "He said to tell you, and I quote, 'We have a deadline and you're a goddam reporter.'"

The rue de Trévise was the kind of commercial and nondescript Parisian street that no tourist would linger over, but to me its anonymous, ordinary foreignness was part of its charm. The buildings were gray and beige five-story boxes with mansard roofs and red tile roofs, late nineteenth-century speculators' handiwork, thrown up more or less hastily when Baron von Haussmann's great boulevards just to the south sent this whole part of the city into a construction boom. I looked up at the sky, already beginning to fade from blue to slate. At this latitude, in another half hour or so, the sun would vanish, and without Edisonian electric lights it would give way completely to darkness and the city in front of me would swim and flicker and be gone. I remembered an old astronomy class from college—if there were no sun, there would be no weather. Weather is solar energy received at the earth's uneven surface and redistributed.

No sun underground, no weather.

At the corner of rue Richer some builder with an artistic touch had put in a glass-roofed arcade, and there was now a little protected café and bar just inside it, with tables under the glass.

"Actually," Cross said, "Deadline or no deadline, I'm as interested as the Colonel, personally. To a desk soldier like me, you know, what you did is fascinating."

Fascinating. I took a deep, cold breath.

"Since the Colonel insists," I said, and we went inside and sat down under the glass roof. I ordered Sancerre, which was a perverse choice because Sancerre is a white wine served chilled and not a winter kind of drink. The Major, to my surprise, in very good French ordered a snifter of brandy.

But if I expected him to begin a systematic biographical question-and-answer, Army-style, he surprised me again by pulling two or three photographs out of his manila folder.

"These are from our British friends," he said. "They're having trouble identifying some of the faces. We thought you might help."

I picked up the first of the photographs. It was an ordinary five-by-eight glossy, black and white, of course, because color wasn't widely available in those days, and wouldn't be for another decade or so.

But then, for this subject you only needed black and white.

The photograph showed perhaps twenty-five men, sitting and standing in three rows and facing the camera. The shadow of whoever had taken the picture fell across the right-hand side and reached almost to the shattered tree trunk behind them. There was the back of an army lorry just in the corner. A wall of sandbags shoulder-high. A dark, gaping space beneath the sandbags on the right, where some learned joker had placed a handwritten sign in Latin, "Facilis descensus Averno." Easy the descent to Hell.

"This chap, for instance," said Cross and put his finger on a face.

When I didn't say anything, after a moment he took a sip of his brandy and remarked in a conversational tone, "Some of you people had remarkably long hair, for the military."

"That was Norton-Griffiths' idea. He thought people talked too much when they went to the barber."

"Ah." Cross made a microscopic adjustment to the photograph, squaring it with the edge of the table, and to his credit offered no comment about my gray hair. "So you knew the famous Norton-Griffiths, a legendary person."

It was an excellent interviewing technique, deliberate or not, almost guaranteed to loosen the tongue. Major John

Norton-Griffiths, known throughout the British Army as "Empire Jack," was one of those colorful, eccentric, and hugely outsized personalities that spring up so easily in the damp, unweeded garden of the English upper class.

Before the war he had owned a civil engineering company that specialized in building tunnels for the London Underground and sewers for the city of Manchester. When the war began he had taken one look at the Royal Geological Survey of Flanders and the Low Countries, imagined somehow what was to come, and soon afterwards formed with his own money a private company of miners, tunnelers, and geologists, all of whom he insisted on calling, to the disgust of the Regular Army, "Moles." I had become a Mole in the fall of 1916, about five months after I had dropped out of my class at Harvard.

"Your job, as I understand it," Major Cross said, "was to dig deep tunnels from our side of the trenches over to the German side, under No Man's Land, and plant bombs literally under their feet."

"'Overcharged' bombs, that's what we called them, even though they were underground. We put them under the German lines, yes, about ten feet below the surface. 'Undercharged' bombs were called camouflets, and those we used to make 'controlled' explosions inside the tunnels, to blow up the German moles, who were digging as fast as they could toward us to blow up our people. The Army has a funny idea of 'controlled.'"

"Quite a sight, I imagine," Major Cross said. "Eight or nine hundred pounds of TNT going off right under a mess hall or a barracks or people just marching calmly across what they thought was terra firma, no warning at all. Nerve-wracking."

When I said nothing to that, Major Cross reopened his manila folder. "You also went to General Leonard Wood's volunteer regiment in Plattsburg, New York, I see, another larger-than-life character, like Norton-Griffiths."

I nodded and watched a girl who looked not in the least

like Elsie Short strolling down the rue Tricher. Just beyond the entrance to the arcade she stopped and hiked her skirt and peered backwards over her shoulder, as only a French girl can, at her very well-turned calf.

Major Cross paid no attention. "And you were born in Massachusetts," he read from a form, "but grew up in Gila, New Mexico. Then Harvard College. An unusual combination."

The girl lowered her skirt, winked at me, and moved on down the street. I picked up my glass and held it to the winter sunlight, and as the poet said, Lethewards sank.

"Well, Major Henry Cross, my father used to claim that New England was a slaughterhouse of ideas, and he couldn't get away from it fast enough. I think he was quoting Mencken. On his twenty-fifth birthday he sold a coffee pot by Paul Revere that he had inherited and bought a silver mine which he named 'the Minute Man,' and from the time I was twelve years old I spent summers working in it, about seventy feet underground, which was why I came to the attention of Empire Jack. And so now you have the story of my war. All my regards to Colonel McCormick."

I stood up and placed two francs on the table, service compris.

Major Cross was cool and unperturbed. He smiled gently. "Oh, I think we've just begun, Mr. Keats."

"Got to see a man about a duck," I said, and left.

Ten

ABOUT TWO PARROTS AND A DUCK, to be precise—Prisoners of the State.

Because seventy-two hours earlier the Paris Police, investigating the death of Patrice Bassot from unnatural causes, had officially confiscated both my mechanical duck and Mrs. McCormick's two ceramic parrots.

Confiscated as state's evidence, police inspector second-class Serge Soupel, had solemnly explained.

Evidence of what? The frustrated Elsie Short had demanded. Police obtuseness? Criminal stupidity?

The French police do not take kindly to American sarcasm even today; they didn't in 1926 or in any other year, for that matter, either. Soupel had raised one bushy Gallic eyebrow in annoyance and, for chastisement, set her to filling out the endless forms and depositions that all French bureaucracies consume by the bushel. Meanwhile he personally escorted me across town to the *Trib*'s building, where I dutifully opened my desk and handed over my miniature aviary. When we got back to the Préfecture, Elsie had signed all her statements, called a cab, and vanished without a word—a habit of hers, as I was to learn.

But Elsie Short was not a girl for the vie silencieuse. On Tuesday she telephoned me three times to see if I had liberated the duck. On Wednesday she called twice and slammed down the phone both times when I said they were still behind bars. Mrs. McCormick had also left an ominous message with Kospoth on Tuesday—She required her parrots no later than Thursday evening at six. If Keats couldn't do this simple errand for her, Bertie would not be pleased.

I had tried my best, of course. I had written and called Soupel. I had reached an assistant consul at the American embassy, who laughed and hung up the telephone. And on Wednesday there had also been a nicely written (if I say so myself) item in the *Tribune*:

> M. Patrice Bassot, 72 years old, a native of Grenoble and dealer in automates and curiosities, was found dead in his shop on the rue Bonaparte late Monday night. Police questioned two American witnesses who discovered the body and have concluded that it was a case of robbery gone bad. Inspector Serge Soupel of the Préfecture tells the *Tribune* that M. Bassot had recently sold his shop and was planning to return to Grenoble. Thieves apparently tried to take advantage of the victim's age and frailty. When Bassot resisted, Inspector Soupel surmises, he was struck a fatal blow. The Préfecture of Police, he added, has committed its full resources to the investigation. Given M. Soupel's formidable reputation as one of Paris's outstanding crime fighters, the *Tribune* feels confident of his success.

On the theory of catching more flies with honey, I had sent Soupel three copies of the paper with his name underlined. In return, at Thursday noon he had sent me a handwritten note granting amnesty to the duck. Not counting the Colonel's rocket from Chicago, this was one of two notes I had received that day.

*   *   *

At the corner of rue Saulnier I looked back at Major Cross, who was still at our table under the arcade, writing in his notebook.

I felt in my pocket and pulled out another slip of paper. This was on plain white paper, not buff vellum, and the handwriting was as round and curved and feminine as a goblet: "Dear Mr. Toby Keats," Elsie Short had written. "If you have finally rescued my duck, which you should not have had in the first place, from the obtuse police, you may bring it to this address today. After seeing your apartment, I will add that admission to the talk is free, since you probably couldn't afford to buy a ticket."

Enclosed was a card with an engraved invitation:

THE AMERICAN WOMEN'S CLUB OF PARIS
announces
a special Christmas presentation

by Miss Elsie Short, Ph.D.:

'Adventures of a Doll Hunter'

Conservatoire des Arts et Metiers,
December 10, 1926, 5–6 P.M.

I looked at my watch. Four-fifteen. Plenty of time to pick up my three birds of Christmas and deliver the duck to Elsie, I thought, and I set out walking quickly toward Soupel's office on the quai des Orfèvres.

If there hadn't been a concert at Notre Dame that afternoon, and several thousand exiting concertgoers blocking my way on the sidewalk, I might have reached the Préfecture of Police before Serge Soupel left for the rest of the week, out on a case in Versailles. But I didn't, and Soupel's sniffy, punctilious clerk announced that he was certainly not about to release official evidence to a civilian on the basis of a handwritten letter, not until the Inspector came back. I sighed and looked at my watch again.

In an open room behind the clerk's desk, swinging gently in a cage on a shelf, Mrs. McCormick's two automate porcelain parrots communed with their thoughts. Next to them, scruffier than ever, head bowed and drooping in the avian equivalent of a hangdog look, was Elsie Short's copy of Vaucanson's Duck.

I took a step in their direction. The clerk had the double beard then in fashion with the police, splitting at the chin and curling up like ram's horns. He stroked both ends and watched me suspiciously. I held up my watch again. Four forty-five. The clerk stood and closed the door.

It is not a good idea, Root had said, to upset somebody whose family owns your place of employment, not to mention twenty million dollars and sixty-six acres of the North Shore of Chicago. In my mind's eye I could see Mrs. McCormick standing in her drawing room at the Ritz, lorgnette unholstered, face of stone. I could also see a trim blonde person, not reclusive, who filled the air with flying shoes and loopy smiles. I looked at my watch, looked at the door, gave the clerk a two-finger tunneler salute, and left.

The "Conservatory of the Arts and Professions" is located on the Right Bank about a block south of one of Paris's tawdrier theater districts. It consists of one part Institute of Technology and one part Museum of Inventions. Some of the inventions were housed in an adjoining Catholic church that the city of Paris had appropriated during the Revolution and rededicated, with a fine French sense of irony, to the Rule of Science.

I stopped my taxi at the corner of rue Vaucanson, mentally

kicking myself for not remembering the name of the street, and hurried past the church and into the Museum.

In Paris in 1926 fewer than half of the buildings had electric lights, but the Conservatory, under the Rule of Science, was practically ablaze with them. Edison would be pleased, I thought. I passed a Bleriot airplane under a spotlight, then a row of illuminated glass cases displaying phonographs, Bakelite radios, and one of Bell's early telephones. I went around a model of Pascal's mystical computing machine and reached the bottom of a staircase where a large permanent sign said, Théâtre des Automates. Next to it somebody had printed in very nice fourteen-point Garamond type: "American Women's Club of Paris. Mlle. Short of New Jersey. 5–6 P.M."

A bored-looking guard waved me on, and I took the stairs two at a time, turned left at what appeared to be an enormous brass weaving loom, and entered a dark, narrow auditorium full of howling children.

Eleven

"I GIVE YOU MISS ELSIEDALE M. SHORT!"

At the bottom of a descending rank of benches, behind a long library table and more illuminated glass cases, Elsie short was looking up at the audience and smiling broadly.

A fat middle-aged man in a red velvet coat and gray trousers stood next to her. He had small pig-like features crowded into the center of a big pink face, he was bald except for a silver bristle around his ears, and he was gesturing toward Elsie with one upturned palm, like a genial Master of Ceremonies.

In front of them both, spilling onto the floor around the table, sat at least a hundred applauding people, American Club women and dozens and dozens of children in costume—elves, fairies, polar bears, one adolescent Old Saint Nicholas.

"Miss Elsiedale Short," the fat man boomed, "of the Thomas Edison Doll Company!"

There was another round of applause, and while it was dying down I edged my way behind the last row of benches and joined a line of what I took to be fathers with their backs against the wall.

At the speaker's table Elsie was stepping forward, smoothing the front of her dress. "A real doll," muttered the man on my left. Elsie looked across the audience from left to right and smiled again. She wasn't wearing her waterproof coat and blue trilby hat tonight. She was wearing a pink and white sheath, tight at the hips, tighter at the bust—no woman in Paris in 1926 wore a bra—and a fleur-de-lys spray on her left shoulder that must have cost Mr. Edison a pretty penny.

"That's Henri Saulnay with her," said my talkative neighbor. "He's a German."

"Boys and girls," said Elsie in a strong, carrying voice. "As Monsieur Saulnay told you, I work for Mr. Thomas Edison in New Jersey, and my job is to go all over Europe looking for rare and special dolls. I'd like to tell you a story about one very old doll that was quite famous. It was an automate. They don't have it here in the Museum. Monsieur Saulnay is a toymaker, and he doesn't have it in his toymaker's shop either. But I can tell you what it was like."

As she talked the fat man opened the illuminated cases and began pulling out brightly colored boxes to stack on the table.

"Miss Short," he said over his shoulder in what I could now place as a faintly guttural German accent, "is writing a book about automates."

Elsie nodded. "This is a story about the great French philosopher Descartes, boys and girls. He lived almost three hundred years ago. One day in the year 1644, Descartes was summoned all the way to Stockholm by the Queen of Sweden, because she wanted to meet him. So he arranged to travel from Paris, right where we are, to Antwerp, Belgium on land, and then from Antwerp to Sweden by sea. He was accompanied, he told the captain of his ship, by his young daughter, Francine. But after two days under sail, neither the captain nor the crew had seen the little girl. She was in her cabin, seasick, Descartes said. Then on the third day a terrible storm arose, just north of the English Channel."

The toymaker opened one of the boxes on the table and pulled out a clay mask, painted brown and white, which looked like the snout of a grinning dog.

"The sailors," Elsie said, "were worried about the little girl. So while Descartes was on deck clinging to a mast in the wind, some of them ran down below, into his cabin, where they found, not a little girl, but a box about the size—"

"Of this box here." The German had a pronounced limp. He put down the dog mask and moved awkwardly a few feet to his right. Then he stooped and heaved a green and red wooden box upright onto the table. It was about twenty inches tall and was decorated with crescents and sparkling silver stars. There were two brass hinges and a golden knob.

Elsie turned the box so that its door faced the children.

"And in that box," she told them, "the sailors found a doll, a life-sized painted doll made out of wax and a wig and pieces of wood and metal. And as one of the sailors leaned forward to touch it, the doll jumped out of the box and began to walk, moving her arms and legs—just like a real person!"

Her hand pulled a lever, the door of the box sprang open, and slowly, mysteriously, into the light lurched a dazzlingly white little girl with golden hair and a red velvet dress moving her right arm stiffly, turning her painted face back and forth. Her eyes rolled. Her mouth dropped open as if to speak.

Some of the children began to scream in terror. One of the mothers cried, "Ohhhh!" and snatched her child back. A patter of applause instantly died away.

"But of course it wasn't a real little girl," Elsie said hurriedly, and stopped the doll in mid-step. She lifted its skirt to show a pair of wooden dowels and two roller balls where the feet should have been.

"It was an automate doll, a toy, a machine that acts like a person. You see, Descartes once did have a daughter, and her name was Francine, but she died when she was five years old, of scarlet fever, and Descartes missed her so much that he made a mechanical replica of her and carried it with him everywhere."

Elsie spread the doll's skirt and flounced sleeves. "She might have looked like this. But our doll was made in 1774 by one of the members of the famous Jacquet-Droz family in Neuchâtel, Switzerland. They also made a pair of life-sized little boys. One of them can draw pictures. The other can actually write 'I think, therefore I am' in French with a real pen and ink. Those are still in existence, in a museum."

"The writing doll is remarkable," said Henri Saulnay, " and very complicated. But this one is simpler." He worked a lever to make the grinning dog's jaw open and its eyes blink comically. "This is an imitation I made myself of an ancient Egyptian toy."

He peered over the toy at a sobbing child in the first row. "I didn't do a very good job, I guess."

"What happened to the Francine doll?" asked one of the mothers.

"Ah." The toymaker limped down the length of the table and put his mask away. Meanwhile Elsie opened another box and extracted, in rapid succession, a blue- and white-striped top, a little metal cowboy on a pony, a red and black bird on a music box, and a top-hatted Pierrot clown with the oversized round face of a full moon. One by one Saulnay began to wind them up.

"I can answer that question," he said. "Poor Francine doll—the sailors were terrified and ran to tell the captain. When the captain saw her, he too was shocked—he thought this was the work of the Devil and must be the reason for the terrible, terrible storm."

Elsie released the cowboy and his pony began to buck. The bird opened and closed its beak and chirped. And the clown began to swing his arms and march in a straight line toward the edge of the table. The children screamed and pointed.

The toymaker ignored the clown.

"It is true, by the way," he said, "that automates can't turn around or change direction. They can only walk forwards or backwards. To change direction and not fall down would require a gyroscope inside, something like this spinning top. But gyroscopes are very large—they use them to steer ships. Nobody has ever made a gyroscope small enough to steer a doll."

He finally looked over at the moon-faced clown as it rocked like a metronome back and forth, closer and closer to the side of the table. Over the shouts of the children he said, "You asked what happened to the Francine doll, Madame? It was a case of Science versus Superstition, you know, and Superstition is always stronger. The sailors took Francine and threw her overboard and drowned her."

He straightened, grinned, brushed the sides of his jacket again, and at the last possible moment his hand swooped out and caught the clown's leg. The children erupted in an earsplitting geyser of cheers.

"Too damn loud for me," said the man on my left, starting for the door.

But I stayed exactly where I was, fists clenched, brow drenched in sweat, mesmerized.

Twelve

IF SOMEONE BELIEVES THAT A DOLL LOOKS "sad" or "angry," that is what the Viennese Doctor Sigmund Freud calls "The Uncanny"— the terrifying feeling we have when we can't be certain that what we are seeing is alive or dead. The Uncanny can be triggered, Freud says, by waxwork figures like those at Madame Tussaud's— and also by ingeniously constructed dolls and automates. A child's innocent desire for her doll to come to life is one thing. But a walking or gesturing automaton may suddenly provoke, in children and adults alike, a deep and unreasoning fear.

Or obsession.

The "Théâtre des Automates" was hardly more than an auditorium tucked into one wing of the Conservatory museum, so I had to wait for Elsie outside in the corridor, in a milling crowd of mothers and costumed children, next to the big brass industrial weaving loom I had passed going in. This time, reading the placard at its base, I was not entirely surprised to see that the loom had been fabricated in the "Workshop of Jacques de Vaucanson" in 1762. I was just leaning forward and squinting into its Lilliputian gears and pistons when the door swung open and Henri Saulnay emerged.

The war had ended eight years ago. But to the French—and the Germans too, for that matter—it was still as fresh and bitter as ever, the bloodiest chapter yet in their centuries-long mutual insanity. Whether it was his intimidating bulk or his German accent, nobody made a move toward him.

"Boche," said somebody in the crowd. Somebody else said, "Hush." The children stared but made no move toward him. Saulnay nodded calmly and limped on by.

Then the auditorium door swung open again and Elsie Short stepped out.

This time most of the children rushed forward to greet her, so that she stopped, knelt, shook hands with two or three dolls held up for her inspection. From her knees she threw me a look of surprise.

"You came! Do you have my duck?"

"No soap, no duck," I said. "Soupel wasn't there."

"But they promised! You promised!"

"My name is Vincent Armus," said a man in a Homburg hat. "I'm with Miss Short."

I had seen Vincent Armus inside, off in a corner, and I had disliked his hat. Now I disliked the rest of him. I nodded brusquely and moved forward to help Elsie to her feet, but Armus stepped masterfully in front of me. He took her elbow and steered her toward the stairs. Like an automaton, I followed.

Vincent Armus, Elsie explained over her shoulder, was a family friend. He lived in Paris. She was staying at his house. And he was very upset that the police had taken her duck—Mr. Edison's legal property—for no good reason at all.

"And I am too," she added. "You told me you would get the duck today. And you spoke such good French to the police, I thought it was just a formality."

"What in the world were you doing interfering, Mr.—"

"Keats," Elsie said. "Toby Keats. I told you that." We were out of the museum by now, passing through the courtyard by the church, into the bright lights of the rue Vaucanson. "Like the poet, 'Hail to thee, Blithe Spirit.'"

"That's Shelley," Armus said, giving me either an amused or a disdainful look. "Keats wrote, 'For many a year I have been half in love with easeful death.'"

There were really only two kinds of Americans in Paris in 1926, apart from the drunken vacationers reeling around Montmartre on what the French called "Whoopee Tours." There were the vaguely literary, vaguely bohemian expatriates like myself and Root, mostly poor and hung over, who had left home for all kinds of personal reasons, including a deeply felt discontent with life in Mr. Coolidge's America. And then there were the older, richer, decidedly un-bohemian residents, mostly in business, who never thought of themselves as expatriates, who lived in private hôtels and grand apartments along the boulevard Haussmann or the Champ-de-Mars and who could summon with a flick of the finger, as Armus did now, limousines out of the dark.

"There's no need for you to be involved further, Keats," he said. A long, thunderous Mercedes, big enough to have a steam engine under the hood, rolled elegantly up to the curb.

"I know some very competent lawyers," he added. "Miss Short is an American citizen, a completely respectable person. I've advised her to turn this matter over to them. You should never have let them take her property away, certainly not as 'evidence' in a so-called crime."

"I think so too," Elsie said.

"It was obviously the work of some kind of juvenile gang or common thug."

Out in the cold night, under a street lamp, I could see Vincent Armus more clearly than I had upstairs in the museum. He was thin, angular, slightly hawkish-looking, in his late forties or early fifties. Under his topcoat I could make out a stiff white shirt collar whose creases bit into his neck, and a red silk tie and diamond stick pin that would have cost two years of a *Trib* reporter's salary. I do not like thee, Doctor Fell, I thought, the reason why I cannot tell.

Elsie was already in the backseat of the big car, under a lap robe that the chauffeur had given her. She was saying something else to me, but her voice was frozen out in the cool precision of Vincent Armus's. "What did you say was the name of the French police inspector, Keats? I'll call him tomorrow."

"Kospoth. Blaise Javier Kospoth."

He gave me a dismissive nod and turned to step into the car.

"I don't really need a ride," I said to his back. "I'll be fine walking."

As the Mercedes slid away effortlessly into the traffic his long pale face flashed at me through the window like a ceremonial knife.

I stood for a moment in the cold night air, contemplating the brightly lit arch of a Métro entrance half a block away. Then I jammed my hands in my pockets and started to walk toward the theatre district, where I knew there would be a cab. And for no reason at all, except that I saw the signpost again, I said aloud, "Funny coincidence that the old man on the rue Bonaparte was born in Grenoble, isn't it, Toby? Where Vaucanson was born?"

At the sound of my voice a dark shape on the sidewalk turned and I recognized the imposing figure of Elsie Short's comrade on the stage, the German toymaker Henri Saulnay.

"I enjoyed your presentation tonight, Monsieur," I said in French. "Most informative and entertaining."

He inclined his big head slightly.

"You would know a good deal about Jacques de Vaucanson." I pointed at the street sign. "Given your profession, I suppose."

There was a big red metal disk hanging from the next street lamp a few yards further on, the Parisian sign in those days for a bus stop. He craned his head to look at an approaching Number 92 bus, which of course didn't go anywhere near the rue du Dragon.

"I know very little about him," he said, "no."

"Vaucanson's famous duck," I said. "According to our mutual friend Miss Short, it was destroyed in a fire back in the eighteenth century. But Robert Houdin made a replica around 1880. She wants to copy it as a toy for the Edison Company."

The big green bus came hissing and bumping to a halt twenty feet away, headlights blazing. Henri Saulnay smiled very faintly and started toward it. "If that's what she told you," he said.

Thirteen

IT'S IMPOSSIBLE NOW, I SUPPOSE, to say what Paris really looked like in 1926 or 1927.

The old newsreels wash it all out into a grainy, flickering black-and-white metropolis that appears faintly comic, decidedly quaint—the narrow streets around the Place de la Concorde, built for horse-drawn carriages, crowded with old-fashioned black cars and omnibuses; women in cloche hats and bobs, wearing long beaded necklaces and flapper dresses so short they had to powder their knees; grinning men in funny straw hats and moustaches, all of them going across the screen with the odd, jerky motions that Mr. Edison's cameras always gave them, somehow making a whole city walk like Charlie Chaplin.

It was probably an advertising man who first called the twenties the "Jazz Age," a term without much meaning for the seven or eight million young French widows and orphans the Great War had left behind in its wake, or the dozens of legless, armless, or sightless young veterans I passed every day on my way to work, sprawled on the sidewalk, wearing the "Mutilé de Guerre" placards that a compassionate government had issued as their license to beg. The French themselves afterwards called it "Les Années Folles," the Crazy Years, which might have been better. Nobody ever called it the Age of Reason.

"Do you speak German?"

Bill Shirer leaned across the table and studied me with his usual faintly humorless intensity.

"Not a word." I was having coffee and a cigarette, the soldier's breakfast, according to Remarque, and he was still mopping up the remains of a very handsome omelette aux fines herbes, which had cost, my treat, the rough equivalent of a nickel.

"I thought maybe, since you were in the war, and saw a lot of the Germans, and Root said . . ."

"I was trying to kill them, Bill, not open a salon."

"I know, I just thought—I'm studying German now, that's why I asked."

He pushed his plate away and signaled our waiter for another coffee. Then he pulled out a pipe, a leather tobacco pouch, and various shiny metal tools for loading, tamping, ballasting, and igniting it. Pipe smokers ordinarily carry more equipment than a coal miner. Young Bill Shirer had only taken up his pipe a few weeks ago and still hadn't mastered all of its subtleties. He had started it, he told me, to look older and impress French girls, but in fact Bill Shirer's main ambition in life, as everybody knew at the *Trib,* was to be posted away to eastern Europe, where he was convinced the next great war would start, and he was certain that a pipe and a trench coat would do the trick.

I signaled for another cup of coffee myself and squinted through the window at the rain.

"I'm taking it from a guy in my hôtel," Bill said, between noisy puffs, "Jewish guy. He works as a clerk at J.P. Morgan, but he speaks German, and I give him English lessons back. Did you see this?"

He handed me a copy of that morning's *Tribune* and pointed to a story about a Montmartre artist's model who had been arrested as a spy for a "Foreign Power." She was caught taking photographs at a French military airfield. The government wouldn't identify the foreign power, but the story (byline "Wm. S. Shirer") strongly hinted that it must be Germany.

"Well, I wouldn't believe everything you read in the paper, Bill."

There was always a kind of two-beat pause with Shirer, while he decided whether you had made a joke. He puffed, then smiled.

"What I don't understand," he said, "is how you and Root are such good friends." He pushed the paper aside and handed me a little stack of note cards and two fat brown envelopes. "You're not really alike at all. You're like a monk, compared to him. This is what I could find so far."

I looked at the note cards first, but they were in Shirer's tiny crabbed handwriting and would need to be deciphered later, when I was alone. The two fat envelopes each contained a copy of a different scholarly journal, both of them stamped "Property of the American Library of Paris." The first was the "Bulletin of Modern European History," published by Columbia University Press, and the second was something called "Publications of the American Anthropological Association."

I turned the pages of the first one, while Shirer talked with his pleasant midwestern earnestness about the German menace to world peace, which he and many other students of world affairs—but not the French—devoutly believed in. The French were still too busy rebuilding after the war to do much more than sneer at the defeated and sulking Germans, which they did constantly and nastily. To call somebody like Henri Saulnay "Boche" was actually pretty mild. Two years ago, in 1924, they had self-righteously banned German athletes from coming to the Olympics in Paris.

But like most of us they had no idea of what victory had actually cost. Over his desk at the *Trib*, Shirer had tacked a translation from a speech by the National Socialist leader Adolf Hitler: "It cannot be that two million Germans should have fallen in vain. No, we do not ask for pardon. We demand—Vengeance!"

One of these days, Shirer liked to say, Hitler and his so-called 'Nazis' would be all over Germany like snakes coming out of a drain.

But on December 11, 1926, in a little café I liked on the rue Montmartre, what I was thinking about was not the accelerating future, but the distant and placid past.

The article Shirer had marked in the "Bulletin of Modern European History" was titled "The Automatons of Jacques de Vaucanson," the production of someone named Parvis Mansur, who was an Assistant Professor at Bryn Mawr. I had read only the first two or three paragraphs before Shirer finished his coffee with a loud gulp and tapped his watch.

"You said we ought to get there before nine," he reminded me, "while Mr. Hawkins is free."

Reluctantly I tucked my journals and note cards away. Then I led Bill Shirer out into the rain.

We were going four or five blocks south on the rue du Louvre, which was at that hour a busy, fractious, wildly overcrowded commercial street, one of the main arteries into the great fruit and vegetable market at les Halles. It was also the street that housed the offices of our main rival newspaper, the *New York Herald*. Eric Hawkins was the *Herald*'s Managing Editor and Bill Shirer wanted to meet him as a favor in return for the journals he had brought, probably with the idea of angling for a better job.

But Eric Hawkins and every other newspaperman in Paris would have been amused by the thought that the *Herald* and the *Tribune* were rivals. In 1926 there were three English-language papers in Paris—us, the tiny *Paris Times,* which was a four-page spin-off of its granddaddy in London; and, leading the pack with a daily circulation of almost 20,000 copies, as Gertrude Stein was supposed to call it, "the dear dear dear old *Herald*." It was rightly said that the *Trib* was so far behind the *Herald* that we had to give away free copies in hôtel lobbies, but that was actually a trick the Colonel had borrowed from his circulation wars in Chicago. As far as I knew the Colonel stuck with nothing that wasn't showing a profit.

"I come to the markets here with Root sometimes," Shirer told me. "He knows a restaurant here."

Which was what they would put on Root's tombstone, I thought, pulling my collar up against the rain. "He Knew a Restaurant."

A policeman on a huge chestnut-colored horse was directing traffic at the chaotic western gate to les Halles, and we stopped in the middle of the slippery cobblestones. I looked at the horse's great wet haunches rippling with tension, like muscles under a silken tent, and thought of all the horses I had seen in the rainy fields of the Marne, hauling or feeding or lying blown apart in the mud.

I like open-air markets, I always have. I like the sprawl, the noise, the general air of unorganized energy that does not march, or counter-march, or bivouac. I understand the impulse that makes tourists finish up their revels with a pre-dawn visit here to quaff raw, dauntingly alcoholic farmers' red table wine and slurp thick onion soup with a spoon the size of a ladle, while they watch the market stalls open.

We paused for a line of stooped, burly-shouldered men to pass in front of us. These were called les forts des Halles—the strong men of the markets. Back then they didn't use motorized dollies or scooters to move the merchandise around. The forts just piled their loads onto wooden frames that looked like shelves, and strapped the frames to their backs with canvas belts.

They didn't use crates either—this was long before people hid their vegetables and fruits behind wooden slats. At les Halles they carried them off the trucks or horse-drawn carts and stacked them loose on the ground in the long barn-like pavilions. Outside on the pavement, Shirer and I had to navigate our way through what looked like an exploded cornucopia. Even in cold, drizzly December there was French abundance—white beans from Normandy, carrots and cauliflowers from the rich black fields to the east, oranges and lemons from Provence.

Root had written a quite beautiful article on les Halles, the kind of thing that was so good and unexpected in a newspaper that it made you think the Colonel actually had his eye on something besides the profit line. I still remembered one sentence by heart: "Unpackaged vegetables and fruit covered the sidewalks, arranged by skillful and loving hands into colorful masterpieces of edible architecture—red pyramids of radishes, green cubes of cabbage, purple parallelpipeds of eggplants."

"It's not as grand as I thought," muttered Shirer when we stopped at a shabby three-story building marked number 38, rue du Louvre. He peered at a modest polished brass sign, "NEW YORK HERALD PARIS EDITION."

"Upstairs is better," I told him, and pulled open the door.

Fourteen

LIKE THE *TRIB,* THE *PARIS HERALD* had arranged its premises vertically—printing presses down in the basement, a spacious, well-lit composing room on the first floor, and next to it a number of smaller storage and mailing rooms. The editorial offices were just above the composing room, on a mezzanine with a wall of towering two-story windows in the grand French manner, looking directly down on the rainy parallelpipeds of les Halles.

When we reached the top of the stairs I watched Shirer's startled reaction to the massive polished mahogany table that dominated the city room. This had apparently been built according to the exact specifications of the paper's legendary founder, Commodore James Gordon Bennet (title courtesy of the New York Yacht Club), a man of such spectacular eccentricity that he had been exiled from New York society for urinating on his fiancée's grand piano. The table had space for more than a dozen deskmen, each sitting beneath a dangling electric lightbulb. There was a U-shaped slot in the center of the table, reached by lifting a flap, and the Managing Editor presided at the open end, facing the windows and the market.

Or in the case of this morning, facing the top of the stairs and tamping tobacco into his pipe with his thumb.

"The pipe is a good sign," I said, and presented Bill Shirer to Eric Hawkins with the odd feeling that they both might promptly vanish in a burst of smoke.

Hawkins greeted us warily, probably because he disapproved of what he had once called my "habitual lack of seriousness." In any case Hawkins was an old hand at sizing up and putting off ambitious young newspapermen who wanted a job. Hawkins himself had come over from Manchester, England, in 1915, and stayed with the *Herald* through the whole four years of the War, during which time the *Herald* was reduced, like the *Trib,* to a single sheet of daily newsprint. He now ran a full-time staff of twenty-five or thirty journalists. He had an encyclopedic knowledge of the business and no sense of humor whatsoever, being famously baffled by the American slang his reporters liked to slip into their stories (once changing, people claimed, "So's your old man!" to "Your father is also!").

"If you came to see your friend Billings, he should be back in his lair," Hawkins told me, giving the last word a pleasant little North England burr. "Or he will be soon. Did you see this?"

For the second time that day somebody showed me a paper. This one was that morning's *Herald,* folded over to a two-paragraph page four story about one Professor Robert L. Goddard of Clark University in Worcester, Massachusetts, who had fired the world's first liquid-fuelled rocket back on March 16 and was now firing another one, bigger, better, farther. I looked down at the gray rain whipping endlessly back and forth across the striped awnings of les Halles and thought of a leaden sky filled with exploding rockets.

"And nobody pays any attention," snorted Hawkins, who was something of a student of popular science. "Not even us—page four, no less. Of course he can't steer the damn things yet, he just points them and fires, but they can already go for miles and miles."

"The Germans pay attention," said Shirer, earning himself a quick, thoughtful Hawkins nod. "They have a full-scale rocket program. And the Russians too. Last month the Russians invited Goddard to speak at the Tsilovasky Institute."

"Ah," said Hawkins wisely, "the Russians."

"What he really needs to invent," Shirer said, "is a way to steer them."

I left them puffing smoke at each other like a pair of locomotives and worked my way along the back of the mezzanine, past an open door where four tickers on private leased wires spun out the *Herald*'s cables from New York and London. Any one of them would have put our old Rube Goldberg contraptions at the *Trib* to shame. At the end of the mezzanine a corridor led down a row of offices to the photo archives.

My friend Eric Billings—known at the *Herald*, because of Hawkins, as Eric the Minor—was about my age, a Cornell graduate, and another veteran of 1914–1918. He had been badly gassed by the Germans toward the end, somewhere on the Somme, but no worse, he liked to say, than when he covered Congress for the Associated Press. We had met two or three years ago at one of the bookstores on the rue Saint-Jacques, both of us reaching at the same time for the same copy of Baudelaire. Once in a while we had lunch at the Camargue and talked about books, never about the War.

He wasn't in the archives, of course, because on cold, stormy days his lungs worked about as well as two wet paper bags and he stayed home and drank brandy. But he had left a brown envelope with his secretary, labeled as always, according to his instructions, "To the Poet Keats."

I took the envelope and my canvas bag and a cup of coffee back into his private office, sat down in his chair and pulled out two photographs of Vaucanson's duck.

Maybe.

These were copies, it goes without saying. The originals were lost. But Bill Shirer had seen a mention of them yesterday in his research. And I had written Eric Billings, who had run his fingers through the superbly well-stocked archives of the *Herald*.

I shook out a cigarette from a pack of Gauloise Jaunes, which would have been my second cigarette of the day, my fourth of the week, thought of Eric the Minor's lungs, and put it back. The two photographs staring up at me from his desk blotter had a brownish, washed-out antique quality that suggested they had been made in the previous century, perhaps by daguerreotype.

I shifted in the chair and corrected myself. Daguerreotypes had come in around 1840 and were one of a kind, they couldn't be reproduced in multiple copies. That was why they never appeared in old newspapers and books. These looked like modern photographs, taken, in the usual way, from negatives.

The first one showed what seemed to be the skeleton of a featherless bird constructed out of bent wires and coiled springs. It was perched on a tree stump. You could see right through the spaces in its springs and wires to a painted background of sky and cloud. Its neck was long and arched, like my duck's, its beak partly open, its wings flung back at an exhausted angle, as if it had just flown two hundred years and passed through a furnace.

The second photograph showed the same duck skeleton from the front, but resting this time on a big wooden frame. A metal drum suspended inside the frame bristled with levers and wires that went up through the duck's legs.

There was a typed note in French stapled to the bottom. It said, "Images of Vaucanson's Duck, received anonymously from Dresden." Then a little string of question marks and somebody's faded handwriting: "Dated 1911. Found in a desk drawer, Musée du Louvre, April 13, 1922."

Shirer knocked on the door and stuck his head in. "I'm going to scram," he said. "Catch you later."

"Did he offer you a job?"

He looked at the neat row of metal filing cabinets behind Eric Billings' desk and studied the labels. "I'll see you back at the office," he said, and closed the door.

There was one more item in the brown envelope. It was the torn-off masthead of the left-wing Paris newspaper *Le Canard Enchaîné* and a scribbled question from Eric the Minor Billings: "Poet, what the hell are you up to?"

I leaned back in his chair, lit my Gauloise Jaune after all, and opened the first journal.

Fifteen

WHEN I WAS TEN YEARS OLD I was allowed to borrow a book from my father's library for the first time.

I remember the day very well—I remember the library itself, a spacious wood-paneled bay with three big windows that had been specially added on to our old ranch house and lined from floor to ceiling with his books. Even then I think I recognized that it was a little slice of his much-despised New England recreated in the arid, brown, faintly lunar landscape of southwestern New Mexico. The windows looked west, toward a blue-black mesa some ten miles away where his silver mine began. My father's desk was shoved right up against the center casement, so that he could frown and worry to his heart's content, with nothing but space between him and his underground gamble.

The book I had chosen to borrow was *The Red Badge of Courage* by Stephen Crane, in a little hardback edition purchased, according to the spidery notation under the title, at Lauriston's Bookshop, 9 Tremont St., Boston, April 13, 1896. My father turned it over for a while in his rough, no longer very Bostonian hands, then pulled out a little spiral notebook from a drawer. In the notebook I was to enter the title, author, date borrowed, date returned, and a two-page summary in my own words of the story. He made me do this with every book I borrowed, until the year I went off to college. To this forcibly acquired habit I attributed, among other things, my ability to work four years (so far) for the Colonel and my impatience with the long-winded world of academics like Parvis Mansur.

"The Automatons of Jacques de Vaucanson" took up thirty-six double-columned pages in the *Bulletin of Modern European History,* was packed with information, and based on a dissertation for the University of Pennsylvania. His major points, in order—if you're reading over my shoulder, Dad—were these:

1. Since the time of the ancient Egyptians, people had been making automatons, which were often simply dolls with movable limbs, but sometimes they reached quite astonishing levels of complexity. The Greeks had them, the Romans had them. They worked by means of springs or water pressure or forced air. Usually priests or magicians made them, and such people were often thought to have demonic powers, which led to the occasional stoning or dismemberment when somebody like the Sorcerer's Apprentice brought inanimate objects dangerously to life. Albertus Magnus (1206–1280) was said to have invented a man made of brass that could talk, but Thomas Aquinas became enraged at its blasphemies and beat it to pieces with a hammer. (In early nineteenth-century France, the professor couldn't resist adding, mechanized rubber women used in place of prostitutes were known as "consolateurs.")

2. In the early eighteenth century philosophers called French Materialists began to spread the idea, furiously denounced by the Church, that a human being was really no more than

a mechanical device. In theory it ought to be possible, the Materialists said, to build an automate that could do anything a man could do—walk, talk, digest, even fall sick and die.

3. And finally, Jacques de Vaucanson was one of those unlucky geniuses born before his time. If he had lived in the twentieth century and worked with Bakelite plastic, chargeable electric batteries, and modern chemical techniques, he might indeed have created a sensationally life-like "robot." Some legends said that he secretly did anyway. In fact, a gifted mechanic, a brilliant student of anatomy, though ravaged himself by mysterious periodic illnesses, he had built only three automatons, now lost in the wreckage of time: the Flute Player, the Tambourine Player, and the Duck.

The Duck was his most celebrated creation. By all accounts it had a beak that could masticate food and swallow, lungs to inhale, and a miniature labyrinth of interior brass pipes that worked to digest and then excrete what it had eaten.

Though, alas, the professor confessed, even Vaucanson couldn't truly reproduce the miracle of excretion.

According to the nineteenth-century magician Robert Houdin, who claimed to have seen the original, the Duck was a hoax. It could indeed quack, waddle, flap its wings, and eat—but not truly digest or excrete: a hidden compartment held an already prepared mixture to be discharged after the food was ingested.

All three automates had vanished in Germany or Italy or the south of France, in a well-documented fire that nobody seemed able to document.

I ground out my foul-tasting cigarette against Eric the Minor's metal wastebasket.

Through the window opposite his desk I could see that the rain had stopped and the stalls at les Halles had closed, as they usually did about nine o'clock, except for a few small children picking up scraps of food from the sidewalk. A woman was pushing a cart of old clothes for sale down the street, and even three stories up I could hear her raspy voice as she sang out their prices. Over by the gates a few twentieth-century consolateurs were waiting, hands cocked on hips, for stray customers from the markets. In the ordinary light of day the strange idea that had begun to tickle my brain ought to have drifted away like cigarette smoke. There were no blasphemous automates out there, no shitting ducks or robots.

Only reclusive journalists hammered on the head and antique dealers with their necks snapped.

I frowned at the window and the gunmetal gray foreign sky. Whether it was taken in 1911 or earlier, the photograph was still modern. I picked up another cigarette. Poet, what the hell have you gotten yourself into?

If my father hadn't made me feel guilty for not reading all the way through whatever I borrowed, I might never have opened the second journal.

Sixteen

"WELL, OF COURSE, I LIED," SAID ELSIE SHORT.

I grimaced at the fat black clouds sagging out of the sky over the rue Lamartine and made a show of turning up my overcoat collar. She glowered at me as if she might stamp her foot through the pavement.

"Of course, I lied, dammit, excuse my French, Mr. Toby Keats. Why in the world would I tell you—a complete stranger? That duck is probably worth five thousand dollars—ten thousand dollars, even."

"If it's not a replica."

"Yes, of course, if it's not a replica. Only the original would be worth that much money." She transferred her glower over to Root, who was standing with conspicuous politeness about eight feet away, by our building door, obviously listening to every word. "As you seem to know."

"As I seem to know," I said. I slipped the *American Journal of Anthropology* back in my pocket. That particular issue contained a thoroughly impenetrable article on the private lives of primates, an article on Navajos and rain, which I thought was pretty good, and one quite fascinating article by Elsiedale Short, Ph.D., entitled "Vaucanson's Duck and the 'Bleeding Man.'"

The question was, I thought, who else knew?

Root held up his wristwatch and tapped the crystal with one finger. "One-twenty-five," he said, "if Keats doesn't get upstairs in the next three minutes, my little friends, our managing editor is going to hang him from the yardarm with a typewriter ribbon and I'll have to find a new desk mate, who probably won't lend me money or lose at cards the way Keats does." He walked over to Elsie and raised his hat. "Waverley Root, Esquire," he said. "Enchanté."

"Miss Elsie Short," I said.

She looked at me with a hard, flat, very red face. "I want my duck."

"I don't have it," I said. Truthfully.

"If it's that mangy toy duck with the hangover," Root told her, "it's on its way to sunny Nice, no doubt for the cure. Our boss's mother Mrs. McCormick bought it and wanted to return it, and now she says she's changed her mind and she's going to keep it." He gave her his big moon-faced grin. "Women."

Elsie gave him a frozen stare.

"Anyway," Root said, "I got the duck from the police this morning while Toby was out of the office, and I packed it myself: two parrots, one mechanical duck. I took the whole menagerie à trois to the Gare de Lyon"—he tapped his watch again—"about four hours, forty-two minutes ago."

"I don't believe you."

Root shrugged. "Hôtel des Anglais, sunny Nice, undoubtedly a first-floor suite."

Elsie glowered at him, at me, then turned on her heel and marched off down the sidewalk.

"There's a divinity that shapes our ends," Root said, tilting his head and studying her walk. "Nice girl, and much prettier than you said."

*   *   *

It was, from the point of view of the newspaper business, an extremely busy afternoon.

The novelist F. Scott Fitzgerald—no, I never met him either—was in town that week and Root was assigned the job of editing his interview down to a mere 1,200 words, after which Kosposth decided in a fit of unreason to run it on the Society Page instead of the Book Review page, so the whole thing had to be re-edited and reset. At home two western Senators had boldly come out for a repeal of the Volstead Act, and Senator William E. Borah of Idaho had gone them one better by calling for a repeal of the income tax ("Borah Nix Tx" in *Trib* cabalese—our term for cable shorthand).

On the Sports Page the tennis player Suzanne Lenglen denied engagement rumors. On the Front Page somebody named Paul Joseph Goebbels had been named Nazi Party leader in Berlin, and a French countess had danced at the Hôtel Meurice with a Negro.

I finished off Senator Borah at five o'clock, Lenglen at six, and at seven I left Root menacing F. Scott Fitzgerald (his photograph) with a pair of scissors and a glue pot. On the stairs down to the rue Lamartine I met Shirer, whom I hadn't seen since nine o'clock that morning, and we exchanged a few words about the Germans and Dr. Goddard's wayward rockets. Then he proceeded on up the stairs without enlightening me at all about any job offers from the *Herald,* and I turned around and literally stumbled into Elsie Short.

"I want to apologize," she said.

I looked past her to the street. It was dark and undoubtedly bone-pinching cold outside. Somebody's quilted jacket shoulder slid by on the far sidewalk, and I stiffened and felt a sensation of ice in my throat. Then the jacket was gone.

Elsie Short folded her arms across her chest and repeated whatever she had been telling me.

"I said, Mr. Armus called the hôtel long distance for me and what you said, or what Mr. Root, Esquire said, turned out to be true. Mrs. McCormick did go to Nice."

I rubbed the back of my hand against my eyes. "Did you speak to her?"

"No. The hôtel said she was out. In fact, they said she was registered, but was about to go on a yachting trip with the Prince de Condé and wouldn't be back for at least a week. Mr. Armus is going to try again tomorrow anyway."

"You know, Miss Short—Elsie—Elsie Short—" I stopped rubbing my hands across my eyes and stared at her.

About three months ago a Parisian chemist named Paul Baudecroux had introduced the latest fashion sensation, rouge à levres baiser, which translated roughly as "lipstick that would not leave a mark when kissing." Our fashion editor had written three consecutive stories about it. Minor riots had broken out at the cosmetics counters of La Samaritaine. Elsie Short was wearing her green waterproof coat, of course, and the blue trilby hat with the feather. But she was also wearing, unmistakably, rouge Baudecroux. I peered at the folded slip of official Army notepaper in my hand, which was a reminder from Major Cross of his deadline and a request for another of "our talks."

"You look tired," she said.

Major Cross had said seven-thirty. Root had said nine. Oh what a tangled web we weave, I thought, when first we practice to deceive . . . which either Cross or Root or both of them would have recognized as being a quotation from Sir Walter Scott's *Marmion,* a tale of beef-witted men and faithless women.

"What are you thinking?"

I took Elsie Short's arm and led her toward the door. "Just getting my ducks in a row," I said.

Seventeen

Two-page Summary of the Article "Vaucanson's Duck and 'The Bleeding Man,'" by Elsiedale Short, Ph.D.

Jacques de Vaucanson was a very sick man.

Or thought he was.

All his life Vaucanson suffered from periodic bouts of illness, real or imaginary, associated with his bowels and his digestion. It was this morbid preoccupation with the fragility of his own body that would lead ultimately to his remarkable friendship with the king of France.

He was, of course, a mechanical genius—as a toddler he studied a priest's clock while his mother was at confession, and at the end of a month he had memorized its design and built a perfect copy of it. As a student in the monastery of the Minime monks he invented a mechanical boat that could cross a pond on its own and also two "androids" that served dinner and then cleared the tables. The monks were scandalized—to make a mechanical boat was one thing; to make a mechanical man was blasphemous—Vaucanson was toying with the Lord's prerogative to create, he was coming very close to the creation of—it didn't seem an oxymoron to anybody in the eighteenth century— artificial life.

From the monastery Vaucanson went to Paris and then Rouen, where he studied anatomy with the oddly named Claude-Nicholas Le Cat, a surgeon notorious across Europe for his self-proclaimed project of building, in his own words, "an automated man in which all the primary functions of an animal economy will be duplicated, including respiration and the circulation of the blood."

With Le Cat, Vaucanson actually built a very crude android, but it proved not to do any of the functions very well. The rather haughty young student abandoned his teacher and returned to Paris. There, despite more bouts of illness, he exhibited on February 11, 1738 his own very well-functioning automatons: the famous Flute Player, which looked like a marble statue come to life, and one year later his Tambourine Player and his Duck.

Historians have long believed that he sold all three automates to traveling exhibitors when he went to work for the king in 1741, as Inspector of the Royal Silk Manufactures. All of them disappeared; none of them survived their creator.

But this may not be true.

The two musical figures were evidently destroyed by a fire in Naples in 1780. How they got to Naples nobody knew.

But it is very possible that Vaucanson secretly bought back his old Duck in 1763, from a Lyonnaise glove maker named Dumoulin, though if he did, he never showed it in public again. Nonetheless, a "canard mécanique" was in the inventory of his daughter's possessions at her death in 1834, with the mysterious descriptive tag, "le vrai original." Which mechanical canard was then sold by the daughter's estate to an Alsatian physician named Gottfried Beireis, who kept it in his private collection in the city of Metz.

But in late May of 1918, the German and American armies clashed in a furious artillery battle at the nearby village of Cantigny—Colonel McCormick's Medal of Honor battle. Beireis's grandson fled in terror, and the castle was overrun and pillaged by deserting soldiers. If it was indeed "le vrai original," Vaucanson's Duck finally disappeared for good that month from the historical record, another unsung casualty of the Great War.

"It's more than two pages long." Elsie Short handed my notebook back to me and picked up her wine glass.

I remembered that all any writer really wants, even a Ph.D., is loud, constant, and unconditional praise. "I thought it was too good to cut short," I said. "No pun intended."

She wrinkled her rouge Baudecroux in a fleeting smile. "And I notice you didn't even get to the part about the Bleeding Man."

I flipped my notebook open and showed her. "It took up a fourth page."

"Do you think I could have another of these?" She held up her glass, and I signaled the waiter, who was listening to a radio turned down low so it wouldn't bother the customers.

Then I leaned forward and said out loud what both of us had been dancing around. "So you think the duck you found could actually be the one from Metz?" I liked one of Shirer's newer bits of slang. "The Real McCoy?"

"I think," she said carefully, "Mr. Bassot bought it or found it in a shipment of old toys, but he didn't know what it was, so he foolishly sold it to me. And it's legally mine now, I don't care what your boss's mother says."

"No Robert Houdin? No replica? Vanished like your nephew Conrad?"

"Oh, yes. Robert Houdin made a replica. He even tried to pass it off as the real one for a few years. Back then people were always doing things like that. Magicians used to bill themselves all the time as 'Vaucanson the Second.' I'm going to put all of that in my book. The book I'm writing about automatons. That article's just a chapter."

She leaned back while the waiter filled our wine glasses again. The music now coming from the radio was Don Giovanni, and pleasantly enough the scene when the old General's marble statue, like Vaucanson's Flute Player, comes to life.

"When I first visited Paris," I told Elsie Short, "before the war, people used to listen to the opera on their telephones—you had to pay a special subscription. It was called 'Theaterphone,' and it was the only time in history that their telephones worked."

Elsie was not interested in my reminiscences. "I want my duck, Mr. Toby Keats."

Who. What. Where. When, they taught you. I slipped the notebook in my pocket and asked the journalist's fifth question: "Why? So why did Vaucanson buy back his duck and keep it a secret all those years?"

She drummed her fingers on the table. "I don't know why. He was a strange and disagreeable man. Maybe he wanted to give it to his daughter—he adored his daughter. Or maybe he thought it would bring him luck after the silk workers' riots in Lyon. He was evidently very superstitious. Or maybe he was just one of those people who has to have a secret—I've known collectors like that. Why are you smiling?"

"My father used to say he belonged to the school of 'No Single Explanation.'"

"I want my duck."

"Is Mr. Edison really going to pay you five thousand dollars for that little hunk of rusty metal?"

"He might. If I could get it authenticated. A museum might

buy it. Private collectors might buy it. Mr. Armus is a collector. He might."

It was my turn to drum my fingers on the table. "Mr. Armus is a collector?"

"He has a very good amateur collection, yes. And he knows a lot about the history of automates. He went to Yale."

"Some people do. Does he know what you think?"

"About the duck?" Elsie found something interesting in the bottom of her wine glass. "I suppose he thinks it's just a Houdin replica. That's what I told him." She raised her head and looked me in the eyes. "I don't like being deceitful. But to answer your question, nobody else knows that I think it may be the real Vaucanson's Duck, only the two of us. And you only know because of a crazy mixed-up delivery and a couple of ceramic parrots."

"If the duck is worth all that money," I said slowly, "maybe somebody else does know."

Her face went blank.

"Maybe somebody else saw it in the shop window, too," I said, "and thought the late Patrice Bassot still had it. Another collector, for example."

She drained her wine in one gulp and stood up. "That," she said as she shook on her coat, "is most unlikely. The police were very clear. He was an old man alone in his shop. There was a robbery. Pure coincidence."

"Somebody did hit me on the head," I reminded her, "that same day."

"I'm surprised it doesn't happen every day. You're a very exasperating man."

"They hit me while I had the duck."

"Which you had in a wrapped package that nobody could see inside. And you were coming out of the incredibly expensive Ritz, not your awful room on the rue de Beast."

"Rue du Dragon. An English synonym for bad-tempered person."

I handed her the blue trilby hat and she began buttoning her coat perversely, from the male point of view, from bottom to top. My mother had done it all the time.

"Tell me about Henri Saulnay," I said.

Her fingers stopped moving. "There's nothing to tell. I only met him two days ago, because he's a toymaker and they use him sometimes to repair the automates at the Conservatory. I needed somebody to help with the talk. I didn't really like him very much."

"You know, the first time I saw you," I said, "it was on the rue Lamartine and a man—"

She finished buttoning the coat with an impatient twirl of her fingers and jammed the hat on her head like a sock. "Like many men I've known, Mr. Keats, you seem to confuse conversation with autobiography. Fascinating as your Parisian memoirs must be, I'm really not in the mood. Right now I'm thinking maybe I should just go see Mrs. McCormick in person, myself. I could probably take a train to Nice first thing in the morning and be waiting on the dock when she comes back from her cruise."

I stood up and pulled back her chair. "Well, she's not that easy to talk to," I said. "I'd let Root handle it. She likes him. He can make a long-distance call on a *Trib* telephone and if we're lucky she won't put up a fuss and he can have it shipped back to Paris, as she likes to say, toot sweet."

Elsie put her hands in her pockets and cocked her head. "Why do I think, Mr. Keats," she said, "that there's something you've forgotten to tell me?"

I put my hands in my pockets and cocked my head the other way. "Nothing at all. Absitoively, posilutely."

The same ghost of a smile crossed her lips, and for just an instant her face relaxed and softened. Through the window behind her I could see the short, straight figure of Major Cross coming down the sidewalk.

"You talk funny," she said, and turned and left.

*   *   *

Major Cross was a career librarian who had metamorphosed
into a military man. Or vice versa. He, at least, didn't confuse
autobiography with conversation. From West Point in 1918, he
told me, he had gone straight to General Pershing's staff for
the battle of Saint Mihiel, as record keeper and logistics officer,
and from there to President Wilson's staff of archivists and
historians at the Paris Peace Conference. But that was really all
he wanted to say about himself.

We sat down at my table and ordered, at the Army's expense,
a plate of cheese and a bottle of 1923 Santenay and he explained
that since it was a Friday night and I undoubtedly had social
engagements to pursue, he only wanted to give me copies of a few
sample interviews he had already conducted with other Moles.
After I'd read them, he thought, we could schedule a formal
meeting at his office with a stenographer. Then he would edit,
send it to Washington, and I would be officially quits with the
Army, if not with Colonel McCormick.

"Next week?" he said, pulling open his manila folder and
holding his pen poised above a little calendar grid. "Say, Monday
afternoon?"

I swirled the wine in my glass and watched the snowflakes
beginning to fill the air outside, earlier than predicted in the *Trib,*
little silent distant artillery puffs of white.

"So what do you know about Dr. Robert Goddard and his
liquid-fuelled rockets?" I asked.

"Not familiar."

"He's invented rockets that can go twenty miles or fifty miles
or a hundred miles, longer than any artillery shell anyway, and
carry a warhead. He teaches at Clark University in Worcester,
Massachusetts, and if he can figure out how to steer the things
accurately to a target, somebody can sit in Paris, say, and lob them

right onto Trafalgar Square in London. Or the Alexanderplatz in Berlin. It's funny. Here you are, worried about the history of the last war, which was fought, as far as my experience goes, about ten feet underground, but the next one is going be fought in the sky."

Cross shook his head.

"'Without Contraries is no Progression,'" I said.

He did his paper-cutter smile and put down his pen. "William Blake. 'The Marriage of Heaven and Hell.'"

I filled my wine glass again, thinking you never know what is enough unless you know what is more than enough, also William Blake. "At Saint Mihiel, you saw a good deal of the machine gun in action."

"The Maxim machine gun, yes."

"Which was aimed by adjusting the angle of the barrel relative to the fixed firing platform and tightening or loosening the transversing screw."

"Yes."

"And the gunner made it sweep back and forth by what the Brits called a 'two-inch tap,' which laid down a stream of bullets so dense you could literally see them shining in the air, like a metal curtain. Six hundred rounds a minute. Nobody in the world could walk upright in front of a machine gun."

I finished my wine and reached for the bottle again. I had visited the American cemetery at Saint Mihiel. There were more than four thousand graves. Major Cross's face was very flat and quiet. "The machine gun," I said, "emphasis on machine, more or less made the business of killing automatic. It's a kind of an automaton, in fact, wouldn't you say? Except that it still requires a human being to aim it and feed it and whisper sweet nothings in its ear. A Goddard rocket doesn't even need that."

"An automaton," said Major Cross, pushing the sample reports across the table to me, "by definition looks like a person or an animal. This is my card with the address. We have an office up on the rue Taitbout. Say, four o'clock Monday?"

I slipped the card in my shirt pocket. "I'm just one of many soldiers, Major—why are you and the Colonel so damned eager to have my interview?"

He was already getting up and preparing to go, and Root had just that moment appeared in front of the café window, peering in like a rakish moon.

Cross shrugged himself into a warm-looking camel's-hair topcoat and began to button it, from the top down, of course. "I can't speak for the Colonel, but as far as the Army goes, you're an anomaly, you know, Mr. Keats. There were thousands of Americans who fought with the British and Canadians, probably as many as nine or ten thousand. But in the whole war only twenty-seven Americans were actually assigned to the British tunneler crews, and despite your Professor Goddard and his rockets the Army is very interested in the underground war."

"Always looking backwards, the Army," I agreed. "Twenty-seven of us with our heads in the ground."

"You're the only survivor," Major Cross said, and turned and left.

*   *   *

Root and I had dinner in another café over by les Halles, a somewhat pricier establishment with cloth on the tables and curtains in the window, and we ate escargots in their shells and then lamb for the main course.

Root looked at the next table, where a couple had also ordered lamb. "Sheeps that pass in the night," he said.

As we ate he told me about the food shortages during the Prussian siege of Paris in 1871. At one point, people grew so hungry that there was actually a shortage of rats to eat. Toward the end, the government slaughtered animals in the zoo for the starving populace, and, according to Root, the famous chef César Ritz promptly invented a new recipe—elephant trunk, with sauce chasseur.

When we scattered our coins on the table for the bill, he sighed and allowed as how Herol Egan had just made twenty-five dollars writing an English-language brochure for a brothel on the rue de Louvois. He could dig up similar work for us, Root said, if we wanted. I shook my head. He patted my shoulder and left for a party at the Hôtel Lisbonne.

It was past ten o'clock when I reached the rue du Dragon. In my room, despite the cold, I opened my window and watched the long Paris night settle in. The sky was filled with snow, not falling exactly, but gently riding up and down on the back of the wind. The golden dome of the Invalides was barely visible. A few blocks away I could hear the trucks starting up the grade on the boulevard Raspail, making the same low growl as the tigers in the zoo. Here and there in windows behind the drifting snow I could see a few flickering pinpoints of Edisonian lights.

I closed the window and sat down in the chair that Elsie Short had used and made my mind work back and forth, like a man excavating a tree stump. Then I pulled out my little spiral notebook.

Two-Page Summary of "Vaucanson's Duck and the 'Bleeding Man.'" Page Four.

After the Shitting Duck came the infamous Bleeding Man Project.

Louis XV had assumed the throne in 1710 when he was five years old. He was an orphan, lonely, as kings usually are, and plagued, like Vaucanson, by inexplicable and untreatable illnesses. As he grew older he studied anatomy with a royal tutor and performed all kinds of surgical experiments on dogs and cats. When he was twenty-nine he was taken to see an exhibit of Vaucanson's automates—taken at the instigation of his Controller-General, a man named Jean Baptiste Bertin. The king was instantly fascinated and demanded to meet the inventor. A year later, following a royal order, Bertin, as front man, hired Vaucanson to reform the national silk industry in Lyon.

But there were other, secret royal instructions as well.

Vaucanson was given a large amount of money to build—in seclusion, in confidence, in total secrecy, especially from the Church—a complete and functioning human being, which the king could use for medical study and experiment.

This "Bleeding Man" was long thought to be mere blasphemous rumor, the work of Vaucanson's many enemies. In fact, exactly one year ago Elsie Short, Ph.D., had come across evidence that this royal secret really existed. She had found in the special collections of Columbia University a previously unknown entry in the proceedings of the Lyon Academy of Arts and Sciences. It was the record of a conversation during which Vaucanson, evidently drunk, described to the Director of the Academy his project for an Homme Saignant—a "Bleeding Man." This was to be an automate, Vaucanson said, like his celebrated Flute Player. But this time he planned to build a full-sized model of the human body—no flute. It was to be shaped in semi-transparent wax, with visible intestines, a heart, a stomach, and rubber veins and arteries through which real human blood could flow. A man, anatomically correct and complete to the last detail. Or as close to completeness as eighteenth-century science could manage. When finished, the Bleeding Man would be able to catch a fever, eat, excrete, move his arms—in short, "enjoy all the functions of an animal economy," just as in Le Cat's and Vaucanson's early dream.

But toward the end of his life Louis XV began to suffer from prolonged and terrifying bouts of dizziness. For weeks at a time he could scarcely stand or walk.

And after a disabling fall, Vaucanson himself started

to experience the same symptoms. (They probably both suffered from Menière's Disease, an affliction of the inner ear that destroys the sense of balance.) As a result, the king changed his goal. He instructed Vaucanson to build a man who would not only bleed, but also do what the king could scarcely do now by himself—rise up from a sitting position, walk forward, turn, turn again, walk sideways, never once blundering into the walls or furniture or losing its balance or growing dizzy. For this new wizardry he was apparently prepared to pay—in secret, through Bertin again—a huge fortune in gold and jewels. No other documents, or gold or jewels, have ever turned up.

Louis died suddenly in 1774 and Vaucanson, bedridden and immobilized himself, died a few years later.

As far as History knows, the Bleeding Man was never built.

Or if built, never found.

I put down the notebook and poured myself a medicinal glass of brandy from the bottle in the letter box on my desk. Or if built, never found.

Except in the minds of two slightly hysterical eighteenth-century hypochondriacs, I wondered, did the Bleeding Man ever really exist?

And if it existed once, was it still around somewhere, tucked away and forgotten in a dark corner of the great scattered and jumbled family attic that was post-war Europe?

And what possible value would it have now?

It was a funny thing, but for the first few years after the war ended there had been a surge of sightings of mythical beasts. This had interested Colonel McCormick, so the *Tribune* often ran stories about the harebrained expeditions sent out to spot such creatures as the Australian bunyip or the African rackabore, or, my personal favorite, the cross-feathered snee. Why not one more?

I shifted my chair around to look at the bookcase. Amid the magazines and trashy French novels on the highest shelf there was a three-volume set of *Oliver Twist*, recently purchased for two francs, fifty centimes on the quai Voltaire. Next to it was a paperbound almanac for the year 1925. Next to it an edition of *Macbeth* in French. And sitting in a shoe box on top of the *Macbeth*, looking down with envy at my brandy, was a small, bedraggled, copperish creature that once upon a time had eaten, digested, excreted (maybe), and otherwise enjoyed all the functions of an animal economy.

Fair is fair, and fowl is fowl, I thought, raising my glass to *Macbeth*, which is a play about witchcraft and magic and murder, and men not of woman born.

I swallowed and sighed. Then, because a vague and alcohol-addled notion was slowly taking shape in my mind, I raised my glass again to Vaucanson's Duck and showed him the notebook pages about the Bleeding Man and murmured very softly in French, so as not to wake the dead, "And what else do you know about this, my fugitive friend?"

Eighteen

WELL, OF COURSE, I HAD LIED.

In the first place, I told myself, I was a newspaperman and therefore skeptical by nature and training. And therefore still far from convinced that the sad-faced little metal contraption on my bookshelf was in fact Jacques de Vaucanson's own long-lost glorious creation.

By general consensus, after all, the "Shitting Duck" had been Missing in Action since either 1770 or 1912 or 1918, depending on whose scholarly article you believed—Elsie Short herself had told me that the skies of the nineteenth century had been thick with Vaucansonian replicas and faux canards. Who was to say that Elsie, a roving "doll hunter," of all implausible things, wasn't simply another in a long line of tricksters and fortune seekers, aiming to put one over on a gullible public? or a wealthy and gullible collector? or a gullible and senile Thomas Edison?

This seemed like so muddled a piece of reasoning that I stopped in the middle of the pont Royal and took off my hat and shook my head to clear it.

Because who would go to so much trouble for a bizarre little excreting automaton? Five thousand dollars was a lot of money, but not a duck's ransom.

Too much brandy, I thought. Too little logic.

It was quarter to eight in the morning, Saturday morning, and the snowstorm, our fourth of the month, was just twirling its great white billowing skirts in farewell and rising slowly to dance away to the east. We get snow in Paris about every third year, for a few weeks at a time, rarely sticking to the ground, nothing at all compared to the iron-cold winters I still remembered from the eighth and ninth circles of Hell that were Boston and Cambridge for a New Mexico boy.

Even so, during the night a good half an inch had managed to accumulate on the rooftops and the streets. The familiar hulking black shoulders of the Louvre were still covered with a soft, unlikely crest of white, like epaulets. The trees in the Tuileries Gardens looked like ranks of white-haired soldiers in a row. Over to the east, the dawn sky was low and gray and sunless, and stippled everywhere with silvery bits of down, still falling gently.

I watched a few early buses churn by in the snow. Somewhere off to the left children shouted. I heard dogs bark from one of the pet stores down by the quai du Louvre. Otherwise, Paris was so still and silent you might have thought its heart had stopped.

And in the second place, I thought, starting on again toward the Right Bank, somebody had very definitely taken a fist to the side of my head, in the alley by the Ritz, while I was burdened with duck, and not much later the unfortunate Patrice Bassot had turned up dead in his shop. And though Root had snorted dismissively and quoted Thoreau to the effect that the world was simply a Tissue of Coincidences, there was no point at all in exposing anybody else to possible danger, Elsie Short included.

This was marginally more plausible, and I congratulated myself and crossed over into the Tuileries, whose name didn't come, as most Americans imagined, from the tulips planted in its flower beds every spring, but from the sprawling factory that used to dig up its red clay and make roof tiles (tuiles) back in the days, I thought, of Jacques de Vaucanson.

This morning it was still too early for anybody but a crew shoveling the paths, and a pair of ragged clochards on a bench, sharing a bottle. I exited the gardens by the rue de Rivoli gate and turned left through its long, chilly gallery of arcades.

And finally, I told myself, shifting the weight in my overcoat pocket as I approached the much brighter and breezier place Vendôme and the Hôtel Ritz—finally, in the third and last place, there was some little part of me that thought once I handed over the duck, that might well be the last I would ever see of small, blonde, rather splendid Elsiedale Short.

Unlike the *New York Herald,* the *Trib* put out a Sunday edition. But it was a laughably thin affair and consisted mostly of advertisements and an occasional travel supplement, along with various "soft news" features that we either copied shamelessly from the home Chicago edition or wrote ourselves for an extra stipend from the Colonel.

It was almost nine o'clock by the time I reached the rue Lamartine, and the city room was still empty except for B. J. Kospoth and the French copy boy, who were sitting at opposite ends of the long table drinking coffee from paper cups and staring at each other.

A skeleton crew would drift in later to lay out pages and check the cables, in case the weekend in America produced something important enough to stop the presses. Meanwhile I sat down at my desk by the window and thumbed through my files. The French copy boy came by, smirking around a foul bituminous Gitane, and told me that the snowstorm had knocked out the electricity from Montmartre to the Faubourg Saint-Antoine and likewise all the telephone lines in Paris. But the pneumatique, he said with an admiring shake of his head for the genius of France, was immune to all possible weather and functioning just as well as ever.

With which he lifted up a wire basket of fat little copper cylinders and dumped them on my blotter.

The pneumatique seems incredibly quaint now, but in those days it was the last word in urban communication, and in many respects the very practical Parisian response to their moody and unreliable telephones.

An X-ray photo of Paris in 1926 would have revealed the system to an onlooker: an amazingly complex web of two-inch pneumatic tubes and pipes under the city's skin, strung all over the central arrondissements, beneath the sidewalks, over buildings, through the Métro, like two thousand miles of veins and arteries in a gigantic Bleeding Man. You could find the pneumatique in businesses, hôtels, embassies, even in some private residences. The copper cylinders that I was unpacking on my desk were about six inches long, the shape of a stubby candle, and they twisted open at either end to allow a rolled-up paper message to be inserted. Air pressure propelled the cylinders at remarkably high speed, like underground rockets. If your correspondent didn't have the pneumatique, you could pay an extra thirty centimes and fire your letter off to the nearest post office, which promised to deliver it within two hours, and often did.

I knew so much about the system because I had written a feature three months ago for a particularly slow Sunday edition. Kospoth had run it uncut and asked for more, and the following week I had written a piece about the first private bus line in Paris (it was started, since you ask, in 1684, when an entrepreneur named Villiers bought twenty big horse-drawn freight wagons called carrosses, installed backless benches in them, and hired the philosopher and mathematician Blaise Pascal to work out the most efficient and profitable routes).

As if on cue, Kospoth finished his coffee and worried his way down to my desk.

"This is okay," he said, handing me a dummy of tomorrow's page three. "I'm actually bumping the Paul column to Tuesday, so you get an extra inch."

"Give a man an inch," I said, "and he thinks he's a ruler."

Kospoth rubbed the back of his head and grimaced, because putting out a newspaper was the single most serious and important thing in the world and not ever to be joked about. I turned the dummy page around to look.

This week I had written about a uniquely Parisian enterprise I had stumbled on one evening when I was wandering near the Bastille. It was called the "Blanchisserie des Imprévoyants," which translated more or less as "The Laundry for Those Who Don't Plan Ahead," and it consisted of two bare, steamy rooms on a backstreet just beyond the ancient pile of brick and rubble where the French Revolution had begun. In the front room about a dozen men were sitting in chairs around the walls, naked from the waist up. Some of them were reading, some were playing cards. Most were just smoking and staring out the window. In the back room a stooped and wrinkled Corsican, old enough to have been there when the Marquis de Sade lodged in the prison, was slowly and methodically washing and ironing their shirts while they waited. The only shirts, in fact, that most of them owned. He charged thirty centimes an item, same as a pneumatique. Collars cost extra. I thought the name of the place was a bit unfair.

"The Colonel likes this stuff," Kospoth informed me with a sniff. Kospoth had been a brand-new reporter on the *Des Moines Register* when a hurricane and fire in 1894 killed five hundred people in Hinckley, Minnesota, and thus he tended to equate news with disaster.

"I was thinking," I said, "of a story next week about French automates."

"What? Like Horn and Hardarts?"

"Little machines, automatons, toys that look like people and wave their arms and roll their eyes just like you."

"Those things give me the creeps," Kospoth said, and picked up the dummy page and took three steps back toward his sanctum. Then he turned around and came back to my desk.

"The Colonel says you got no ambition," he said. "You know that?"

I nodded and opened the last of my cylinders.

"You could get out of this if you wanted to—" Kospoth's arm took in the big, shabby city room, our run-down building, presumably the streets, and the gray and alien city outside. "You're so good," he said, "you write so clean and fast, you could be in New York, Chicago—"

"Paris," I said.

His face went hot and red, as if it had burst inside. "You make a joke out of everything, Keats. But you don't fool me. You're hiding out from the war, off in your miserable little Left Bank apartment and you don't talk to anybody but that nut Root. You want to know who's a goddam automaton?" he said. "You are!"

Somewhere a telephone rang, and we both looked around, startled. Then Kospoth leaned over and rapped the side of my desk with the edge of the dummy. "Bulletin just in," he said, "the fucking war is over!"

I watched the door of the sanctum slam shut, then swiveled my chair around. People were starting to wander in now. One of the financial reporters was at the oval table, typing. Herol Egan was standing in a corner, reading Le Monde. I swiveled back and sat quietly, looking at nothing. Slowly my hands stopped trembling. I lifted them carefully from my lap and placed them flat on my desk. I heard myself inhale and exhale gently, the way Buddhists do when they learn to meditate.

There were seven pneumatiques on the blotter, five of them press releases from the various fashion houses along the avenue Montaigne, which, since snow was still falling all over Paris, were naturally getting ready to announce their spring lineups.

The sixth copper cylinder, however, had clearly materialized straight from the great universal Tissue of Coincidences. In it was an envelope addressed to Mrs. Millicent Cubbins, Society Editor, not of the lowly *Chicago Tribune* but the exclusive and fashionable *New York Herald*. Her name, however, had been partially crossed out and over it a familiar hand had printed in loud caps, "TO THE POET KEATS."

I opened the envelope and took out an expensive-looking creamy bond note card that fell just short of being a press release. It was a personal invitation to Mrs. Cubbins and it read: "Mr. and Mrs. Vincent Armus will be receiving guests Sunday, December 14 at their spacious home on the rue Jean Carriès, from 8 P.M. to midnight. Light refreshments will be served. And as a special treat of the season, Mr. Armus will be displaying the latest addition to his colorful collection of French automates—the celebrated nineteenth-century creation 'Bird Bush and Clock,' by Bontems."

Across the bottom of which Eric the Minor Billings had scrawled in rude blue pencil, "Curiosity killed the Cat—E."

The seventh cylinder held a single folded sheet of paper that simply said in French, "Perhaps I do know a little about Jacques de Vaucanson's Duck. I'm at home anytime. Henri Saulnay."

Nineteen

IN THOSE DAYS THE AMERICAN LIBRARY was on the Right Bank, on a side street by the French president's residence, and it was open on Saturday afternoons if you had a membership key.

I skipped lunch and at a little past two o'clock sat down in one of the library's second-floor alcoves, looking out on the shops of the rue du Faubourg Saint-Honoré, where the morning snow flurries had turned to rain and it was already dark enough for the cars and buses to turn their headlights on.

In front of me, on a carrel desk, I arranged my copies of the two scholarly journals and alongside them every book and encyclopedia volume I had been able to find with information about Jacques de Vaucanson—it was a little like a treasure hunt, I thought as I started to wander up and down strange scholarly alleys, in and out of footnoted byways and pedantic dead ends. I was no Bill Shirer as far as memory went, but I read fast, the old-fashioned eighteenth-century French was brittle and clear, and bit by bit as the afternoon wore on, the city below me faded into the shadows and an earlier, grimmer Paris came into focus.

Jacques de Vaucanson, everybody agreed, had been a tall man, gangly, thin, with a classic beaklike nose and a large black mole under his left eye, which he was in the habit of picking at and scratching when he was angry, which was often. He had a lifelong stammer, frequent diarrhea and asthma, possibly the pox. He suffered from constant sore throats and may have been deaf in one ear, and one night in Lyon the rioting laborers chased him through the streets till he fell and wrenched his leg so badly that he walked with a crutch for the rest of his life. Not much later he had fled Lyon disguised as a monk, and when he got back to his Paris workshop he designed a silk weaving loom that could be operated by a donkey, proving, he said, that an ass can make more beautiful cloth than a man.

"The reverse of the duck," I wrote in my notes, "not excrement from the end of an animal, but silk."

Then I leaned back and stared at the yellow headlights prowling up and down the street like cats' eyes in the dark. After a time, I took out Henri Saulnay's pneumatique and read it again. The truth was, I thought, it wasn't the duck that interested me now.

If his body was soft and fragile, given to collapse, Vaucanson's personality was hard and cruel. He desperately wanted to be a gentleman. He wore a sword from the time he was twenty. He was greedy for money. In his private hôtel and workshop on the rue de Charonne—something like Thomas Edison's famous Invention Factory in New Jersey—he kept an entourage of several dozen workers, but he paid them badly and worked them too hard. Except for a man named Hervé Foucault, his employees usually left quickly, in disgust. "All his genius," wrote Foucault to Henri Jacquet-Droz in Switzerland, "is in his fingers. His soul is closed off in a locked box. When he leaves off work, he's more a machine than the machines he makes."

There was more like that, much more. Vaucanson was known to dabble in secret codes, according to some scholars. He briefly interested himself in mechanical languages. There was a spooky, almost occult quality to what he did—the fingertips of his Flute Player were probably lined with human skin, his Talking Head had a dog's tongue. His spoiled daughter was flighty and had an affair with Hervé Foucault, whose grandson would inherit the family talents and devise the famous Foucault Pendulum. He would also invent the children's toy gyroscope.

Once, and once only, Vaucanson made a joke about his most famous creation: "If I had devised a shitting man," he wrote Foucault, "instead of a duck, what a grand Prometheus I would be!"

Not much of a joke.

There were two more descriptions of the proposed Bleeding Man, which I tracked down from footnotes in Elsie Short's article. Both descriptions were the same—a full-sized human body with a glass or wax torso through which you could see its organs and intestines, rubber veins through which real human blood could flow, a heart that would pump it, legs that would lift the body and move it about. Everybody thought the king had promised him a fortune to build it. Nobody thought it had ever been built.

It was six o'clock by then, and the library attendants were coming through the stacks with their carts. I shuffled my notes together, piled up the books for them to collect, and made my way out into the twentieth century.

Halfway down the rue Royale, I went into a nearly empty café and ordered a marc. On the other side of the zinc bar, in a big floral mirror, I watched myself drink. On the second glass I turned around and watched the cars and trucks on the street drive up and down through my ghostly reflection on the window.

What none of the academics got, I thought, was *why* Vaucanson built automatons.

Why, Toby? Do tell us.

Well, all of his automates, it seemed clear to me, even the shitting duck, were mirrors of his own diseases, reversals of his own weaknesses. Why else build an animal with bowels of steel and digestion like clockwork? Why else build a Talking Head that doesn't stammer and have sore throats, a statue that stands up straight and walks without a limp and plays the flute and doesn't choke and strangle with asthma? When you're flawed and damaged, you make yourself over, if you can, if you know how. You make yourself whole. You fix what's broken. You try to create yourself the way you were before . . . before you broke down.

In the wavering light of the cafe window I could see my own body, but not my face.

Across the way, in front of a toy store, a street mime in a top hat and red velvet cape stood on a little wooden box, arms akimbo. His face was weirdly white with makeup, his head cocked at an unnatural angle, clicking slowly from left to right as if on a ratchet. He was a person pretending to be a machine.

If you want to write a good story, Root likes to say, it's very simple—you give somebody an obsession, then wind him up and turn him loose.

Sunday was much better. The weather was cleaner, warmer. I went for a walk in the Luxembourg Gardens and watched the boys play with their sailboats in the fountain. In the afternoon I sat in the Café Edmond Rostand and listened to two students from the Sorbonne perform scenes from "Cyrano." An old couple from Lille bought me tea and talked about General Pershing. At six o'clock I started to walk.

People sometimes ask me, frustrated Americans thumbing their pocket dictionaries, how long do you have to study before you really start to understand French? And speak it so they don't wrinkle their noses and walk away?

In my case it happened in the spring of 1917, when I worked

six tempestuous weeks as the liaison between Norton-Taylor's 23rd Tunnelers Group and General René Lanrezac's 222nd Field Artillery. Get it straight, Norton-Taylor had instructed me grimly, because any mistake or mistranslation could turn the big French guns the wrong way and point them toward our tunnels instead of the Germans. And in those days a fifteen-inch howitzer shell weighed 1200 pounds and would drive six or seven feet into the ground before it exploded. Every tunnel below or beside it would simply collapse into a long, dark coffin.

Nothing concentrates the mind, Dr. Johnson said, like the prospect of being hanged. Or, he might have added, suffocated.

Root told me his French came to him one night in the Métro, when he suddenly realized, like switching on a light, that he understood every word the pretty girl beside him was saying. But I don't take the Métro.

It was five minutes to seven when I turned off halfway down the boulevard des Invalides and walked up a quiet tree-lined street toward the severe eighteenth-century facade of the École Militaire.

This part of the 7th Arrondissement was one of Paris's wealthy quartiers. The long rectangular Champ-de-Mars was its green park, with the Eiffel Tower and the Seine squaring it off at the north end, the École Militaire at the south. On either side of the Champ-de-Mars, in an elegant grid of side streets, ran two or three rows of handsome, very expensive modern apartment buildings, uniformly six stories high, topped with penthouse gardens. In the dark, except for the mansard roofs and the cat's-eye yellow headlights on the passing cars, you might have thought you were on the Upper East Side in New York.

That, of course, and the faint Parisian smell of urine on the street from the vespasienne at the corner.

I sat down on a bench and watched the spotlights revolve on the Eiffel Tower, a sight I very much enjoyed. Hard to believe now, but the Eiffel Tower had originally been painted red. Then the second year of its existence it had been repainted a bright, eye-curling yellow. Three hundred artists and writers had signed a petition to tear the tower down, on the grounds that it was the single ugliest structure in Europe. But then the war came and the Army had galloped in to the rescue, and now it served as the world's largest military radio antenna and the artists and writers were off in the outer darkness, gnashing their teeth as usual.

Even harder to believe now, of course, is that in 1925 the Citroën car company had placed the name "André Citroën" in great luminous letters on all four sides of the tower. The letters were in six colors and twenty meters high. People said they could be seen forty miles away.

I looked at my watch and noted with obscure satisfaction that the first two letters of the "André" facing me had burned out. Originally, the École Militaire had used the park for troop maneuvers and drills—hence the "Mars" in Champ-de-Mars— but all that was gone with the days of the musket and the saber. My grandfather had come to Paris for the Universal Exhibition of 1878 and told me that he had been on the Champ-de-Mars when a well-known Irish courtesan named Lee d'Asco went up in a balloon, wearing men's clothes and carrying a revolver. She came back down perfectly naked, except for the revolver, having thrown out her clothes piece by piece to lighten the basket. It was my grandfather who taught me my first words of French.

Somewhere nearby a municipal clock struck a sluggish seven bells. Around me shoppers were still going past with their Christmas packages. A few soldiers from the École drifted by in kepis and mufflers. There were no armed ducks, no academic bounty hunters, no thuggish persons with billy clubs and quilted jackets. No ghosts, no Moles.

I watched a dog running back and forth on the snowy grass, and slowly, slowly the same nagging question began to circle around in my head again, like a scrap of paper in the wind.

I was a rewrite man. I edited stories and tried to figure out what people really meant to say, consciously or not, and I was usually not too bad at it. And right from the start Elsie Short's clearly written but oddly illogical essay had set off a blinking light—she hadn't written about the Flute Player, or the Tambourine Player, or Vaucanson's remarkable silk weaving looms, which in the great historical scheme of things could be said to have started the Industrial Revolution in France. Those were clearly far more important than a few mechanical toys.

She had written about two things only, not logically linked. "Vaucanson's Duck and the Bleeding Man."

And what in the world did the one have to do with the other?

I pulled my right hand out of my overcoat pocket and saw that I had made it into a fist.

At seven-twenty-two Root came bounding up from the Métro like a six-foot rabbit popping out of its hole, and we set out across the park for Vincent Armus's party.

Twenty

THE RUE JEAN CARRIÈS RUNS AT RIGHT angles to the Champ-de-Mars, on the southwest side, about a third of the way down toward the river. In the lobby directory of number 8, I was not surprised to find that Armus lived on the penthouse floor.

There was an elevator, but in deference to me, Root and I walked up the stairs. Root found the hall light and knocked, and a butler in correct evening dress opened the door.

"You are . . .?"

"Gentlemen of the Press," said Root. He gave a confidential pat on the head to the boxy black camera he had lugged all the way from the rue Lamartine. "Here early, to take some pictures for the Society Page."

The butler looked from Root to the camera to me. "I'm Mr. Pulitzer," Root said. "This is Mr. Hearst."

"Who is it, Nigel?" said a female voice in the hallway. Nigel took a step backwards, swept a white-gloved hand in our direction, and murmured, "Mr. Pulitzer and Mr. Hearst, madame."

The voice gave a throaty chuckle, said, "Then I must be Jenny Lind," and materialized in the form of a tiny, sharp-nosed, dark-haired middle-aged woman. She was dressed in an ink-black silk Chinese jacket and trousers, and she looked, as Root would say later, like one half of a pair of crows. But she gave us each a quick smile and said, "Well, this must be one of those sex-change operations you read about, or did dear old gray-haired Millie Cubbins just split in half like an amoeba?"

"We're from the *Tribune*," I said. "Not the *New York Herald*, I'm afraid."

"And you're selling subscriptions door to door, like a troop of Boy Scouts?"

Root has a way with older women, which he modestly attributes to a certain mischievous handsomeness (his phrase). He lifted the camera and tripod up to his shoulder like a soldier with a rifle and switched on a dazzling, if slightly piratical grin. "This is Toby Keats," he said. "Lost soul, solemn recluse, harmless drudge. Possibly the second-best writer in Paris. He wants to do a long, brilliant story about Mr. Armus and his automates, and I'm Waverley Root and I like to eat and I just wanted to crash the party."

Mrs. Armus kept her expression blank for a long moment while somewhere behind her Nigel coughed like a sheep into his glove. Then her face opened into an equally roguish smile, and she stepped aside with a little mock bow. "Well, then come right in," she said, "and feed."

We followed Mrs. Armus down a hallway and into a living room three times the size of my flat. It had a thick brown carpet, a fireplace whose gray stonework ran up to the ceiling, and it was sparely but handsomely furnished with a dozen or so glittering rhomboids and triangles in the most up-to-date Art Déco manner. Directly in front of us the Eiffel Tower was framed in a balcony window. Off to the right, we could see the tops of the plane trees in the park below and the silent traffic circling the École Militaire. At the far end of the room, behind a pair of chromium parallelograms posing as sofas, two maids were setting out chafing dishes on a long buffet table.

"If you'll wait right here," said Mrs. Armus, "I'll go find the Lord of the Manor."

Root leaned his camera and tripod against a chair and started toward the buffet table. I walked over to the big balcony window and craned my head to see the place du Trocadéro behind the Eiffel Tower. The rich are very different from you and me, Scott Fitzgerald was supposed to have observed one day with his usual breathless amazement at the obvious. To which his friend Ernest had apparently muttered, Yes, indeed, they have more money.

"An absurd mistake," said Vincent Armus from the doorway. "I don't know who sent you that notice. We normally deal with the *New York Herald* only."

He paused for a moment, glanced at Root by the buffet table, and then advanced three steps toward me. He was wearing a creased black lounge suit with a gray vest and a narrow silver-colored tie that emphasized the hawk-like intensity of his features, and in the sharp reflected light of all the chromium and steel he looked every bit as angular and rigid as his furniture.

With an expression of disloyal amusement Mrs. Armus handed Root a plate.

"But Miss Short tells me it might possibly help in her job," Armus added flatly. "I know that the Edison Company positively courts publicity."

Behind him Elsiedale Short, Ph.D., stepped into the same doorway, looking surprised and curious. Her blonde hair was freshly clipped and shaped and she had on the same tight-fitting sheath she had worn on Wednesday, and as she walked around one of the sofas, to my eye she was the only curved thing in the room.

"Elsie's staying with us now," said Mrs. Armus from the buffet table. "She moved in last Tuesday. She's a dear girl. We used to know her father in New York."

"Tuesday?"

"We didn't like a hôtel," Mrs. Armus said, "for a girl alone, after what happened."

I brought my gaze back to Armus and his perpetual frown. "No, of course. Well, about our being here. I have a friend at the *Herald* who told me about the party. I'd already talked to my editor about a Sunday feature—'Automates in France'—something about the history of them, automates and toys and the Christmas season. He wants to start with a local connection. It's a nice hook—nineteenth-century French machines, a twentieth-century American collector."

"You don't have the Duck yet, do you?" Armus said.

"Mrs. McCormick is still at sea."

"Who is that person by the table?"

"Waverley Root is his name, Vincent." Elsie was wary, but helpful. "He works at the *Tribune,* too, with Toby Keats."

"He brought a camera," I said, "if it's all right with you. He's a very good photographer."

Root waved a knife and a piece of bread. "It is a far, far butter thing I do," he said.

"If it weren't to help Miss Short and her job," Armus muttered. When nobody said anything to that, he made a show of pulling back his cuff and looking at his watch. "If you really must see the automates, they're in the next room," he said. "We have just enough time before people arrive."

Twenty-One

THE NEXT ROOM WAS, IN FACT, three doors down the hall and faced into a courtyard, not the Champ-de-Mars. Elsie Short pushed open the door and stood back and I stopped dead on the threshold.

On the left-hand side of Vincent Armus's Collection Room, reaching about to shoulder height, were two big aquarium tanks, filled with what seemed like blackish-green water and speckled like a pointilliste canvas with bright, silent patches of color, rising, falling, gliding away out of sight.

I stared at the fish for a moment, then turned to the right-hand side of the room where a bookshelf covered the wall. In front of the books, on three rows of rectangular black pedestals, stood the main items in Vincent Armus's collection. There were perhaps two dozen automatons altogether. Some of them looked like the toys Elsie and Henri Saulnay had displayed at the Conservatoire—colorfully dressed clowns with big round white faces like the Man-in-the-Moon, a monkey with a violin, a monkey with a cigar, a minstrel with a banjo. But most of the automatons were representations of birds, and most of the birds were in small brass cages.

"When I first started, Mr. Keats," said Vincent Armus, clearing his throat behind me (in his little kingdom he was, if not warm and friendly, at least markedly more civil). "When I first started out, I was living in Berlin and I collected any sort of antique automate I could find, though I particularly liked the clowns. Clowns are not, of course, the sort of thing the Germans do well. When we came to Paris, I discovered the French sub-specialty of birds and I decided to concentrate on them."

I opened my notebook and he began to walk down the first row of pedestals, reciting names, dates, and brief, crisp technical descriptions. I was suitably impressed. Armus didn't know what Elsie knew about Vaucanson's Duck, but otherwise he did Yale proud.

Probably the first automates in history, he informed me, were singing birds. The Egyptians made them. Then the Greeks did. The painted wooden cuckoo clock in the farmhouse kitchen, so ordinary and familiar, was a lineal descendant, by way of the eighteenth-century and Switzerland, of the ancient automate-maker's art. There was an old castle at Hesdin where all the birds and little animals in the garden were still automates, set in motion by hydraulic power from a fountain.

But no one, in Armus's opinion, had ever made mechanical singing birds to rival those of Gustave Bontems of Paris, who started his business as a teenager in 1831 and created his last great masterpiece in 1890, when he was crippled with arthritis and nearly blind.

"And this is it," Armus said. He led us around the bookcases and into a scallop-shaped alcove that contained exactly one black pedestal. On top of the pedestal was a brightly colored, three-foot-high enamel thorn bush, populated by what looked like a dozen tiny birds peering out from its paper leaves like Christmas lights on a tree.

We stood in front of it, studying the trunk and the birds and the sharp, realistic thorns. He had had to repair some key parts of the apparatus himself, Armus said, which were broken when he bought it. He was, he allowed, not a bad amateur technician. Then he reached around the base and turned a key. There was a pause of a few seconds. Something metallic and unseen clicked twice. Slowly, in random sequence, the birds began to move their beaks and chirp, and a moment later their wings began to open and close, and their tail feathers lifted and fell in an irregular, jerky rhythm.

What I disliked most about it—what made me back up and rub my sweating palms against my jacket—was the fact that one by one the birds started to hop from twig to twig as they sang, their bead-like little eyes bright with what might have been life, but was only reflected light from the lightbulbs on Vincent Armus's ceiling. I felt spooked and nervous, I felt exactly the way I had felt when Elsie's clown at the Conservatoire had started to walk.

"It's called 'Bird Bush and Clock.'" Armus tapped the small clock dial in the center of the base. "People often say 'Bird Tree' instead of 'Bird Bush.' I hope your newspaper gets it right, Mr. Keats."

I was still rubbing my hands against my jacket. "Hope," I said for absolutely no reason I could think of, "is the thing with feathers," and Armus turned and studied me coldly for a moment, then raised one eyebrow and smiled. I realized then that I had no grip whatsoever on his character.

Root was slow in getting his camera and tripod around and into place in the little alcove. Arriving guests could be heard in the big living room down the hall, and one or two wandered into the Collection Room, plates and glasses in hand.

"He began as a taxidermist, you know," Elsie Short said, coming up beside me as I stood in front of the fish tanks. I looked over at

Armus. "Gustave Bontems did," she said dryly. "As a boy Gustave Bontems was apprenticed to a taxidermist, and according to the story, one day a customer said how life-like his stuffed nightingale looked and he burst into tears and said, 'Yes, but it doesn't sing!'" She frowned at me. "Shouldn't you be taking notes on all this?"

I pulled out my notebook and obediently opened it to a blank page. "Thank you for interceding with the host," I said. "I wasn't sure he was going to let us stay."

Elsie kept her attention fixed on the Bird Bush, where several older men, American by their voices, had now gathered around Armus. Next to him a tall, mannish-looking woman in her early forties had just arrived by herself.

"As you might have guessed," Elsie said, "Bontems was fascinated by sound. He used to get up before dawn and go out in the fields and listen to the birds coming awake. Then he would file the teeth on his music box over and over until he got them exactly right and duplicate them with cams."

"A cam is a little curved wheel, right? Like a pulley?" I asked.

"More or less. In automates they have teeth to engage the gears and make the tines in the birds' throats bend and vibrate like the ones in a music box. They also turn the heads and open the beaks. There are fourteen birds on that Bush, seven different species, and believe it or not, each one is singing a precise, scientifically accurate call." She tilted her head in my direction and added in the same dry voice, "As for interceding, I just thought I should keep an eye on you, Mr. Toby Keats, seeing that you still have my property, so to speak."

"Birds of a feather," I said proudly and wrote it in my notebook. "How do they jump from branch to branch?"

"You have wires that run to the cams and wheels in the base," she said, "behind the clock. I built something like it once when I was a girl, my father and I did, down in our basement, but on a much bigger scale, of course. I was something of a tomboy."

"William Peyton Short," I said. "Descendant of the diplomat

William Short who was Thomas Jefferson's private secretary right here in Paris when the French Revolution began. I knew there was something about your name, and I had a human encyclopedia in our office named Shirer look it up. Your father was an engineering professor at Columbia, and he had two or three patents in mining technology, one of them with our friend Mr. Edison."

Her face turned unexpectedly pensive. "My father was quite a wonderful man," she said. "My mother died when I was four and he brought me up by himself. He wanted me to be a professor too, like him."

"Except—?"

"Except—have you tried to find a university teaching job in New York, Mr. Keats? As a woman? My father died two years ago. The last thing he did was introduce me to Mr. Edison, who gave me a job out of charity. But I'm not going to be a doll hunter all my life. Not if I publish my book."

I put away my notebook. "My editor says, 'Don't get it right, get it written.'"

Her laugh was spontaneous and irresistible. But then she put her hand on my sleeve and asked, "Who is that woman?"

I had already recognized the new arrival. She was wearing a hipless gray "flapper" dress that might have come off the cover of that month's *Vogue,* along with a silver tiara and a white fur fox piece draped around her shoulders, and while she smiled she kept one large bejeweled hand resting in a proprietary fashion on Armus's left shoulder. "Her name is Natalie Barney. She's a scandalous American expatriate."

"She certainly seems to be charming Vincent and those other men. Libby won't like that."

"Actually," I said, "she won't have the slightest interest in Vincent."

Elsie looked at me, then at Natalie Barney, who had just then turned her gaze in our direction. "Oh," she said. A faint pink blush colored her cheeks. "Oh."

"Mr. Keats the reporter." Natalie Barney crossed the room in three brisk steps, shook my hand with a firm, masculine grip, and showed her large, predatory teeth, not to me, but to Elsie. "I'm Natalie Barney, Mr. Keats. We've met at various oh-so-dull American Colonist functions, and I read you every day in the dreadful old *Tribune*. Now I understand you're going to write about poor Vincent's toys."

She extended her hand to Elsie and repeated her name, and Elsie, descendant of a diplomat, smiled and shook hands and appeared not to notice that Natalie had maneuvered us both around to one side of the aquarium tanks and still had Elsie's one hand in both of hers.

Natalie Barney was one of the wealthiest, most intelligent, most uninhibited of all the American expatriates in Paris, and incidentally its most prominent lesbian, though she was reputed to have once seduced Bernard Berenson, out of curiosity. Her house on the rue Jacob was notorious for its all-female soirées, which usually culminated in what admiring Parisians called the "rites of Sappho." There was a small Greek temple at the bottom of her garden, Root had told me, which the ladies reached on a path strewn with flower petals by a small boy hidden out of sight.

"I adore Mr. Keats's hair," she told Elsie. "Don't you? If I ever go gray"—she patted her own raven-black cloche—"I mean to dye it the same color exactly."

"It makes him look young," said Elsie the Ironist.

Natalie chuckled. "You must be a writer too. What I like about the writer's art," she added, looking at me, "even in newspapers, is the way good literature so naturally divides everything into two opposite parts, like the body and soul. Or male and female. Here, for instance, Mr. Keats, you have on one side of the room the organic, living world of the fishes, silent but alive."

She smiled at her own wavering reflection in the aquarium tank. "And on the other side of the room the dreadful automates —not alive, mechanical, but somehow capable of singing. Toys to keep a drowsy philosophe awake." She leaned forward confidentially. "That's much too imaginative a contrast for our host. The fish tanks came with the house, I think."

"I think I'd better go help him with the Bird Bush." Elsie finally pulled her hand free.

"I didn't know you were friends with the Armuses," I said to Natalie, who had turned to watch Elsie cross the room.

"I adore them both, especially the wife, Libby." She stroked her bare throat with one hand. "I always say that the burdens of marriage are too great to be borne by two people alone."

"Ah."

"That rather unnerving creation must have cost Armus quite a pretty penny."

"He told me two thousand dollars."

"Then he must have stolen it," said Natalie Barney, "because I know for a fact that he hasn't a sou. Come and see me sometime, Mr. Keats." She patted my shoulder and looked at Elsie again. "But not by yourself."

At a quarter to ten Elsie Short led us out to the front hallway and held open the door. The sounds of the party were growing louder in the other rooms, and I had pretty much run out of journalistic excuses for staying.

"Your friend Miss Barney," Elsie murmured, "just invited me to the rue Jacob for chocolate."

"Natalie Barney," Root told her, grinning, "is a fine and friendly person, and her chocolate is good."

"Are you really going to write a story about the Bontems?"

"I still have," I said carefully, "a lot of questions about automates."

Root made little rude snorting sounds as he folded his tripod and hoisted it over his shoulder. We were all in the foyer outside the apartment now. "I'm going to say good night, young people," he told us, going down the hall toward the elevator. "Veni, vidi, video—I came, I saw, I photographed."

We watched him clamber into the elevator, which was a polished iron cage designed for someone half his size, and wave cheerfully as it started to clatter and wobble and sink out of sight.

"That is very bad Latin," Elsie said, "video," and we both looked at the door to the Armus's apartment. I put my hand on the knob and closed it. I have no idea why you and Root are such good friends, Bill Shirer had said, you're more like a monk than anything else. You don't even chase girls. But I hadn't always been a monk. I looked at Elsie's bright, upturned face, the glossy rouge Baudecroux on her lips, the curve of the pink sheath where it cradled her breasts, and like an idiot I asked her about Vaucanson's Duck.

"Those songs that Bontems made for his birds—they're created by cams, you said?"

"Very small, very precise."

"So you could change the cam and change the song whenever you liked. You could make a nightingale caw like a crow if you wanted to."

"Well, they're interchangeable, yes." Elsie's smile was faint and cautious. "But I don't think anybody has ever tried to make a nightingale caw."

"And Vaucanson's Duck could do something like that?"

"We'll have to see," she said. Her smile was completely gone. "When you give it back to me."

I walked two paces down the hall to a window that looked down on the trees and the lighted footpaths of the Champ-de-Mars. The test of a first-class intellect, Scott Fitzgerald is supposed to have said, is the ability to hold two different ideas in your mind at the same time. I couldn't do it.

"Why do you really want the duck, Elsie?"

"I beg your pardon?"

She had reopened the door to Armus's apartment and Nigel the butler was peering curiously out at us.

"Look," I said, "I admit the duck is interesting, fascinating—the whole world of dolls and automates and strange mechanical gadgets that walk and talk and defecate, though God knows only a Frenchman would have thought that last one up. I didn't know anything about them before you came." I looked hard at Nigel and he moved back inside. Elsie took a step inside the door. I thought of Eric the Minor's wrecked lungs. I thought of the artificial legs and arms I had seen on soldiers in England after the War, the big iron contraption I had seen in the Brompton Road Chest Hôpital that closed around a man's torso like a cage and squeezed his chest in and out, hissing and sighing, to make him breathe, or sing.

"The duck knows the way to something else," I said.

"No."

I began to walk toward her. My head pounded and hurt like a real and living knot of flesh and bone. "Does this have something to do with the Bleeding Man?"

She closed the door and was gone.

Twenty-Two

MAJOR CROSS: People are always telling me about the mud. I suppose you have some vivid memories of it too. I've read a few of your articles in the *Tribune*—you have a way of sketching scenes.

SERGEANT KEATS: Well, a lot of the English regular soldiers still wore old-fashioned spats over their boots, at least in the early years. The mud just latched onto those and pulled them apart. Sometimes it was so thick and gloppy that when they ran across a field the mud even sucked their boots and socks off and they had to keep charging the Germans barefoot.

MAJOR CROSS: But not you tunnelers?

SERGEANT KEATS: In the tunnels you usually wore just socks anyway, for the silence, or you went barefoot by choice. The Germans wore boots. We could hear them. We were used to mud underground—but upside, I remember seeing two Corpsmen bending down and trying to lift a stretcher that was on the ground with a wounded soldier on it. All that happened was the stretcher stayed where it was and the two Corpsmen started to sink down into the mud, first their shoes, then their knees, all the way to their waists.

MAJOR CROSS: And the horses in the mud?

SERGEANT KEATS: The horses would sink to their bellies and whimper and cry like a dog. For days at a time in the winter you couldn't haul a wagon, anything. Except Norton-Griffiths had a Rolls Royce that he had somehow got over to Belgium and he went everywhere in it, with a chauffeur. It was nearly hit once by a German shell. The concussion blew off all of its fenders and doors, but the motor kept running and he kept going. Mud was different in different places, you know, according to the geology. In Flanders we dug our tunnels through blue clay mostly, which was like a slimy soap. After a shift of working underground you were covered with it, your hair and clothes and face. But it didn't stay blue. It had an odd property of turning white as it dried, so that by the time we crawled back to the surface we looked like a parade of ghosts climbing up out of a hole in the ground.

MAJOR CROSS: And in the Somme?

SERGEANT KEATS: In the Somme you had either red clay or chalk. The chalk was so bright sometimes that the men wore dark goggles underground. You could get a tunneler's version of snow-blindness.

MAJOR CROSS: *[consulting notes]* Tell me about the listening stations.

SERGEANT KEATS: *[no reply]*

MAJOR CROSS: You had to be so quiet in the tunnels, I understand, because the Germans were also digging tunnels from their trenches toward yours, to plant their bombs and mines under our people, and any sound would give away your positions. They would detonate a bomb and bury you. Or vice versa. But you had advanced technical devices to hear them coming.

SERGEANT KEATS: *[slowly]* In the beginning we used the advanced technical device of a bucket filled with freezing cold water and set on the floor. You put one ear into it and listened as hard as you could, on the theory that the water magnified sound vibrations. Or sometimes we used the old Roman way of holding a stick between your teeth and pressing it into the wall, same reason. Later we had doctors' stethoscopes. Early in 1917 somebody devised a "geo-listening" device with earphones that wasn't bad. But a good listener still depended on his own ears mostly. You reached the point where you could distinguish footsteps from spades, feet from knees. The best listeners were the Welsh—

MAJOR CROSS: *[chuckles]* The Welsh always claim special powers.

SERGEANT KEATS: Sometimes to fool the Germans we would dig a side tunnel, away from the main one, and set up a mechanical device that bumped against the clay a couple of times a minute like a shovel.

MAJOR CROSS: How deep underground were you?

SERGEANT KEATS: *[speaking rapidly]* You have no idea—nobody could have any idea—what it was like to crouch by yourself, alone, in a completely dark tunnel about a shoulder's width across, crouch there in the mud and the dripping water and do nothing but listen. We had three-hour shifts. The Germans could be inches away, on the other side of your wall. The end of a tunnel was often stuffed with ammonal and gunpowder cotton that would detonate at a pistol shot or a blow with a hammer if we needed an explosion. We mainly used hand signals. If you had a cough or a cold you couldn't go underground. After an hour of utter silence you could hear your heart beating, every single motion, function, breath you took was magnified so much—like the man in the Edgar Allan

Poe story—men frequently went insane, they hallucinated and started to crack up and that was the end of them as tunnelers.

MAJOR CROSS: Everybody in the Army had hallucinations, from what I hear. One of my interviewees talked about seeing an angel on a white horse, waving a sword. Another one told me his captain ordered them to march up to a castle across a stream, but there was no stream, no castle, there was nothing at all, just endless flat Belgian countryside. And it was like that underground too?

SERGEANT KEATS: The problem with hallucinations, Major Cross, is that they can be real. Not far from Metz, forty feet underground, I saw disembodied hands sticking out of the mud and clay. For a minute I thought they were like the dragon's teeth in the story, that turned into men. Then I saw that the Germans had fired a camouflet next to one of our tunnels and collapsed it. Those were our people buried in the mud. I counted three hands and then turned out my light.

Cross scribbled a note in his ever-present manila folder. "And faces?" he said. "One of the reports talks about your seeing faces?"

I poured another glass of his good brandy and said nothing. I stared at the wall behind his head and said nothing. A fat black winter fly such as you get in a city, never in the country, was buzzing around his window curtain, beyond which, I assumed, was still the rue Taitbout and the bright shops and gay clothes and inexpressibly pretty French women. I swallowed more brandy and didn't say anything about faces. Instead, I told him that sometimes when tunnelers were killed underground their bodies were pulverized by the explosions, and then the chalky water that oozed through the tunnels, all the way back to the entrance, was reddish-white with blood.

"And in April, 1917?"

"In April 1917 we had a counter-blast from the Germans that killed dozens of men and nearly sealed off our tunnel. We started digging through the wet chalk and clearing timbers and after about thirty feet we heard voices and tapping on the other side of a collapsed wall. They were our people and they were still alive, but of course, without fresh air they wouldn't last long."

"Because of the poisonous gases in the tunnel, yes? From the explosion?"

"The captain in charge ordered us to push a pilot hole toward them, extremely low and narrow, no beams to support the walls, and we took turns digging forward as fast as we could. You were wriggling on your belly like a worm, clawing at the wet chalk with your hands, and passing it back along your body to the man behind you, and the top of the tunnel was scraping your head and pressing down on your shoulders. We had gone about twenty feet when I turned on my flashlight and saw two men straight ahead of me. I knew them both. Welsh miners from Cardiff. They were about another ten feet ahead of me and they were lying face down on the floor, pinned by the broken timber beams."

"Alive?" Cross closed his folder.

"The broken timber," I said, "was what had saved them. It was keeping the weight of the collapsed chalk off their heads and chests, but the rest of their bodies were buried in chalk. And right behind them, dammed up by the mud and wood, was a rising pool of water. I could feel the tunnel tightening around my own body, it was like being squeezed to death in a great white fist. I had a moment, one moment—how long is a moment by Army standards, I wonder? Ten seconds? Fifteen? After that it was clear the water would rush over the mud dam and flood us all. I didn't move. I stared at Harry Lewis's face and he stared back at me and then somebody behind me began to pull my legs because I couldn't move or wouldn't move and my flashlight beam was still on his face and they dragged me back out of the pilot hole just as the water burst over the timbers and the last thing I saw was their two faces staring at me, and then the chalky water came over and they gulped it and were gone."

Cross wrote something else. Then he said softly, "That still wasn't the worst thing, was it?"

The fly landed on the left arm of my chair and sat perfectly still. I raised my right hand, held my breath, and then snatched it from the air as it rose. I could feel it beating frantically against my palm, trapped. Then I opened my fingers and set it free.

"No," I said, and stood up to leave.

PART THREE

The Toymaker

Twenty-Three

ELSIE LIKED VINCENT ARMUS, SHE SAID. He had been a friend of her father, and if he hadn't exactly dandled her on his knees as a baby, she had seen him now and again with his family in New York, from her school years on. People misunderstood Armus, she thought, because of his money and his rather grand, impatient manner, which concealed a sensitive and scholarly nature. He was a born worrier. To her the curious thing was that, with his brains and sensitivity, he hadn't become a professor like her father.

To a reporter, however, the curious thing about Vincent Armus was that nobody knew where he got his money.

Or more precisely, when his money would run out.

As far as the public records went, Vincent Armus had worked for the Chase Guaranty in Paris as a gentleman banker until they closed their branch two years ago. Since then he had evidently lived on his savings, which were not inconsiderable, given that in 1919 he had inherited well over $150,000 from his father, who had owned three hardware stores in Connecticut.

One hundred and fifty-thousand dollars was a princely sum for a *Trib* employee. But not all that much when you had no regular job but kept an apartment on the rue Jean Carriès and drove a Mercedes car. He had a personal checking account at J.P. Morgan Bank, which was eight hundred dollars overdrawn that month—this was highly illegal to know, but came courtesy of Bill Shirer's friend the German-speaking bank clerk. Armus also had a second mortgage from J.P. Morgan, which would come due next June, and it wasn't obvious from the books how he could pay it. Or in other words, as usual, Natalie Barney's information was correct and he didn't have a sou.

But lack of income so far hadn't changed Armus's high-living style. In addition to automates, Elsie's new landlord, I learned, also collected expensive silver cow creamers, first editions of the writings of Samuel Johnson, and, according to the amazing Shirer's notes, something called "pornographic snuff box lids" painted by an eighteenth-century Englishman named Richard Cosway.

"Of whom," said Root, "regrettably I have never heard."

We had just then reached the corner of the rue des Capucines, where a short snaggle-toothed old Frenchwoman known universally as Madame Charlotte kept a cart of fried potatoes for sale. It was six-fifteen on a cold Monday night, three days before Mrs. McCormick was due to return from Nice, and Root was carrying a single blue chrysanthemum, which he had liberated from a florist's trash can near the *Trib* and which he now presented, with a little bow, to Madame Charlotte.

Madame Charlotte, Parisian to the core, blushed like a schoolgirl as she took the chrysanthemum and held it up to the street lamp, and Root added something I didn't quite catch, in his own curious brand of French—he himself described it as more fluent than accurate—and she grinned broadly, as people did when they talked with Root.

There was a pile of newspapers on an upended crate beside her.

She picked up the top sheet and rolled it deftly into a cone. Then she shook out some potato slices that were cooking in a can of oil and flipped them into the cone. A dash of salt, a splash of vinegar, and she handed it over to Root, who gave her one franc, which was too much, and murmured (I think), "Ma déesse culinaire,"—My culinary goddess.

He was just finishing the last of the potato slices when we entered the lobby of the Hôtel Ritz. He wiped his fingers on the newspaper cone and dropped it in an ashtray. I took a heavy brass key from the man at the desk and with what I liked to imagine were condescending nods to the porter, we mounted the stairs to Mrs. McCormick's suite.

"Did you notice, by the way?" Root asked as we entered the living room. "In his apartment Armus had a Yale medal on the wall where nobody could miss it."

"I saw it. Class of '96." I walked over to the closet by the bedroom door and reached high up on the shelf.

"There is," he said, clearing a space for me on the coffee table, "a brothel on the rue Chabanais that has a blue and white banner right over the piano: 'For God, Country, and Yale.' They claim it brings in business."

Then he stood back and I placed the duck carefully on the coffee table. I had gotten the idea early on Saturday morning, looking out my window at the snowfall and thinking of Mrs. McCormick in the south of France, because she, in the careless, imperial way of the very rich, had of course kept her suite at the Hôtel Ritz while she was away. Both Root and I were known at the desk. We could come and go whenever we wanted, I had thought, on the pretense of doing Mrs. McCormick's errands. And for the safekeeping of stolen mechanical ducks, as all the authorities agree, a suite at the Ritz is better than a bank vault.

"What time is your appointment?" Root asked.

"No appointment. I said I would be there sometime after eight."

"It ain't gonna fly," he said, and shook his head sadly at the duck, which I now had on my lap. I pressed one finger down on its skull and its neck stretched slowly out full-length and its black dopey eyes stared sadly up at me, as if I were measuring it for the gallows.

I was not bad with my hands, for a Harvard man. In my father's silver mine you worked with machines, and machines broke, and in the outer reaches of southern New Mexico, seventy feet underground, you learned how to fix them yourself.

I picked up a tiny flat-headed screwdriver that a jeweler around the corner from the *Trib* had sold me. If you raised the wings of the duck one at a time, I had already discovered, the head would bob and some kind of inner spring would turn in the neck and make a swallowing sound like a metallic gulp.

It was amazingly realistic. The wings, Vaucanson had claimed to the king, duplicated the bone structure of a real duck's wing. They moved up and down with perfect smoothness, and as they moved they worked a kind of suction cup or inverted bellows in the throat, exactly like sinews and bones.

"Is this the book?" Root held up a tiny duodecimo volume that I had checked out of the American Library on Saturday, the only book Jacques de Vaucanson had ever written. It was published in London in 1742 as *Le Méchanisme du Fluteur Automate* and had an English translation in the back, "The Mechanism of the Flute-Player Automate, with a Note on Vaucanson's Duck."

Root balanced himself on the arm of one of the Ritz's handsome horsehair sofas and flipped to the next to last page. "'I believe,' he read, 'that Persons of Skill and Attention will see how difficult it has been to make so many different moving Parts in this small Automaton of a Duck; as for Example, to make it rise upon its Legs and throw its Neck to the Left and Right.'" He paused and looked at the duck. "Can it do that now?"

"No."

"'They will also see that what is sometimes a Center of Motion for a movable Part, at another Time becomes movable on that Part, which Part then becomes fix'd. In a Word, they will be sensible of a prodigious Number of Mechanical Combinations.'"

"There was a pedestal in the picture," I said. In the second of the photographs that Eric the Minor had given me, the duck stood on top of a waist-high pedestal, with a drum-shaped wind-up engine beneath it and rods attached to its feet. "The engine made the rods go up and down like pistons in the body, but you couldn't see them because the pedestal was covered with a sheet of plaster."

"'This Machine,'" Root turned the page, "'when once wound up, performs all the different Operations of a living Animal without being touch'd any more.'"

He kept on reading. I closed my eyes and tried to imagine what it must have been like in the eighteenth century, back when Vaucanson himself was a "living Animal." The past, I had been taught by my best professor at Harvard, is a foreign country, under permanent quarantine. We can't really go there, even in imagination, and if we could go there, we wouldn't like it. We wouldn't like the smells and the dirt, the diseases, the sewage, the violence, the extraordinarily rough and clawed-up texture of everyday life.

But then again, I thought, I had been a long time in a foreign country.

Jacques de Vaucanson was thirty years old in 1739, the year he first exhibited the Flute Player and the Duck. All the books agreed that he was a tall, underfed hypochondriac from the provinces, uncomfortable in Paris. He was invariably overdressed in a powdered wig and a gentleman's fine laced surtout that he couldn't afford. One year earlier he had borrowed a huge sum of money to rent a workshop and an exhibition space in the Hôtel de Longueville, the "Salle des Quatre Saisons," a famously beautiful room covered with mirrored panels and gilded ornaments and newly painted frescoes over the doorways and windows. And even though he was struck down in the autumn by yet another of his mysterious illnesses and had to direct his workmen while he lay feverish on a couch. By the time spring rolled around he had seventy-five visitors a day lined up outside the Hôtel de Longueville to see his automates perform. Each visitor paid three livres admission, a week's wages for an ordinary laborer, and Jacques de Vaucanson was on his way to wealth and fame and the Bleeding Man.

None of which explained why twenty years later he had secretly repurchased (possibly) the Duck and (possibly) given it to his daughter.

"'The End,'" Root read, and then closed the book. "'Finis.'"

I picked up a wrench from the table and then, trying to ignore the feeling that the duck was giving me a look of pained indignation, I undid the rust-coated plate that served as its belly, which was as far as I had yet dared to go in tinkering with it.

"You know what Natalie Barney said to me?" Root watched as I pulled the belly plate away. "She said she thought Armus's automates were boring, and I said why? And she showed me those enormous crocodile teeth and said, 'Because I don't enjoy innocent pleasures.'"

I grunted and pried the plate down and a bit of screw and rusted flange dropped out. The screw was a dry ancient greenish-brown in color and clearly not machine-tooled as it would have been in the late nineteenth century or the twentieth century. Hand-turned on a metal lathe in 1738, if Elsie Short was right, by M. Jacques de Vaucanson himself.

"She also said—this was while you were chatterboxing with your young lady—she said, 'You men are interested in women only from the waist down, while my interest in men is only from the neck up.' She hates Gertrude Stein, did you know that?"

I did know that. Americans all over Paris knew that. I also knew that, notwithstanding their mutual dislike, Natalie Barney and Gertrude Stein often sat side by side for hot chocolate at Rumplemeyer's. I also knew that Gertrude Stein's favorite piece of music was "The Trail of the Lonesome Pine," which she played over and over on a phonograph during her salons for Hemingway and the boys. But at this moment I wasn't thinking about what Root called the scribbling tribe. I was peering inside the bowels of Vaucanson's glorious duck and seeing nothing but a corroded metal cobweb of miniature struts and springs, some of them loose, some of them barely attached to the walls of the body.

"Give up?" Root had gotten on his knees beside the coffee table and was squinting into the duck. I rocked back on my heels and rubbed my eyes.

Outside the windows of Mrs. McCormick's suite, down on the place Vendôme, the sounds of automobile traffic had faded. There was a tourist's horse and carriage just below us, and briefly, just as if we were truly transported back to the eighteenth century, all I could hear was the slow clop-clop of its hoofs on the cobblestone, faint clicking noises that made the suite sound like a roomful of clocks.

"I see eight extra cams I can't figure out, really small, four hooked into each wing," I said. "Right at the shoulder joint. There must be twenty more cams on each side to move the wings."

"What's a cam?"

"This thing. Elsie explained them to me." I showed him a tiny copper disk about half the size of an American dime. "It changes the direction of a gear. And on the throat there's a metal bar with teeth like a comb that clicks onto a gear. But these cams aren't attached to a gear or anything else. I don't get it."

Root brushed his knees and stood up with a little wheeze. "Toby Keats," he said. "You ever hear of Captain Ahab?"

I had, but I didn't like the question. "No."

"It's late, it's dinnertime in Paris, you have made the acquaintance of a charming blonde person, and instead of being outside enjoying it all, you're down on the floor on your hands and knees, sweating and red-faced, like a man who's been chasing a white whale all day. Or a metal duck." He bent forward so that I had to look at his face. "What the hell do you want, Toby?"

"I don't know what I want."

"You still think there's something hidden in the duck, don't you? Something Elsie Short won't tell you about—diamonds, rubies, a Golden Turd."

"I think," I said, holding up a cam from the wing and turning it slowly in the light, "I think that Jacques de Vaucanson was a very strange man. And I think," I said, "that there's something here that I can't quite see. I'd like to find it."

Root snorted and grinned. "You just want to impress Elsie Short." I squinted at the cam.

"Love," he said, "is blonde." And somebody knocked on the door.

We looked at each other and Root's grin faded to a frown. He bent down and scooped up the duck and walked into the bedroom.

I counted the dislodged cams, eight of them, and slipped them into my jacket pocket. Then I went to the door.

There is a certain kind of elderly woman in Paris who grows shorter and denser with age. Their perfectly silvered white hair looks like coiffed marble, and they sprout small hard bits of jewelry everywhere on their bodies, like barnacles.

"You're not Mrs. McCormick," said the specimen in front of me. She spoke English with a British accent and she leaned forward and adjusted her eyeglasses for maximum penetration. Behind her one of the Ritz bellmen peered over her shoulder at the room.

"Mrs. McCormick is away on a trip. She won't be back till Thursday. I work for her son."

"The Colonel McCormick," said the bellman. "This is Monsieur Keats."

It was remotely possible, I thought, that Root would have a sneezing fit, or the duck would come to life and start quacking and splashing in the bidet. I stepped outside into the corridor.

"I am Gwyneth Crawford Gleeson," she informed me, pausing ominously between each name. "One of her oldest friends. From London. I had a message from Mrs. McCormick. I most certainly thought she was here. She should be here."

The door behind me swung open and Root handed me a medium-sized cardboard carton, fastened across the top and sides with electrician's black tape. "You're going to be late," he said to me, "if you don't hurry. Number sixteen rue des Minimes. Which," he added to Gwyneth Crawford Gleeson, "is in the Marais, you know, a district of Paris I dislike very much."

"It is," she said, staring at the carton, "rather dangerous there."

"But what can you do?" he said. "Mrs. McCormick ordered cuff links for the Colonel, a little Christmas gift, and they sent her a bunch of painted snuff box lids by mistake. If you want to come in and wait, Keats is just leaving."

Twenty-Four

MORE DANGEROUS THAN MRS. GLEESON KNEW.

At a quarter past eight I stepped off the bus in front of the church of Saint-Paul and Saint-Louis on the rue Saint-Antoine, the triple play of sanctification as Root called it, and promptly took two wrong turns in the winding medieval streets of the Marais and ended up at the northwest corner of the place des Vosges.

Here I stumbled and nearly fell over a metal bar in the sidewalk that people once used to scrape mud from their shoes—"Marais" sounds very fine, but it really just means "swamp" in French, which is what this part of Paris was in the fifteenth century, a narrow marshy bog stretching roughly from the present-day Bastille to the Hôtel de Ville. At one point in the sixteenth century it was highly fashionable to live here. But swamp has a way of trumping fashion, and gradually, as the houses sank and the water rose, the private hôtels and luxurious apartments had been abandoned. For the last two hundred years or so, the Marais had been nothing but a damp, crooked, and labyrinthine refuge for the social outcasts of Paris—Jews, bandits, prostitutes. Toymakers.

At the dark and muddy rue de Béarn a city crew on overtime was digging utility ditches in the street. I turned left by a corner café, gave fifty centimes to a pair of beggars who staggered up out of the shadows, and one minute later entered the west end of the rue des Minimes.

Henri Saulnay, born "Heinrich Zell," was fifty-seven years old, German by citizenship, but a native of the French-German region of Alsace—I knew this because, having metamorphosed now into amateur historical researcher, I had just spent two profitable hours that afternoon in the *Trib*'s modest little business library.

Saulnay was also, according to the *Almanach de Commerce,* one of a vanishing breed of little-known European craftsmen: a toymaker who designed and built by hand, in his own shop, each and every toy he sold.

There were, our business editor had told me, perhaps a dozen of his kind left now remaining in all of France, aged Davids struggling against the American Goliaths that mass-produced toys by the tens of thousands from pre-cut and pre-stamped metal sheets and Bakelite plastic. The best American manufacturer was called the "Humpty Dumpty Circus Company of Philadelphia," and some of their toys were designed by a young artist named Alexander Calder, who had spent some time in Paris studying design. Calder liked to make toys that have moving or articulated parts like automates—he preferred the word "mobile"—and in an interview published several years before in the *Trib* he had said he thought Henri Saulnay was a true artist in his field. Too bad, Calder had said, about Saulnay's German politics.

"If you'll wait right there," said the bored young man who opened the door, "I'll tell him you're here."

I don't wait very well anymore. I shifted my package under my arm and followed him down a hallway and into an open courtyard. He glowered at me over his shoulder, but said nothing. Together we squeezed along a narrow passageway on the left and stopped in front of an ancient wooden door with a sixteenth-century spy grille at the top and a Yale lock on the side.

Any old structure in the Marais has certainly been flooded many times by the Seine, in the slushy brown days before modern dams tamed the river. In winter every crooked alley and house in the district gives off a notorious clammy odor, a cold, green, reptilian sweat that comes through the walls like a fungus. I tipped up my collar and held my breath while the bored young man fumbled through a set of keys.

But if I expected to step through the door into something like the leaking hold of a ship, I was pleasantly surprised. The room directly in front of me was about twenty feet long and ten feet wide, brightly lit and almost dry, almost modern. There was a big, hardworking Franklin stove at the far end, and a cluttered table in the center, where my guide abruptly sat down.

"In here, Mr. Keats, if you please." Henri Saulnay himself appeared, in his fat man's red velvet jacket, at a door just beyond the stove. He limped out two steps and waved me forward.

The clutter on the table, I saw as I passed, was largely made up of exquisitely tiny wooden body parts—dozens of dolls' heads and legs and arms scattered about at random. More body parts were stacked in a kind of Lilliputian boneyard in the center, under a lamp. There were paintbrushes, paint pots, Christmas ribbons and wrapping paper, a flat tray of screws and screwdrivers and tiny hammers the size of my thumb. Through an open door I could see one more room. A slope-browed man in a leather apron stared at me from beneath a swinging lightbulb. Then he turned out the light.

"A disconcerting sight, I suppose," said Saulnay in his guttural French, shrugging in the direction of the table. He ushered me into his workroom. "All those poor maimed creatures. But this is our busy season, you know, as much as a three-room workshop with almost no customers can have a busy season. The French don't like to buy German toys, so I have to sell bits and pieces to French shops, where they put on their own name. I'm told that this time of year the Edison Doll Factory in New Jersey looks like a butcher's shambles on the grand scale—barrels and barrels of arms and legs, buckets full of glass eyes and painted lips. But that's the American way, is it not? Everything on the grand scale, even slaughter. Shall we speak English?"

Saulnay closed the door, turned the lock, and cocked his oversized head at me.

I looked at the locked door for a moment. Then I set my carton on the workbench that filled the center of the room and pulled up a stool. "English is fine."

"Good. Good. Zehr gute." He removed his red jacket and hung it from two hooks on the wall, where it billowed like a sailor's hammock. Then he drew up a stool for himself at the table. "You must forgive my forced humor, Mr. Keats. I was in our Great and Mutual War, in a modest way of course, because of my age, and it was an American artillery shell that gave me my limp"—he paused long enough to adjust the swinging lamp over the table. "And my notoriously Teutonic point of view, of course. I am, you may say, unrepentantly German. Is that package for me? Let me have a look."

I don't like impatience, especially in strangers. "In a minute, I think."

"Oh?" The toymaker cocked his head the other way. I glanced around the room.

Most of Saulnay's work space was filled with the same jumble of tools and toys as the outer room. On a shelf behind him sat a Punchinello marionette and two tiny brass birdcages like the ones at Vincent Armus's house. Propped against some ledgers was a framed photograph of a younger Saulnay in the uniform of a German corporal. But my eye was drawn irresistibly to something else.

I stood up and walked over to a side table and bent forward to look at the single item on it, a beautiful porcelain doll about ten inches high, wearing a golden-colored silk gown. She had bright blue eyes and a little puff of blonde hair and she was seated at a tiny dulcimer piano. All the strings inside it were visible. The doll's hands held two little felt-covered hammers.

"If you touch the lever on the bench," Saulnay said, "the lady will play for you." I stretched one finger toward the lever. There was the usual delay and metallic whirring I had come to expect, then the lady on the bench began to move the hammers rapidly over the strings and a silvery bright whirl of musical notes filled the room. As she played, the lady turned her smiling face from side to side and her eyes moved back and forth from Saulnay to me.

"That was built by a watchmaker named Kintzing, a German," Saulnay said. "About 1780. It may have belonged once to Marie-Antoinette. There's an even better one in Neuchâtel, a girl who plays original melodies on the organ. Her chest moves up and down while she plays, and the very first spectators thought she was breathing, like a living person. Most of them ran away in terror."

I watched the hammers fly across the strings. The lady's eyes lingered on mine as she smiled.

"In Paris, you know," Saulnay said, "some of the first spectators at the cinema fled screaming from the theater—it was a kind of a riot—such is the fear we have of artificial life. The musician in Neuchâtel was created, incidentally, by Henri Jacquet-Droz. I wonder if you've heard of him?"

Reluctantly I stepped back from the lady with the dulcimer. She turned her head away. "You mentioned him in your talk. He built a boy who could write with a pen and ink. You said the boy could write, 'Je pense, donc je suis. I think, therefore I am.'"

"Very good, Mister Keats."

"And Jacquet-Droz was a protegé of Jacques de Vaucanson."

"Very good again. He studied with Vaucanson and then returned to Switzerland and started his own workshop. The Writing Boy is one of my favorites. I wish he could talk as well as write, of course. Then he would be perfect. Many of those old craftsmen were interested in sound, you know, sound and music. Which is something they have in common with your Mister Edison, I suppose, being deaf as he reportedly is. I understand that, with a nice sense of irony, he's working on a motion picture that can talk—imagine the riots then!"

The doll's delicate hands slackened their speed, stopped, the music leaked slowly out of the room.

I found that I was breathing hard myself. I wiped my hands on my coat and sat down again at the worktable. "I thought you might be able to tell me something about this," I said, and pushed the carton across the table.

He pulled it close to his belly and picked up a small bone-handled knife.

"Your pneumatique to me at the newspaper said you know a good deal about Jacques de Vaucanson."

The toymaker was extraordinarily deft with his hands. I watched him quickly slit a strip of tape on the box with the knife. Then just as quickly, as if he were pulling a bandage from a wound, he yanked the tape away and dropped it into a trash basket beside his stool.

"Not a good deal," he corrected me, and wiped the knife blade on his sleeve. "I know a little something. I grew up in the Alsace, you see, and spent my boyhood summers at a family farm not thirty kilometers from our Jacques's old family home. Our friend Miss Short visited me there not long ago. My grandfather knew people who had actually been acquainted with Vaucanson. And there were still some around when I was young who remembered the family—his daughter moved there to enjoy her widowhood. There was one of Vaucanson's Paris proteges named Hervé Foucault, who evidently contributed much to her enjoyment."

He slit a second strip of tape and opened the two cardboard wings of the carton. Then he leaned back on his stool. "You have an interesting face. Elsie Short said as much at the Conservatory. She saw you in the audience. An interesting face."

"She said that?"

He nodded. "She also said you write for a newspaper, which is how I found you."

"All the moues that's fit to print."

Saulnay wrinkled his piggy nose. "I disapprove of puns," he said dryly, "if I don't think of them myself. Before the war, let me say, Mr. Keats, I owned a small but thriving business in Dieuz, which is in Germany despite its French name. I had twenty-six employees and an annual profit of around seven or eight thousand of your dollars. The American Army burned it to the ground in 1918, and all but one of my employees was killed. So I picked up what little I had left and changed my name and came to Paris, where the craft is still thriving—not the easiest thing in the world, to move to your enemy's capital. But I thought art—and craft—are above politics and I could reestablish myself here, where the business is."

There was a distant rumble of thunder, which I felt even through the thick walls of the workshop. "And so you have."

"Hardly. I'm poor and not truly thriving, as you can see. But in the years right after the Peace it was worse. I was a very bitter and unhappy toymaker, I assure you, and I made certain angry speeches, led certain angry manifestations in the street that I now regret. Things are bad in Germany, Mr. Keats. It was a very bad peace you Americans imposed on us. I have considerable sympathy for Herr Hitler and his followers. But an old man's speeches and posters don't change anybody's politics. The world falls apart no matter what we think. I say all this because, along with your interesting face and handsome gray hair, I sense a certain wariness in your posture toward me. I imagine that as an American you may have formed resentments against Germans. German soldiers."

"No."

"No? Ancient enemies like ourselves? Very saintly of you. Well, I ramble on." He suddenly turned the carton sideways and switched from English to a clumsy Alsatian French. "'Certains ne trouvent leur vie intéressante,' as Jules Renard says, 'que lorsqu'ils la racontent.' Some people find their lives interesting only when they talk about them. This looks like Vaucanson's Duck."

I stood up abruptly. "The real one?"

Saulnay had the duck completely out of the carton and was revolving it in his big, careful hands. His face had a look of genuine surprise.

"I thought, I was told—I understood from all the books. I thought you were bringing me a toy. No, it wouldn't be the real duck, of course. The real one disappeared a long time ago. But this is certainly very old."

There was a flush on his cheeks and a new energy in his movements. He set the duck in the center of the table and reached for his tools. In a matter of moments he had the stomach plate off and he was greedily lifting the two side plates of the torso, swinging them up where they hinged at the spine to reveal its drooping tangle of curved greenish-crusted metal tubes. Most of the tubes were no bigger than a pencil. Some teeth-like struts must have been ribs when the duck . . . when the duck was alive, I thought like an idiot, and bent to peer over his shoulder.

"That," Saulnay said. "Please. Now." He pointed down the table without looking up and I handed him a jeweler's loupe, which he fixed in his left eye. In his right hand appeared the tiniest pliers I had ever seen.

"Elsie Short says this was a replica of Vaucanson's Duck."

"Yes, yes, I know her ideas. She claims there were dozens of nineteenth-century replicas made. Robert Houdin made at least one, an Englishman named Babbage made another—not a very good one. Hervé Foucault probably did, others, the Jacquet-Droz brothers. The test is always the wings, you see, the most complex part." He rocked back on his stool. "Mister Keats, forgive me—I don't work well with somebody staring at me. In the other room, there is wine, bread—if you'd give me ten minutes alone, twenty?"

I straightened slowly and my eyes must have traveled across the little workroom, checking for doors and windows, because

Henri Saulnay's small pig-like features tightened and he placed his hands on the table.

"I won't," he said, and his smile reached no further than his lips, "steal your duck."

Twenty-Five

IN THE NEXT ROOM THERE WAS, IN FACT, a bottle of red wine on one of the back shelves and a set of six unmatched glasses. Nobody else was in sight. Thunder boomed overhead, and a lamp flickered off and on in the corner. The front door looked locked and bolted. I could hear the angry hiss of rain sweeping across the ceiling, and feel the cold night air rubbing around and around the corners of the ancient building like a cat. Some days in Paris it failed to rain. The door to the third room was closed.

I don't like thunder, I don't like locked doors. I don't like it when the power goes off and the lights start to flicker.

Miss Short had visited our family farm, he said, in Alsace.

But Elsie Short said she had just met Saulnay a week ago. She had only just come over from New York.

I turned around. "No," I said.

The door to Saulnay's workroom had not quite closed. At

the table I could see the pale bristly dome of his head bent over the duck, whose worried black eyes seemed to be fixed on mine, pleading.

"No," I said and stepped back into the workroom. Before Saulnay could move I pushed the empty carton to one side and picked up the duck. "No," I said, as if third time were a charm, "I've changed my mind, I think. I'm taking it back."

Slowly, slowly Saulnay rose from his stool, spilling shadows. His head bumped the swinging lamp. His big shoulders spread out like a cape.

"You are," he said, "a quite stupid American."

I backed into the main workroom and felt my hip touch something. More thunder rumbled above us, and the electric lights blinked on and off. When I turned again the other workroom door was open and a burly man in a dirty gray quilted jacket was coming through it. I looked at him, looked at the Yale lock on the front door. Saulnay limped closer.

"You want the duck," I said, "because you think it's the real one, too." And then I added the thought that had been skating about somewhere in my mind since the moment I met Elsie Short. "And more than the duck, you want the Bleeding Man."

His face hung in the dim room, bald as the moon, and a second, fainter look of surprise came and went with the wavering lights. "There is no Bleeding Man, Mister Keats. There never was a Bleeding Man. Pure legend. Pure stupidity." He leaned against the table and held out his hand. "But I do want this automate, never mind why."

He lifted his chin toward the man in the quilted jacket. "This is my nephew Johannes, my sister's son. He knows very little about toys. He knows a good deal about rougher things."

The French version of the Yale lock works from the outside by a key. From the inside your thumb alone can turn a latch to

move the tumbler. The nephew in the quilted jacket started
toward me. I took a step back and as I fumbled with the door,
Saulnay shoved the big table forward into my belly and the floor
seemed to rock like a boat.

"Get him!"

I staggered sideways. My right arm swept a little army of dolls
and doll parts from the table, and the nephew's shoes went out
from under him. He landed in front of me on one knee, so close I
could smell the garlic and grease on his jacket. He fumbled on the
table for a hammer.

I held up the duck.

"Stop!" Saulnay's big palm shot forward. The lights in the
room flickered on and off again. Johannes came forward in quick
stroboscopic jerks, like film running backward, his hammer raised.

"If he comes any closer," I told Saulnay, "I'll smash this thing
like an eggshell."

Saulnay lowered his hand. He limped a step toward me. "You
are in," he said, "very far over your thick American head."

I flipped the lock and opened the door.

The cold, wet Paris night oozed into the room like a
waterlogged ghost. There was a metal working chisel on the floor
beside my shoe. My eyes fixed on Johannes, I stooped and picked
it up with my left hand. Then I straightened, turned, took two
steps through the door, and slammed it shut.

Outside, I shifted the duck's weight and jammed the chisel into
the door frame above the lock.

The courtyard I had come through was dark and slick with
rain, and completely empty. By the time I reached the street I
could hear the door splintering behind me. The street lamps were
out, of course, on the rue des Minimes and the wind was whipping
the black sky up and down like the flap of a tent.

There were some parts of Paris I knew by feel and touch like a blind man, but the dank, labyrinthine Marais wasn't one of them. I slipped and staggered, squeezed the duck's bony wings into my chest, and broke into a run—and found myself directly in front of yet another new utility ditch. This one was a monster: deep, crazy deep. As far as I could tell in the dark, it extended the whole width of the street. The pit in the center was a jumble of sawhorses and sewer pipes. Right over the center was a sloping sheet of plywood that stretched across the ditch and blocked out the sky like a roof.

Like a tunnel.

I stood on the edge of the ditch, swaying. A peal of thunder turned over and over on its side, like a body rolling down a hill.

If I hadn't been able to see a thin gleam of light beyond the plywood roof I would never have moved, I would still have been wobbling back and forth in the rain when Johannes skidded into sight at the end of the street.

But I did see it, and so after hesitating one more beat of my pulse, I plunged down the slippery mud and under the plywood roof, shaking, stumbling, eyes fixed on nothing but a watery glow thirty yards away. The thunder pealed again and I counted backwards from ten the way they had taught me, hunching my shoulders against the unimaginable weight of earth and stone that was about to come down across my back.

Then my shoes hit pavement, cold rain pelted my hair, and I burst white and flailing out of the ditch like a swimmer exploding out of the surf.

There was electricity here. The place des Vosges was straight in front of me, ringed by street lamps, its long arched arcade bright and shimmering in the rain. Two cars were coming from opposite directions, and I skittered somehow between them, over to the dark fenced garden that filled the center of the square. Behind me Johannes scrambled up into the light.

If you put up a table and a chair, the French will eat outside in a snowstorm. At the farthest diagonal corner of the place des Vosges, a small indomitable café had four or five tables set out under the stone arcade, and at one of the tables a waiter and two customers were staring in my direction.

I glanced at Johannes, on the opposite curb. Then I ran along the fence.

By the time I reached the arcade, he had vanished. The waiter, incongruous in a tuxedo jacket and white apron, was marching toward me, frowning.

"Monsieur! Attention!" He stopped under a fluttering electric light and folded his arms over his chest. Behind me Johannes's face reappeared between two arches as if we were playing Hide and Seek. Cat and Mouse. Duck-Duck-Goose.

"Téléphone, s'ils vous plaît?" I said.

The waiter studied my wet hair, my soaked overcoat, the strange metallic duck tucked under my arm, bobbing its head.

"Pas de téléphone ici, Monsieur."

"Dommage," I said, and shifted the duck so that I could reach in my pockets. The first bill I came to was a crumpled ten-franc note, pink and soggy from the rain and, like all French paper money, about the size of a beach towel. If I sat down right there, I thought, and ordered a twenty-course meal, Johannes and Saulnay would still be waiting in the square when I finished, two against one.

"Dommage," I said again, shoved the ten-franc note in his apron, and from the couple's table picked up a wine bottle by the neck and smashed it against the wall.

Then I held up the jagged end of the bottle up so that anyone at all could see it, and stepped around the corner and into the rain again.

At the rue de Rivoli there were many more people on the street, shoppers laughing and walking in the rain, shoppers huddled under awnings, a little armada of shiny black umbrellas sailing up and down the sidewalk. I dropped the broken bottle in a trash can and heaved myself up onto the platform of a number 41 bus, going west.

The rue de Rivoli is the second or third longest street in Paris, and the 41 bus goes all the way down it to the end of the Tuileries. I made my way inside and squeezed into a seat on a wooden bench. I closed my eyes and wrapped my coat around the duck and tried to imagine the Bleeding Man in a cold Paris rain, the Bleeding Man in pursuit of me, running fast, catching up like a rocket, swinging gracefully onto the bus, never once, not for a moment, stumbling or losing his balance.

Because of a gyroscope, I suddenly thought, and opened my eyes to see Johannes sitting on the opposite bench.

Twenty-Six

PARISIAN BUSES IN 1926 WERE GREEN and yellow and divided, like all things in Gaul, into three parts. There was the open platform in the rear for standees; then a second-class section with wooden benches; then, separated by two vertical black wooden panels with leafy gold lettering, a first-class section that contained exactly 17 leather seats, a front door, and the driver's chair. By law nobody could be standing in either the first- or second-class sections when the bus started to move—you had to be in a seat—and there was always a ticket taker in a Napoleonic admiral's uniform ready to enforce it.

I leaned forward until my knees touched Johannes's.

"What's your last name?" I asked in French. "Is it Saulnay, like your uncle?" And then, even though I had told Bill Shirer I didn't speak it, I repeated the question in German.

His skin was less swarthy than I remembered it, washed out in the dim interior light of the bus to a milky blue, but up close, under the dirty wet jacket, the shoulders looked as broad and hard as a railroad tie. I saw the glint of something metallic in his belt. He smiled just enough to show two gold teeth.

"Johannes Saulnay."

"You can't have the duck, Johannes," I said in German again, then forgot the words for 'Get off the bus and go to hell,' though it didn't really matter, because at the sound of German being spoken half a dozen of our fellow passengers craned around and scowled, and the young woman next to Johannes actually drew her skirt up as if it were about to drag in the mud. The French had lost a thousand soldiers a day in the war. Nobody forgets a number like that.

Johannes wasn't interested in an international popularity contest. He said something rapid and guttural, the only words of which I understood were "for a higher good"—Das alte Gute—and spat on the floor, which was, I remembered, a very German thing to do.

Then he stood up and grabbed the lapels of my coat.

The bus was just then slowing for a turn. I shoved him back with the flat of my hand and in the same continuous motion stood up myself and walked into the first-class section.

Behind me the benches had erupted in a collective howl of disgust. In front of me the ticket taker shouted till he saw the coins in my hand. Then he waved me toward the last empty seat and positioned himself in the center of the aisle, between the two wooden panels.

There is something about a uniform to a German. Johannes was on his feet again by now, swaying with the bus, but the ticket taker, all gold braid and shiny leather cap, stretched a "Complet" sign across the doorway, folded his arms, and told him to sit down at once.

I had no illusions about the deterrent effect of a cardboard sign on a piece of rope. Ahead of the driver I could see the towers of the Hôtel de Ville. Alongside the bus, under my window, a long panoply of umbrellas, wet, multi-jointed like the carapace of a Chinese dragon, was unwinding along the sidewalk. You don't have to be Jacques de Vaucanson, I thought, to understand how a lever works. As the bus slowed again I shifted the duck in my hands, reached over the driver's shoulder, and pulled the front door open.

Out on the rue de Rivoli there was the usual bedlam of Paris traffic going in a thousand directions at the same time. For an instant I could see Johannes bulling forward, a blur of quilted jacket and shoulder, and the ticket taker tumbling backward. The driver was furiously wrenching the door closed again. Then the bus lurched forward and I was on my home ground, the center of Paris, the labyrinth I knew, and I gripped the terrified automate close with both hands and started to run.

Halfway to the place Vendôme I stopped in front of a closed hairdresser's window and stood for a long cautious minute. The window had a Josephine Baker doll for sale and a display of "Bakerfix" pomade for sale, but no Johannes Saulnay in the reflection.

I looked up and down the street. A passing car's yellow eyes crawled up the window and disappeared. The sky was a narrow gray stripe of cottony cloud. As long as you can see the sky, Norton-Griffiths used to say, you're not really in trouble. But I was.

It was nine-fifty-two on the dot when I spotted the stone-cold figure of Napoleon on the top of the column in the center of the place Vendôme, and two minutes after that when I walked under the big red awning and entered the lobby of the Ritz.

Around ten o'clock the lobby of the Ritz is almost always jammed—the late boat train from Le Havre gets in at nine, the "Mistral" and two or three others from the south of France rattle into the Gare de Lyon about the same time. Consequently steamer trunks and valises are piled everywhere, from the two revolving doors all the way to the last potted palm before the bar—suitcases, hat boxes, Moroccan portmanteaus, not to mention their train-weary owners, porters, valets, bellhops, and the higher class of pickpockets (the Ritz charged nine dollars a day minimum for a single room—I had no idea what they charged for a suite).

I wrapped my coat tighter around my own bedraggled baggage and navigated through a crowd of ermine collars and waterproof coats, wincing at the high-pitched skreaks and honks of English travelers braying at each other. If I—or the duck—had worn a monocle and top hat and spats, we might possibly have slipped through without anyone taking notice. As it was, however, heads turned disdainfully in my direction. My muddy shoes left a wet black trail across the blue Persian carpet, and over on the left, behind his golden cage one of the clerks looked up, recognized me, and frowned.

I gave a little salute and hurried on toward the elevators, which, then and now, were three in number and stood just opposite the dark noisy cave of mirrors that was the Ritz bar.

In fact, in those days the Ritz had two bars. The one on the left was small and undistinguished and reserved exclusively for gentlemen. The one on the right, where Root was a fixture, was brighter, often crowded with women, and served little plates of olives with their cocktails.

I took one step inside the one on the right and caught the eye of the bartender Frank, who shook his head. No Root tonight.

I turned and looked at the elevators. My pulse was finally slowing. My heart was no longer pounding my ribs like a hammer. But my duck was dripping rainwater and making a puddle. An exotic traveler in a green turban and turned-up slippers stared at me curiously. Root, I thought, would have laughed and showed him the duck and announced he had just arrived on the Canard Line. I wasn't Root.

An elevator door slid silently open and the operator's face peered out. I shook my head and started up the stairs on the right.

In the corridor on the first floor I paused at a window with a view of the place Vendôme down below. Its Christmas lights and banners swung and glittered in the rain, people standing by the Napoleon column in the center had champagne bottles and umbrellas. They may have been singing, but I couldn't be sure, because the Ritz insulates its corridors and rooms very well. I pulled the automate free of my coat and wiped its long springy neck with my sleeve and realized that I had no name for it, only Vaucanson's Duck, which seemed a feeble and inadequate thing to call something that had already caused—

My pulse might have been slowing, but my mind was still bumping wildly up and down, caroming like a pinball. I needed Root, I thought as I reached suite Eleven, I needed to get to a telephone, to a typewriter—I would call the police. If I could figure it out I would write one hell of a story for the *Trib*. I reached for the door handle and turned it. I would call the duck—

"Keats," said Mrs. Katharine McCormick as she swung the door majestically open.

Twenty-Seven

"YOU MAY COME IN, MR. KEATS. In-Tray," she added in her personal version of French, and swept the folds of her dress to one side and stepped back.

She was wearing a black hat with a wide brim and a wet feather, a jacket and long green traveling dress made of some stiff, heavy material I didn't recognize, steel wool probably, and, behind her jeweled lorgnette she was wearing an expression of severe and icy displeasure. On the coffee table sat a small Tartan carpetbag with a railroad tag tied to its clasp.

"He looks surprised," said Mrs. Gwenyth Crawford Gleeson from the couch.

"He looks guilty," said Elsie Short.

"That damned duck has nine lives," said Root. He was seated on a window divan behind the couch, overlooking the place Vendôme, and he raised an imaginary glass to me in a sardonic gesture of fellow feeling.

"Language, Mr. Root," said Mrs. McCormick and closed the door. "I would like to know, Mr. Keats, what precisely has been going on in my suite? What has been transpiring? This young woman"—her lorgnette dipped like a scepter toward Elsie—"has been telling me a most extraordinary tale."

"I thought," I said, gripping the duck in the crook of my arm, "that you were still in Nice, Mrs. McCormick, until Thursday."

"I telephoned the *Tribune* and told Editor Kospoth that I was returning early. He was to telephone you, both of you, to let you know."

"The Problem of Communication," said Elsie maliciously.

"She says," Mrs. McCormick placed her hat on the table and moved across the carpet toward the fireplace, where, as always when she was in residence, a little cairn of sea-coal was burning merrily on the grate. "She says that one or both of you told her that I had taken this wretched automat to Nice with me and that I was going to keep it for myself."

"Yes," I said. Elsie was standing at the far end of the couch, next to the seated Mrs. Gleeson. She was wearing a simple cotton dress of the kind you would buy off the rack at the Samaratine. It was navy blue, with a white belt and the big shoulder pads then in fashion, and a kind of chevron of pleats down one sleeve. Her blonde helmet of hair was sparkling, not with barnacles and jewels like Mrs. Gleeson's, but with a little lacework of crystal-like raindrops that must have been shaken out when she took off her hat. Her cheeks were flushed a bright healthy pink, no makeup, not even lipstick tonight. Her nose was small and pert and ordinary and next to her, I thought, all the other women in Paris were as plain as cabbages. "Yes, that's pretty much correct."

"Actually," Root said from the window, "I was the one who told her that. I remember it well. It was last week outside the *Trib* just after lunch—"

"Be quiet, Mr. Root." Mrs. McCormick inspected him through the lorgnette. "You would say that, of course, to help Mr. Keats. The two of you are inseparable, Heaven knows why, but you are only the follower and Keats is the moral and intellectual leader."

Root and I both stared at her in amazement.

She gave a brisk, imperial nod in the direction of Mrs. Gleeson. "That is what Bertie always says. 'Damaged goods,' he calls Keats, because of the War, he says. But not hopeless."

"Well, the automate is mine, thanks to nobody." Elsie stepped around the coffee table and held out her hand. "I've shown Mrs. McCormick the receipt," she said. I took a step backwards. "She knows all about the mix-up at the store and the murder and robbery and Mr. Edison's plans for the doll factory."

"Mr. Edison is a friend of Bertie's, you know."

"She doesn't want the duck," Elsie said. "But I do." I took another step backwards, and her face tilted and softened just as it had in the café when she told me I talked funny. "Toby?"

There was a rapid series of thumps behind me. Mrs. McCormick raised her palm for silence and turned with the slow majesty of a gunboat turret toward Root. Grumbling under his breath, he stood up and walked past Elsie, shrugged at me, and opened the door.

"A thousand times apologies for the delay," said somebody in professionally mangled English, and two young men in the gray Cossack uniforms of the Hôtel Ritz porters staggered in, lugging a small mountain of suitcases, clothes bags, and Christmas packages. Behind them, in correct evening dress and carrying nothing, came a Ritz functionary of the management caste.

"In there," said Mrs. McCormick, pointing to the bedroom door, and indicated to the rest of us with a nod and a pursing of her lips that we should all remain in mute and frozen tableau while the servants were present.

"When were you in Alsace?" I said to Elsie Short.

"What?"

"Mr. Keats," intoned Mrs. McCormick, my boss's mother and owner of one quarter of the *Chicago Tribune*, Paris edition.

"When were you in Alsace?" I said. "You told me you'd just

arrived in Europe, but Henri Saulnay said you had come to his farm, you talked to him about Jacques Vaucanson—"

"Saulnay," she said, and grabbed for the duck.

Behind her now the two porters were craning their necks in curiosity, management was frowning. Mrs. Gleeson bolted up like a catapult.

"Keats!" cried Mrs. McCormick. "Give her that ridiculous toy!"

"No."

"Give it to her!"

"No." The person who had Vaucanson's Duck was going to be directly in the path of Henri Saulnay and his thuggish nephew, and I had fought many more Germans than Elsie Short. The person who had Vaucanson's Duck—

"Toby!"

Root held Elsie's arms while Mrs. McCormick advanced toward me, flames shooting out of her eyes.

"Give her the goddam duck!" Root cried. At which point Elsie broke free, the porter behind her toppled sideways in an avalanche of luggage, and I pulled open the door and took French leave.

At the bottom of the stairs I threw one glance toward the crowded lobby and then ran straight ahead, into the gentlemen's bar.

A waiter leapt out of my way, the bartender shouted. I dashed out the side exit and into the cold, dark street.

It was the rue Cambron, some idiotic part of my mind remembered, and it ran three short blocks north and south, toward nowhere in particular. Both sides of it were lined with parked cars and delivery vans. I turned automatically right, heading in the general direction of the rue Lamartine and the *Trib,* where I might or might not still have a job, and started to trot along the sidewalk, weaving in and out of the parked cars. The rain had stopped completely, but the wind was still shrieking up and down the street. Far overhead it had punched and torn the night sky into a ragbag of frayed clouds and frozen stars.

I heard the bar door slamming open and voices calling my name. I swerved right at the first corner I came to, looked back for a heartbeat over my shoulder—and ran headlong into Johannes.

Vaucanson's Duck flew out of my hands like a ball. As I fell to the pavement, I saw it tumbling in the wind. It smacked into a puddle under a street lamp, head bobbing frantically, one brass wing flapping.

For an instant everything was what Mrs. McCormick had wanted—a mute, fixed tableau. I lay sprawled on my chest on the sidewalk, my empty right hand stretched out in front. To one side, balanced on a knee and a fist, Johannes was staring at the duck. To my left a tramp sat on a bench with a wine bottle halfway to his mouth. Two yards ahead the duck tumbled over one last time in Edisonian slow motion and landed on his feet.

And Johannes took three quick steps and scooped him up.

By the time I scrambled to my own feet Johannes was thirty yards away. I saw him dodge around a knot of people coming out of a restaurant. I felt blood on my cheek, heard blood pounding like a cannon in my ears. I was the ultimate automaton, I was the Bleeding Man. I dropped my shoulders and charged straight forward, through the same knot of shouting people, over a curb, off a lamppost—we were on the boulevard des Capucines, I realized, wide, bright, horrible, dancing with Christmas lights and banners, swarming with cars and taxis.

Ahead, rising up like a steamship from a sea of light, was an enormous green and white facade—he was running for the Opéra, he was going to lose me in the great crowd of Christmas revelers and opera goers now streaming out of its six golden doorways, flooding the sidewalks and street.

I watched Johannes disappear behind a taxi. Over the boom-

boom-boom of my bleeding ear I heard a gendarme's whistle. Amazingly, even as my legs pumped up and down, I somehow swept my gaze left to right across my whole field of vision, going up and down by systematic quadrants just the way they had trained me, just the way you did when you were trapped in a tunnel and had to find your target. And at that moment Johannes bounced into sight again and dashed to his right and I saw that it wasn't the Opéra he was running for after all, but the Métro.

It was too much. After everything else—after Elsie, after Saulnay, Mrs. McCormick, the rain and the cold and the wind—it was far too much.

There was light behind me, light all around me, moving, floating, pushing away the night air. But at the bottom of the Métro entrance, twenty feet down a set of wet and slippery concrete steps, I could see green wooden doors and behind them . . . and behind them, I thought. I stopped on the topmost step and gripped the handrail. Behind the green doors there would be no light, behind them there would be the long black throat of the Métro tunnel. Facilis descensus Averno. Not ever, I thought. Not ever again.

I took one step down.

Just in front, Johannes turned and looked back at me.

I took a second step, trembling from head to toe like a man in a fever, and lurched for the duck. It was too wet and slick for either of us to hold, and it went skidding out of my fingers onto the ground, between the legs and feet of the crowd coming out of the doors. Johannes's face turned hard and flat, and he yanked the metallic glinting thing out of his belt, which some crazed part of my mind noted was a Webley .38-caliber officer's pistol, the kind the British had used in the War.

I heard people scream, and I must have seen him snarl and step toward me, but by then my thoughts had shut down, my feet had stopped.

I forced myself one more step back into the War and felt

the tears running down my cheek, the Weeping Man, and then Johannes, too scornful and cruel to waste a bullet, clubbed me three times in the skull and face with the barrel of his gun, slowly, casually, as one might slap a coward, and I rolled over and over down the steps and hit the doors with a sob.

When I opened my eyes it was starting to rain again and a policeman in the only city I had ever loved was shaking my shoulder and Waverley Root was wobbling into focus just as before, holding the shattered pieces of Vaucanson's Duck in his hands.

"Damaged goods," I said, and then I was gone.

PART FOUR

On the Rue Jacob

Twenty-Eight

IN THE ARMY WE USED TO CUT OFF the suspenders of captured German soldiers, so that they had to use both hands to hold up their pants and couldn't run away.

Something like that, I assumed, must have been in the minds of the good Sisters who ran the little Hôpital Franco-Britannique out on the rue Barbès in Neuilly, where the French police had finally taken me on the night of December 22nd and where, for the first three days, they dressed me in a knee-length blue hospital gown with no underwear and only paper slippers for my feet. Not that I was going anywhere.

Ordinarily, of course, with Root and Elsie on the scene and my *Tribune* press card in my pocket, the police would have carted me off to the American Hospital about a mile down the road from the Franco-Britannique, where there was undoubtedly a bulk-rate contract for concussed reporters. But the American Hospital had been closed since October for renovations.

Actually, I didn't mind the Franco-Britannique at all. It was small and had an interior garden laid out in the bristly concentric geometric patterns the French find so soothing. It also had a library and a "Letter Room" looking out on the garden that reminded me of the "Talbot Service House" we used to go to in Ypres, a sprawling Belgian mansion that the Reverend Tubby Clayton of Oxford had bought with his own money and fitted out for soldiers on leave from the trenches. The Service House was open to both officers and enlisted men—the Reverend Tubby had placed a sign over the door: "Abandon All Rank, All Ye Who Enter Here"—and had a piano, a laundry, and a room where you could use an actual toilet, and I had spent three days there (not in the toilet) in the spring of 1916, not long after we blew up Messines Ridge.

"'Some days in Paris it failed to snow,'" muttered Root, which I took to be a revision of his unpublished story. He eased himself into a roomy leather chair and handed me a folded copy of the *Trib.* "I see they finally trusted you with a razor."

It was late morning, January 5, 1927—I had more or less slept through Christmas and New Year's, like Rip van Winkle—and out in the garden it was indeed snowing lightly. I was abruptly put in mind of the day in April 1918 when a freak blizzard had swept over the forward lines, and while I was down on my hands and knees repairing a pump, a troop of Brits came marching by in the snow and singing the Eton Song, "Jolly Boating Weather."

Enough with the war, I thought. Kospoth is right, the goddam war is over. "Stitches coming out tomorrow," I told him, and tapped the fat white bandage under my left eye. It's surprising how much damage the barrel of a pistol can do when somebody swings it full force into the side of your head. The first time Johannes had hit me, in the alley outside the Ritz where he tried to steal the duck, he had just given me a headache. This time he had left me with a mildly fractured skull, a shattered cheekbone below my eye socket that had taken the surgeons an hour and a half to repair, and a harsh off-and-on buzzing sound in one ear for which the euphonious French word was tintement.

"And by the way, you owe me dinner, Biff." Root took the paper out of my hand and pointed to an article halfway down page 3, "Annual Quat'z Arts Bal in Montmartre." This had taken place on New Year's Eve, when an expatriate American playboy named Harry Crosby had rented a dance hall near the Closerie des Lilas and one of the bare-breasted art students had been seen wearing a live snake around her arm and a necklace of dead pigeons. Herol Egan had written the story, and I had bet Root fifty francs that Kospoth wouldn't print the word "nipple." In fact, as I saw now, he had only cut "dead pigeons."

I grunted and turned to the front page, where I learned, first, that nobody knew yet whether Calvin Coolidge the Silent was going to run for a third presidential term next year—he refused to say—and second, that the young American aviator Charles Lindbergh had put off his transatlantic flight attempt till May.

I leaned back and read while Root got up and wandered around the Letter Room in his usual restless, bear-in-a-cabin manner, picking up books and putting them back, turning an empty ashtray upside down to read the label on the bottom. At the door he made a kind of semaphore signal with his hands that he was going to find coffee for us, and I turned back to the window. In the center of the garden were two stone cupids squirting water into a basin, and a great stone turtle between them. All of them wore the green patina of a Paris winter, and they were gradually disappearing behind a veil of blowing snow.

Johannes and Henri Saulnay had also disappeared behind a veil of something, though that wasn't news I would find in the paper. That, in fact, I had learned from Criminal Inspector Serge Soupel, he of the bushy eyebrows and the affair of the late Patrice Bassot. He had come out to the Franco-Britannique the day after New Year's, looking grim and red-nosed, and had spent two and a half hours, until the nurses sent him away. Most of the time he had rubbed his temples and smoked Gauloises and poked a stubby, impatient finger at implausibilities in my official statement. Who, he wondered scornfully, would go to the trouble to purloin a beat-up, non-functioning, antique children's toy—a shitting duck, of all things? Much less, kill a harmless old man for it, not to mention assault a foreign journalist, in public view, on the steps of the Métro?

But then, he had sighed, it was true enough that Johannes and Henri Saulnay had completely disappeared. The toymaker's workshop on the rue des Minimes in the Marais had been closed down, abandoned in a hurry, evidently. A pair of French girls who came in to do the sewing for the toys' dresses had been left to their own devices, without a sou. Nobody had given a forwarding address, nobody knew where Saulnay might have gone, though the German police were supposed to be looking into it at their end.

"Not that they'll expend much energy on the murder of a French citizen." Soupel had ground out his last cigarette on a coffee saucer and started to gather his papers. "And anyway, Henri Saulnay is a decorated veteran of the army, and you know how the Germans are about the army. I doubt they even started a file, if you want my opinion."

I stood up, listened to the faint little sounds of gunfire and tracer bullets tintementing in my ear, and braced myself on the chair.

"He's probably crazy from the war," Soupel added. When I didn't say anything, he snapped his briefcase closed and told me that his grandfather used to say the best cure for depression was to look at large animals, like elephants or hippopotami.

"I'll head for the zoo," I promised, "just as soon as they let me out of here. Meanwhile, I guess Saulnay could be anywhere? He and Johannes?"

Inspector Soupel wrapped his scarf twice around his collar. "They could be anywhere at all," he agreed. He picked up his case and turned toward the door. "They could still be right here in Paris."

When Root came back with the coffee and a cribbage board, it was past eleven, the snow had stopped, and I was lightly dozing, dreaming of large depression-busting animals, a chorus line of hippopotami grinning cheek to cheek. I have some memory of his wheeling me in a chair back to my room, easing me into bed. One of the nurses came in with my morning dose of eye of newt and toe of frog and I asked, apparently, about the forthcoming wedding of Bill Shirer and Elsie Short. I fell asleep, Root told me later, muttering about their children, who would all be automatons or duck-stepping Germans.

On the seventh of January, Kospoth himself came out to the hôpital with a bottle of cognac and a cowboy novel he had picked up in one of the bookstalls along the Seine, which he thought would remind me of happy trails in New Mexico.

Elsie Short had evidently come by the hôpital three different times while I was still too sedated to know her, then she was whisked away by Vincent and Mrs. Armus on a Christmas trip to Normandy. From there she had sent a nine-page letter which alternated between blaming me for deceiving her about Mrs. McCormick and the duck and hoping sincerely that I wouldn't need any more operations, though she was surprised, she couldn't help adding, that anybody as thick-headed as I was could have a fractured skull.

By the eleventh of January I was back in my flat on the rue du Dragon. By the thirteenth, which was Friday, I was back at my desk on the *Trib*, catching up on the Gumps. And by the evening of the sixteenth I was sitting in a tiny restaurant called Chez Paulette at the end of the rue Vavin, over by the Luxembourg Gardens, watching Elsiedale Short, Ph.D., trying to decipher the backward-slanting, nearly illegible green and purple hieroglyphics of Paulette's handwriting on the mimeographed menu.

"I give up," she said, and passed it over to me. "You order.

Libby always lets Mr. Armus order for her. She says it's important to keep the male ego occupied."

The restaurant had only eight or nine tables, all of them empty but ours, so Paulette herself was hovering beside us, setting out a bottle of Beaujolais and a pair of almost clean glasses. I pointed to the sweetbreads and farmer's salad, and she nodded twice and hurried away.

"I think it was Thomas Edison himself, your boss, who actually invented the mimeograph machine."

"He did. I found a nice doll for him in Normandy, by the way, and I think he's going to pay a commission on it. But I'm still going to let you pay for dinner tonight."

"Very correct of you."

"Because I'm still poor, and I'm also still mad at you for hiding my duck and lying about it and getting yourself broken to pieces and scaring us all like that."

"Are you still staying with Vincent Armus?"

"And worse yet, you got my duck broken to pieces too. Don't change the subject, Toby Keats. I'm staying at their apartment, yes, but she's gone back to New York for a visit and he's in London."

I leaned back and let Paulette arrange the two heaping plates of farmer's salad and then take the wine bottle out of my hands and fuss with it. Elsie sat straight in her chair with her head tilted slightly to one side in the way she had, watching Paulette intensely, also in the way she had. She was wearing a pale orange sweater with no collar and a pleated brown tweed skirt with a shiny leather belt—you don't live in Paris without noticing women's clothes— and her short blonde helmet of hair was neatly trimmed, with only a few stray rebellious tendrils around her cheeks. The sweater was tight, in the reckless fashion of the 1920s, and clung to her curves like the skin of a peach, and I found it hard to think of her as a terrier anymore.

"We need to talk," I said as she bent over her salad.

"We are talking."

"About Henri Saulnay and the Bleeding Man." I pushed my plate to one side and thought of Root and Captain Ahab and why "single-minded" was a better word than "obsessive." "And the gyroscope."

At which exact moment, with a deafening blast of noise and cold air, Waverley Root sat down beside me.

Then Bill Shirer, young and drunk, on my left, and Herol Egan with two cigarettes in his mouth next to Elsie, then Kospoth, two more reporters from the day shift, a couple of French girls from Atlantic & Pacific Photos, and three or four more people I would never actually be introduced to.

It was, Root explained with a kind of asthmatic whoop, a party in honor of Shirer, who was going to pay for the wine for the entire evening—he picked up my glass, took a sip, made a face, and held up his hand for Paulette, while Herol Egan pulled both of his cigarettes out of his mouth and offered Elsie her choice. Before we knew it, I had been bustled two chairs down to my right, squeezed between the day reporters and one of the strangers, Kospoth was showing Elsie a photograph of his son, and Paulette and a red-faced waiter were distributing bottles of champagne.

Gradually, as the little restaurant filled with *Tribune* staffers, and people moved, shouting, from table to table, I learned via Root that Bill Shirer had in fact, while I was lounging in Neuilly, been offered a job at the rival *Herald,* but only that afternoon the Colonel, back in Chicago, had cabled a counter-offer with a raise of ten dollars a month and a guaranteed transfer in a year to the Berlin Bureau.

Somewhere during the soup course (our salads and sweetbreads having long ago disappeared), Shirer himself repeated the story and showed me the cable. Then Kospoth stood on a chair and made a toast, more champagne arrived, and the talk, as it always did at a *Trib* party, turned to shop.

I made my way back down the row of tables and reclaimed my chair across from Elsie, just in time to hear Root begin to explain his theories of literature.

"I have begun," he told her solemnly, wagging his glass in front of his nose, "a three-part demolition, starting in Friday's paper, of Dr. William Lyon Phelps, who has made an idiotic list of the hundred best novels in the world."

"He teaches at Yale." Elsie matched him in solemnity. "English literature."

"I wrote—if I may quote myself in advance—" Root said, "'It is a sad commentary on the state of criticism in America that a gentleman respected for his learning should be able to sit down at his desk and soberly, seriously list *Lorna Doone* as one of the world's best novels.'"

"Not soberly," I said.

"Do you know Mr. Hemingway?" Elsie asked him, in apparent innocence.

"Hemingway is a writer," Root said, and held out his glass for more champagne, "with an inexhaustible ability to repeat himself."

"Root sometimes writes fiction," I contributed.

"I used to write poetry," he said sadly, "till I showed some of it to my father and he handed it back the next day and said, 'You don't do much of this, I hope?'"

There was more in this vein, two glasses more at least, and then Shirer stood up at the other end of the row of tables, and proposed a toast to his alma mater, Coe College in Iowa, and afterwards the room fell into one of those abrupt, profound silences that happen in even the noisiest of parties.

That was the point at which one of the day shift men leaned out across his table and called down to me. "So tell us why you're scared of the Métro, Keats."

The room, if anything, grew quieter still. I could hear the faint clink and rattle of pans in the kitchen, Shirer wheezing, the blood slowly draining out of my skin. Up and down the tables faces turned to me, or in the case of Kospoth turned away. Elsie stared at me.

"Why the hell," said the day shift man, "won't you ride the damn thing? Most convenient transportation in the world, the Métro is. I hear you won't even buy a ticket."

"The Paris Métro," Root said, "was begun in 1898, which was later than London and New York, which both had subways from the 1870s on—"

"Kospoth told me," the day shift man interrupted. He was more than a little drunk and glowering and smirking at the same time. "Kospoth told me you were afraid of the dark. When the electricity's off you won't even go down to the basement, a grown man."

"No, he won't," said one of the French girls from the photo office. "I've seen him start down there and then turn around."

Root was tall and slender, but he possessed unusual strength in his arms and shoulders, and he suddenly stood up and slammed his right hand down on the table so hard that the silverware jumped and Elsie gasped. "In the bloody fucking war," he said, "this guy spent two days buried underground in a collapsed tunnel with four corpses, one of them German, only they weren't corpses the first day and he won't ever say what happened or what it was like. He spent two days buried alive with dead men. In a two-foot-high tunnel, a hundred feet underground. He volunteered to go down to rescue them. He volunteered to rescue them." Root looked at Kospoth. "The British gave him the Victoria Cross for crawling down into that goddam tunnel, so if he doesn't want to go underground anymore and ride the goddam Métro, you can let it pass, all of you, you can just give it a fucking miss."

He looked up and down the silent row of tables, then carefully lowered himself into his chair. He wiped his perspiring face with a handkerchief and reached for a bottle. "I like red Burgundy with fish," he said, "if nobody objects."

Twenty-Nine

VAUCANSON'S DUCK—OR THE SEVERAL PIECES of it that were left after my tug-of-war with Johannes—was all this time back in the possession of the Paris Police. Evidence, once again, of a crime.

On his visit to the hôpital in Neuilly, I had asked Inspector Soupel to return it to me. But Soupel had only pinched his eyebrows together and explained that, since the death of Patrice Bassot was now under reinvestigation, the police had no intention of releasing evidence.

Evidence of what? I had asked, sounding exactly like Elsie Short. But he had only tamped his pipe and given an imperturbable Gallic shrug.

It took, in the end, one of the French lawyers that the *Trib* kept on retainer to loosen their grip, and even then, Soupel told me sternly, the said duck was still technically in the custody of the city of Paris. But Colonel McCormick's name carried a great deal of weight in France. (The Colonel himself knew absolutely nothing about the duck or my misadventure at the Métro; and Mrs. McCormick, after sending me a get-well potted aster, had hurried off to London with Gwyneth Crawford Gleeson to rest her nerves).

Which was how it happened that on the 23rd of January, around five in the afternoon, I signed six different kinds of receipt-and-disclaimer, and Soupel handed me a box wrapped in shiny brown oil-paper, pretty much the size and shape of the package I had taken out of the Ritz seven weeks ago. It was raining steadily, just as before, and outside his office Parisian traffic was in its usual state of mechanized lunacy. But this time, I took a number 92 bus, slipped across the Seine without being cudgeled or followed, and carried my duck safely home to the rue du Dragon.

Three hours later, at exactly ten minutes past eight, I climbed the stairs to the penthouse floor of number 8 rue Jean Carriès. For a long moment I simply stood in the hallway, thinking. Shifted my package from arm to arm. Walked to the window and studied the trees below on the Champ-de-Mars, smoking in the rain like true Parisians. At fourteen minutes past eight I raised my hand and knocked at the door.

Even if Vincent Armus and his wife were far away, Nigel the butler and chaperon was very much in. He opened the door almost at once, murmured sardonically "Mr. Hearst," and without another word escorted me down the hall, past the Yale medallion on the wall and the empty living room with the rhomboidal Art Déco furniture.

In the Collection Room the fish tanks were still in place, their golden denizens flickering back and forth in, as Natalie Barney had said, strangely noiseless life. On the right, the painted metallic birds and banjo players and clowns sat on their rows of black pedestals, unmoving. Off to one side of the clowns, Elsie Short, very much alive, sat behind a folding worktable covered with two rows of what looked like surgical instruments.

"You brought it!"

"I brought what's left of it."

Because I was now working full-time again, with assignments and deadlines every day, I hadn't actually seen or spoken to Elsie—with the exception of one brief telephone call—since our aborted dinner at Paulette's, four long days ago. She bounded around the table and liberated the package from my arm. "Nigel—would you mind getting us another chair? And some coffee?"

Nigel looked hard at me and made a silent exit. Meanwhile Elsie was clearing a space among the tools and then carefully, sheet by sheet, pulling the oil-paper apart.

When everything was spread out and neatly arranged under the overhead light, she leaned back and gripped the edge of the table with both hands. "Ruined," she said flatly. "Wrecked, a mess. I can't stand it."

I resisted the urge to tell Nigel that she was talking about the automate, not me. He set out two cups and a pot with quick, flickering gestures, noiseless as the fish in the tank, and left us again.

"Ruined," she repeated. "Look at that—a dozen pieces at least, both feet detached, the head and the neck over here. This is the right wing, I have no idea what this is."

Elsie was far better with her hands than I was. My maternal grandmother had been like that. She had repaired everything in her house herself—my grandfather was a lawyer and limited his manual labor to trimming the nibs of his writing pens—and in my memory she is always bending over the workbench in the little screened alcove next to her kitchen, usually with a broken pot or pan on it and a fistful of wrenches and pliers. Briefly, memorably, Elsie looked like that. With grandfatherly dignity I sat back and poured us both coffee.

"Armus told me he repairs his own automates," I said. "That's an impressive set of tools."

"He's very clever. He fixes all of them."

"The duck still belongs to me," I said. "Legally speaking. Or semi-legally. I signed for it at the Préfecture."

"Vincent knows lots of lawyers." Her left hand picked up a tiny blade. The other hand fit a wing in a slot. "If you're going to be tedious, Toby Keats, he could have them draw up a partnership for us. We could have joint custody until Mr. Edison sends his lawyers. Just like a divorced couple."

I spooned sugar into my cup and watched her work. Four nights ago at Paulette's I had gotten as far as saying the word "gyroscope" to her, but it had been completely drowned out by Shirer's party coming in. Elsie hadn't even heard it. To this moment, "gyroscope" remained my own flea in my ear.

"The other evening," I said, clearing my throat, "just before all Bedlam and Parnassus was let out, I was about—"

Abruptly, I stopped and looked around the room.

Vincent Armus didn't know about Vaucanson's real Duck and the Bleeding Man—so Elsie had insisted. Nobody did, she said, except the two of us and probably Henri Saulnay. Even Root didn't know about the Bleeding Man. Whatever she and I might be thinking, the rest of the world believed the duck was a Robert Houdin replica that Elsie was trying to deliver in one piece to the Edison Doll Company.

But Vincent Armus was different. He was a knowledgeable collector of automates, and a greedy, troubling man, and this was his house, his remarkably expensive apartment. The perfectly balanced organism, the one who would survive the war, Norton-Griffiths used to say, was silent. I started my sentence over.

"I'm still not sure I have the sequence right."

"What sequence?" Elsie scarcely looked up.

"You really do work for Thomas Edison?"

"I really do work for Thomas Edison. And I really am writing a book about automates, though I haven't got very far with it. It's based on my dissertation. As you know."

"So when exactly did you meet Saulnay?"

She fit the second wing into the torso and gently turned the duck's right foot in the proper direction. Then she lifted the tail and fanned it partly open. It didn't look like a wreck at all to me.

"I actually came over here to Europe," Elsie said slowly, feeling for a tool without looking. "I came over to Europe in November, if you must know, when it was clear I wouldn't get a teaching job in New York. So I took Mr. Edison's offer and I went to Germany first, because the Germans make the best dolls, even better dolls than the French. I don't hate the Germans. I wasn't in the war, Toby."

"And that was where you saw him."

"Before the war Henri Saulnay was a well-known toy manufacturer. I never imagined anything else about him. I thought he might still have a few old doll models that he'd never put into production, so I went to his family's farm, it's near Metz, because he was back there on some kind of business. I spent a day and he drove me over and showed me what was left of his factory, which was bombarded and destroyed in a battle—he was incredibly bitter—and we talked about dolls and Mr. Edison and automates. When he told he would be back in Paris in December, I thought he would be a good person to help with my talk. End of sequence."

"Is it Vaucanson's Duck?"

"What's left of it," she said. "Maybe. Probably. All the king's horses and all the king's men couldn't put this together again." She turned the duck's torso upside down and a piece of greenish metal tubing fell out of the open space where, back in the Ritz, I had loosened the plate.

Elsie Short's best feature, Root had told me, was her eyes. Not too big, not too small. They were Delft china blue, sincere and transparent as the day was long. You could see her thoughts like the clouds in the sky.

"If it's the duck," I reminded her, "something about it is connected to the Bleeding Man. Why would Vaucanson buy back the duck in his old age and leave it to his daughter?"

She made a face at the metal tubing. "I have no idea. You know, somebody searched my hôtel room when I was in Metz. I thought it was the maid. But it happened again in Paris, the same day I found Bassot's shop, and I got truly scared. I was afraid some other collector might have seen it first. It never occurred to me that it could have been Henri Saulnay."

"And he came back later to the store with his nephew, to steal it."

"So it was just good luck, as it worked out, that I didn't have enough cash to pay for it then."

"Not for Patrice Bassot."

"Well, no." She lowered her head solemnly and tried reattaching the neck to the torso. With one wing already firmly in place and both feet on the table, it was looking more and more like the ghostly duck in Eric the Minor's photographs. Automatically I felt in my jacket pocket for them, but it was the wrong jacket. I had sent my brown tweed coat to the cleaners the morning I came back from Neuilly.

"And I was truly scared, too," she said, "that other time, right out there at the front door to this apartment, after the party, when you said the Duck knows the way to the Bleeding Man. I was amazed you said that. Because that's what I wonder too. I wonder if that very strange and secretive person Jacques de Vaucanson did finally build the Bleeding Man. And if he did, would he have hidden it somewhere also very strange and put the key to the hiding place in this . . . this—" She looked at the duck and made an exasperated hissing sound, like a wet thumb on a stove.

The duck balanced precariously on its warped feet and did its best to look nonchalantly back at her, but it was headless, of course. Its crown and neck lay directly between its feet on the table, surrounded by more tiny copper tubes, some redundant cogs, broken springs.

"I cannot believe he hid it in this horrible duck," she said, and off to my right, in the clear, glassy silence of the room, there was a metallic whir and a click and I stood suddenly bolt upright, and the Man-in-the-Moon clown slowly raised his walking stick and began to chuckle.

"It's only a toy," she said, and put her hand on my arm.

*   *   *

By eleven-thirty the duck was still less than half assembled—or reassembled. Even Elsie was starting to yawn, and I was rubbing the back of my neck and thinking of how soon I needed to be back at the *Trib* for the morning shift.

Conspicuously, without comment, I retrieved the duck's packing box from the floor and put it on the table.

Elsie stopped in mid-yawn and frowned at the box. "I'm not finished," she said. "We're not finished. We're not even close to being finished. Putting this back together could take days, if we can do it at all."

"Well, we can't leave it here out on a table, for people to see."

"You mean for Vincent to see."

"According to Inspector Soupel"—I picked up the still detached head and neck while she drummed her fingers on the table—"Saulnay or Johannes could still be in Paris. The police aren't looking very hard. And Henri still wants the duck. And right now except for a sixty-year-old butler you're here all alone."

"But the duck will be much, much safer," she said in a voice dripping with sarcasm, "in a one-room flat on the rue de Beast in the custody of a man with no lock on the door and a hole in his head who's already managed to lose the little dear twice."

I turned the duck's head around in my palm till one small black eye was staring up at me. Maybe it would wink. "Madame Serboff has a locked room in the basement that she keeps for storage. It's not the Métro. It has a light. I go down there without any problems. I have a key. You could come and visit the duck whenever you wanted."

"How very kind."

I stood by the table holding the box and said nothing. She paced to the fish tanks and back. "I have to do work on my Normandy doll for Mr. Edison tomorrow morning."

"I can leave the key with Madame Serboff."

She made her face flat and hard. "If you lose it again—"

"I'm a dead duck," I said, and she kept her face rigid for another five seconds before she started to laugh.

At the front door of the apartment Nigel squeezed between us and walked a few steps down the hallway to push the button for the elevator.

"When do the Armuses come back?" I asked Elsie.

"In two days."

"Mr. Armus returns Thursday afternoon." Nigel squeezed past us in the other direction and held the door open for Elsie. "At four o'clock from London." When neither of us moved, he coughed and disappeared discreetly back into the apartment. At the other end of the landing the pulleys and cables at the top of the elevator shaft began to spin back and forth like demented gyroscopes.

"The duck may or may not know the way to the Bleeding Man," I said slowly. "The way it's broken now, we may never find out. But I'm a reporter. I like to go back to why. Why does Saulnay want the Bleeding Man? And why does he want it so much that he would actually kill somebody for it? Two somebodies if you count me."

"Because of the money, of course." Elsie shook her head. "He's after the money, not the academic glory, like me. Not that I would turn the money down."

"The money," I said stupidly, forcing my mind back.

"If collectors would pay five thousand dollars for the real Vaucanson's Duck," Elsie said, "imagine what they'd pay for the long-lost Bleeding Man. You said it yourself in that little café. And remember Saulnay was ruined in the war, he lost his factory and all his money, and his business has never recovered." She cocked her head. "Or do you still belong to the School of No Single Explanation?"

Root claims to be working on a book he's going to call *An American Guide to European Kissing.* The rules, he says, are complex, and if you don't understand them you can wind up looking like a plouc, which is French for "redneck." Italians, for example, kiss each other three times whenever they meet, men and women, once at least in the air with a maximum of noise. German men usually don't kiss a woman's face, but bend over her hand and kiss their own thumb. The French kiss an older woman twice on the cheeks, a younger woman up to four times, depending on the degree of familiarity and the proximity of a husband. The English shake hands.

"You don't really trust me," said Elsie Short in a quiet, rueful voice, "do you, Toby Keats?"

Rules, I thought, are made to be broken, and I touched her lips with one finger as lightly as I could and leaned forward. When she finally drew back, her face was flushed.

"You kiss funny," she said, and she stepped behind the door and pulled it shut with a click.

The elevator had already come and gone again by then. I wasn't going to take it anyway, but I stared at the closed door for a moment, then walked over and stabbed the electric button twice, just as Nigel had done, and watched the wheels begin to turn and the cables move. The little elevator car slid noiselessly up the shaft. I closed my eyes and pinched the bridge of my nose with two fingers and then turned and walked the eight steps back to Vincent Armus's door. Elsie opened it at my first knock.

"And if he's not after the money?" I said.

Thirty

THE GYROSCOPE WAS INVENTED IN PARIS in 1852 by a French scientist named Jean Bernard Léon Foucault.

In Foucault's version the gyroscope was really little more than an amusing novelty, a clever variation on a child's spinning top. I had played with one myself as a boy and remembered the bright chromium frame and the almost hypnotic whir of the spin. Nobody knew how Foucault had come up with the idea, although the Grand Larousse suggested that it was probably devised as a supplement to his famous "Foucault's Pendulum" experiment that demonstrated (to the few skeptics who remained) the rotation of the earth on its axis.

In its original form, and for fifty years afterwards, the gyroscope consisted simply of a frame around a metal wheel, which wheel moved in turn around a vertical spin axis. If you set the wheel spinning, no matter how you tilted or turned its frame, angular momentum would keep the wheel pointing in the direction you had first chosen.

But you can't stop progress. Bigger gyroscopes with electric motors and gimbals were quickly put to work in the war. The gimbals were metal rings that circled the gyroscope and kept it horizontal. At first the Germans used these giant devices to keep their warships on course in rough weather. And then toward the end of the war they used them to stabilize their biggest artillery, especially the Big Bertha cannons, only by now everybody was calling the device a gyrocompass. In 1917 the British and Americans started to use them to aim the gun batteries on their battleships, because those guns could fire a shell the size of a suitcase that would fly almost fourteen miles. And while the ship's deck was rocking and swaying in the water you wanted to keep your barrels always pointed precisely in the same direction, for maximum accuracy and destruction.

These were no children's toys. On a battleship you had a master gyrocompass, about the size of a very large desk, run by a nearby motor and linked to a series of ordinary compasses that sent signals back to it from the deck, the rudder, the engine room, all the arms and legs, so to speak, of the ship.

The problem, as everybody acknowledged, was how to make the gyroscope smaller. Before the war an American engineer named Elmer Sperry, who would later found a company called Sperry Rand, had built a gyroscope that could fit into a wheelbarrow—he tried to sell it to the Barnum and Bailey Circus for a high-wire tightrope act. But that was as small as anybody had gotten.

Why did you want a smaller gyrocompass anyway?

The obvious reason was so you could install one in an airplane. Mr. Charles Lindbergh, for example, was planning, as everybody knew, to fly from New York to Paris without stopping. He would dearly love to have a gyroscope that would stabilize his airplane in the wind and turbulence over the Atlantic and guide it safely to its faraway destination.

Another reason to have a smaller gyroscope, a reason that was slowly dawning on a few progressive military thinkers, was so that it could guide one of Professor Goddard's liquid-fuelled exploding rockets to a target.

*   *   *

"Now the interesting fact about J.B.L. Foucault," I said, and lifted my glass to salute the silent but attentive books on the top of my case. "The interesting fact about J.B.L. Foucault is that he was the grandson of Hervé Foucault. And Hervé Foucault was Jacques de Vaucanson's most loyal and trusted assistant. Are you following this?"

The books maintained their pose of polite attention.

"He was also," I said, "as I have pointed out to Miss Elsiedale Short, the lover of Vaucanson's flighty daughter, so smitten that he followed her to Alsace when she left her husband, and there they lived together in unwedded bliss for twenty years until death did them part."

The books frowned in concentration.

"The same daughter," I said, "to whom Vaucanson bequeathed, oddly and mysteriously, his celebrated duck."

It was five-thirty in the morning now, not quite five hours since I had left Elsie Short at Vincent Armus's apartment. I looked at the brown box on my desk, and poured myself another glass of what Root liked to call one's "breakfast wine," a lesser Chablis in this case. The room was freezing cold, as was the wine, and would be until Madame Serboff turned on the heat about nine o'clock. But I had gotten up out of a warm bed early, partly because my head hurt and my ears were ringing, mostly because, full-time working journalist that I was again, I still owed B. J. Kospoth the second installment of my article on French automates and children's toys. The first part had appeared a few days earlier, to the journalistic equivalent of a massive yawn— two columns of dutiful prose about Gustave Bontems and Vincent Armus, Greek and Egyptian dolls, the cuckoo clock.

"Put some goddam zing in it," Kospoth had muttered, and so

I had now written six more pages covering Vaucanson's Excreting Duck, his Flute Player, and the "Theater of Automates" at the Conservatory where Elsie had talked. Not a syllable, of course, about the Bleeding Man. Nobody in the *Trib*'s readership would be interested in scholarly speculation about two eighteenth-century hypochondriacs—I could hear the Colonel's sardonic, dismissive voice all the way from Chicago. Nobody would care that the Bleeding Man, if indeed he ever existed, could stand up and walk and turn about, going precisely where he was aimed.

Or that he could only do that if he had a tiny gyrocompass in his head and others in his legs.

I stood up myself and hopped three icy steps to the window and pulled the curtain back. Out to the east there were streaks of shivering white light where the frozen sun was trying to hoist itself up over the rooftops. I watched a few gray clouds drift westward toward the tomb of Napoleon and imagined a Parisian sky full of falling rockets.

What was it Mark Twain said?—"History rhymes."

It was possible, Elsie had said when we had gone back inside Armus's apartment. She had sat down behind the table in the Collection Room again, skeptical, doubtful. Barely possible. Jacques de Vaucanson was a mechanical genius, certainly—he could have invented anything, just like Mr. Edison. And Hervé Foucault could have learned enough from Vaucanson's daughter, or guessed, or followed a hint. But still . . . a tiny working gyroscope, a hundred and twenty years old. What were the odds?

On the other hand, she said, warming to the subject, it was foolish to think that those old Enlightenment scientists were so far behind us. We were still using and refining what they had started to uncover in an astonishing burst of creativity at the end of the eighteenth century—the steam engine, she had said, beginning to tick items off with her fingers, 1775. The electrical semaphore, 1792.

The telegraph, 1794. The circular saw, the electrical capacitator, the telegraph, Volta's battery, the fountain pen.

"The guillotine," I had said. "The cuckoo clock. Henry Shrapnel's artillery shell, 1803."

She frowned and patted my hand.

In any case, Henri Saulnay was an embittered and hard-up chauvinist, I reminded her. Suppose he wanted to find the gyroscope and give it to the embittered and hard-up German army? To guide the rockets we knew they were testing—Bill Shirer had already written three stories about them.

She put her chin in her hands. Either motive was possible, she finally allowed. But the fact was, if Vaucanson had ever built the Bleeding Man, and if it did contain miniature gyroscopes to help it stand up and walk, he had hidden it somewhere very secret indeed. Unless the horrible shitting duck could tell us where the automaton was concealed, the motive didn't matter. It didn't matter why you wanted the Bleeding Man, she had said, if you couldn't find him.

I ground out a cigarette and stared out my window at the dawn. In the cool light of day, without Johannes pounding down the sidewalk after me, it didn't even seem barely possible. It seemed like the gyroscopic hallucinations of a washed-up reporter with a hole in his gray-haired head. I shivered and hopped back to my desk to earn a living.

Yesterday I had written eighteen hundred words on the engrossing subject of Charlie Chaplin's impending divorce from his wife Oona. Kospoth had grunted and said that the second installment on French automates ought to be the same length. Which left me, I calculated, picking up my notes, about two paragraphs to go.

I didn't have a typewriter in my room. Much too expensive for what the Colonel paid us. At home I wrote the old-fashioned way, in longhand with a pen and ink on yellow sheets of paper that I brought from the *Trib*.

I sighed, exhaled a white comma of condensation into the cold air of the room, and quickly scribbled three absolutely ordinary sentences about French ingenuity and modern technology. Then I stopped and reread them, wincing faintly, like a tolerant but disappointed parent. Poor things, I thought, but mine own. Some people call writing "self-expression," I suppose, because the ink seems to flow straight out of your fingertips, as if it were squeezed out of your innermost self and onto the paper, as if it were part of you, as if it were in some real sense your life's blood. To write, I thought pompously, reaching for my breakfast wine, was the least mechanical act in the world. No automaton could really do it.

Down below on the rue du Dragon some early riser was out on the sidewalk, sweeping the curb and singing a slow, scratchy song about love and war. There was a whistled refrain at the end of each verse.

I stopped in mid-stretch and stared at the wall. Then slowly and indistinctly, like the tip of a sail on the horizon, an idea began to appear.

Thirty-One

MY UNOFFICIAL WORKING PARTNERSHIP WITH ELSIE SHORT resumed, unofficially, a little past two o'clock that afternoon.

It was, of course, the one time of day that the city room was in full journalistic throttle, as far as the Paris edition of the *Trib* ever was. There were five reporters crowded around the big shabby oval table, three of them typing madly. Herol Egan, feet on his desk, jacket around his shoulders, was shouting into a telephone (the Problem of Communication) while he wrote down racing odds with his free hand (Self-Expression). The copy boy was staggering past him under a tottering white stack of newsprint, and Root and I were grimly facing each other at our rewrite desk. He had just handed me a marked-up page two galley when Egan let out a long shrill whistle that should have broken the windows and pointed his telephone toward the door.

"Bombs away," murmured Root, and took back the galley.

I swiveled around. Ms. Short was standing in the doorway,

blushing furiously. She had on her usual green waterproof coat, but today she was hatless and the coat was unbuttoned and she had clearly spent a good part of the morning in the hands of a first-class coiffeuse. Her blonde hair had been shampooed and expertly clipped to hug the soft curves and strong bones of her face. Somebody had touched her eyelashes with the faintest brush strokes of mascara, making the innocent Delft blue even bluer and much less innocent. Her blouse was white, the skirt beneath the coat was a straight fine red wool, tight as a bell, and stopped very far north of her knees. By the time she reached my desk every male head in the room was turned in her direction.

"Who's that girl?" Kospoth appeared beside Root's chair with a handful of papers and Bill Shirer two steps behind him. He glowered at Elsie and then at me.

"This is Toby's nurse from the hôpital," Root said, standing up and shaking Elsie's hand. "She's come to check his pulse."

"You met Miss Short at Paulette's," I reminded him, "the other night." I had no idea whether to shake her hand or kiss her again like a plouc. In any case, it was unclear that Kospoth, who favored grappa and grenadine when he drank, would actually remember anything that had happened at Paulette's restaurant. He snorted politely and handed me a folder.

"Nice little story," he said, "automates. But those damn things still give me the creeps. You owe me eight hundred words on this for tomorrow, Keats."

Root lifted the folder out my fingers and plopped it on his side of the desk. "He's got to go out and talk with the lady, I think."

Kospoth had an enormous old pocket watch that we called the Turnip. He drew it out of a vest pocket and wiped his moustache with the back of his wrist. "Twenty minutes."

"Absitoively," I said, and picked up my coat.

Kospoth's voice had the carrying power of a battleship cannon. Elsie and I were halfway to the door when we heard him say, "See, Root, that's a nice girl, you ought to find somebody like that."

Root murmured something and then, as I pushed open the door for Elsie, we heard Kospoth again. "Oh hell, Root, the girls you know are as hard to get as a haircut."

Elsie smothered a laugh, the door swung shut, then immediately opened again and Bill Shirer stuck out his head. "Telephone for Toby!"

"Posilutely," I said, and took Elsie by the arm.

We went east to a café near the square Montholon. It was still cold and gray, and the tables were crowded with city workmen who had been out digging holes and repairing pavement. We threaded our way through their piled up shovels and brooms to the far corner of the bar.

"They call the counter the comptoir or the zinc," Professor Keats said as the bartender shoved two cups toward us. "Not elegant, but coffee costs half as much here as it does at a table."

Elsie gave me a dazzling smile. "I have two things to tell you, Toby Keats," she said. "First, it could cost twice as much as at the table. Mr. Edison cabled me this morning—or his office did—and they liked the Normandy doll sample I sent so much that they want to sign a contract with the manufacturer. I have to go to Caen tonight and start the paperwork and then I get the job of staying in Paris and supervising everything. So I'm rich! I have a hundred and eighty dollars a month for six months and all the dolls I can play with."

I grinned and pushed the ticket for the coffee toward her cup. "Congratulations. You can pay."

She pushed it back. "I'm rich, but I'm old-fashioned."

"And the other thing?"

Her smile faded abruptly. She reached into one of the pockets in her waterproof coat and pulled out a folded brown envelope and put it on the bar.

"Last night," she said. "Right after I let you kiss me, I stood there and I thought, what in the world am I doing here with a white-haired old Civil War veteran like you, except that it's true you make me laugh sometimes? Then I thought I really hadn't told you everything, and I should. I hadn't shown you these. Vincent bought them for me when I first came to Paris. They're from a book by Robert Houdin. They're really rare."

I slid two yellowing brittle sheets of paper from the envelope onto the counter. A French coffee drinker to my right pointed a cigarette at two beautifully made drawings of Vaucanson's Duck and its inner workings. "Fucking ugly chicken," the Frenchman muttered.

"These are really detailed, like a machinist's blueprints," Elsie said, ignoring him. She leaned closer so that her shoulder touched mine. "They're either drawings of Vaucanson's Duck itself —our duck—or else drawings of the replica Houdin made for his magic act. It doesn't really matter because you can see the mechanism exposed right here, and Houdin claimed he had copied the original. I got these out after you left last night. If I follow them I can see how to attach both wings to the body just the way it shows—that was always a problem. They might even flap up and down. I know I should have told you."

"What about the drum?" I pointed to the barrel-like contraption in the second drawing, a formidably tall cylinder of wires and springs and levers under the duck's feet.

Elsie's face fell a little. "Harder," she said, and moved away from my shoulder. "Nobody knows if you started the drum by winding a key or using a series of falling weights to turn the wires. Houdin kept that part secret. Sometimes the trickiest thing about eighteenth-century automates is the way they start. It's not always obvious."

Through the café window, on the other side of the street I saw a man about my age step through a doorway and disappear into a hidden court. To an American, someone disappearing through a half-open door into a hidden courtyard is the quintessential European sight.

"What we think," I said slowly, "is that Vaucanson hid a clue in the duck about where to find the Bleeding Man. That's why he bought the duck back in 1763, that's why he left it to his daughter, that's why Saulnay wants it. But now we think we probably have to make the duck quack or waddle or wiggle its ears—it probably has to go into action and do something in order to show us."

Elsie started to drum her fingers on the counter. "That's what we think, Toby Keats."

The door across the street was as blank and solid as if it had never opened. "What do we know," I asked even more slowly, "about codes and ciphers in the eighteenth century?"

Her fingers stopped and a moment later started again, as rapid as gunfire.

It was quieter and much less smoky outside in the square Montholon. I bought two more cups of coffee from a stall on the corner and brought them back to Elsie, who had found a bench opposite a children's carousel. But she was far too restless now to sit still. She took two quick sips, frowned at the silent carousel, and sprang up again, circling the bench and gesturing dangerously with her little waxed paper cup.

Jacques de Vaucanson, she told me, had indeed been one of those Enlightenment savants who dabbled in codes and ciphers and mechanical languages. There were lots of them. There was a seventeenth-century Englishman named Wilkins who had built an elaborate "grammar engine" out of pasteboard flaps and levers. You could supposedly use it to understand any language. The mathematician Leibnitz dreamed up a kind of encyclopedia based on binary signs, every idea assigned a number, some combination of plusses and minuses that a calculating machine could decipher. Later, another Englishman named Babbage actually built two automatons like the Swiss Writing Boy, little English boys who played Crosses and Noughts and had a code embedded in the game. Spectators in the know could read a secret political message when the boys played. It was all a game to puzzle-solvers like that, she said. Vaucanson and his friend Le Cat were playing hide and seek with the Church. But mostly people who liked such devices were just secretive by their very nature. Love of secrecy was what made them think the world had been created in the form of a puzzle, by somebody like them. It was only a clock, a machine that a smart person could figure out and copy.

"I thought," she said, "I really, really thought that somewhere inside the duck he would have scratched numbers or letters or if you pulled the right wires, something would have opened or fallen out, a compartment . . . that's what Mr. Edison would have done."

She handed me her cup. Then she shivered and pulled up her collar and we started to walk around the little park again. At the metal gate that led out of the square a gaggle of French schoolchildren bounced in, jumping, squealing, on their way to the carousel.

"About as far from automates," I said, "as they could possibly be."

Elsie gave a wry little smile and took my arm, and I felt the warm pressure of her weight and inhaled the scent of her blonde hair, stylish and Parisian and bright as toasted gold in the darkening afternoon.

"Some people thought Mr. Edison's first Talking Doll was artificial life, too," she said. "They called him a Mad Scientist. He got all sorts of letters of protest. Did you know that there's even a novel about him—*The Eve of the Future?* He supposedly creates the perfect woman, an automaton, and a young man falls in love with it, like Pygmalion."

We were back on the rue Lamartine by now, passing in front of a pharmacy that had an elaborate display of artificial legs and eyes in the window, a very common display for post-war Paris. I looked at my watch. Norton-Griffiths once told me that we won the war because the Allied troops were equipped with small reliable wristwatches, and the Germans still used big, clumsy pocket watches like Kospoth's Turnip. Over in the square Montholon two grandfatherly old men had started the carousel for the children.

"The Perfect Woman," Elsie muttered, "and the Bleeding Man—what a combination!"

If I had been Root, I thought, I would have made a joke and kissed her again and forgotten the duck. I would have sent B. J. Kospoth a jolly pneumatique and spirited her off to the nearest bistro. But I wasn't Root and I was bothered by the looks of the quilted jacketed workmen coming out of our café. If I weren't truly single-minded and obsessive I wouldn't have lasted two minutes in Norton-Griffiths' goddam tunnels. And besides, just as Root said, I wanted to show off.

"Elsie," I said, and looked at my watch again.

"You have to get back, I know. So do I."

"Listen, this morning I had an idea, first about codes, and then about music."

Most of the smaller parks and squares in Paris have children's carousels. Most of the carousels have a little barrel organ built into the central wheel. Elsie looked at me, then at the carousel, which was revolving faster and faster now. Over the shouts of the children, it was thumping out the opening bars of "Sur le Pont d'Avignon."

"Last spring," I said, "I interviewed a visiting American musician named Gershwin. He was fascinated by the way Paris taxicab horns all sound the same three notes, like a signal. He said he was writing music based on it. You told me Bontem was interested in bird calls. Edison is interested in sound. Vaucanson was interested in sound and music, too. He even tried to build a Talking Head, right? And if Vaucanson didn't put a code in the duck, Hervé Foucault and Vaucanson's daughter could have done it, after he died. What if it's not any action the duck does, but how it sounds?"

"The duck," she said carefully, "doesn't make any noise."

"In the throat there are metal tines that don't make any sense, at least not to me. They look like teeth in a comb. You could tune them like a music box."

She stopped in the middle of the sidewalk and dropped my arm.

"When you were telling me about Bontem's birds," I said, "you claimed each bird had a different song. And you could change the song if you changed the cams."

"But we don't have any cams like that, not that I've seen."

I reached in a pocket of my brown tweed jacket. "Maybe we do."

Thirty-Two

IF I HAD TAKEN MY TELEPHONE CALL, of course, before I left the *Tribune* building, or if I had been a better disciple of Norton-Griffiths and thought before I spoke—but it was late, it was cold and windy and January in Paris and I was far, far too caught up in being clever.

We turned our backs on the square Montholon and hurried back down the rue Lamartine toward the *Trib*.

The idea had come to me that morning, I told her as we walked, when I heard somebody on the street below my window whistling. Then as I was leaving for work Madame Serboff had handed me my jacket, finally back from the cleaners, and with it a card box that contained the strange extra cams that I had taken out of the duck in Mrs. McCormick's suite and dropped in my pocket.

"And you're sure it came from the duck?" Elsie was holding one of them between her fingers but frowning at me. "Not somewhere else?"

"I took it out myself. It's certified duck."

By this time we had reached the front door of the *Trib* and the church steeple halfway down the street was chiming the quarter hour, a short but melodious tune that you heard every day all over the city. Paris was full of sounds, music, I thought—I had forgotten how much. I had spent almost three years in an underground world where you listened to nothing but silence, punctuated now and then, when you did your job right, by screams and explosions.

"In the war," I said, "I remember there was a British chaplain who used to conduct the hymns with a toothbrush. If this thing fits and the duck sings like a swan when we tickle its ears, then surely there has to be some sort of code. We can figure it out."

She was laughing in spite of herself. She put the cams in her purse and raised her hand for a taxi. "Swans don't sing," she said, "and I don't know what kind of code it could be, but it might be a brilliant idea and I can't wait to see you standing in front of a mechanical duck, Toby Keats, with a tuxedo and a toothbrush like Leopold Stokowski."

"Don't go now," I said. "Let's head for the rue du Dragon. The hell with Kospoth."

"I can't go with you. I have to meet Vincent at the train station."

Inevitably, for a girl with toasted blonde hair and a form-fitting skirt, two different taxis swung toward the curb.

"Then come over for dinner and I'll show you my etchings of the duck. "

"I can't have dinner with you tonight," she said as I pulled open the door of the nearer taxi. "Libby is already back and they're having a dinner for me."

She slipped inside, but I kept the door wide open. "Now that you're rich," I said, "are you moving out of the rue Jean Carriès? Or does Vincent want you handy?"

"Monsieur," the driver said, "vous allez entrer ou non?"

The taxi behind us blew its horn, the three short notes, and Elsie looked at it and then at me. "I have to go, Toby."

I squinted through the window toward the other side of the street, where some loitering men were watching us. The taxi driver behind us sat on his horn.

"Better let me keep the cams," I said, but she couldn't hear me over the horn. Her driver stretched one arm impatiently over the seat back and pushed my hand off, and a moment later the taxi pulled away.

On Friday three things happened in quick succession. Major Cross telephoned again and this time I was in. The union printing press operators down in the basement walked out on one of their periodical labor actions—which meant they didn't labor. And on top of the stack of mail the copy boy handed me at noon was a handwritten invitation from Miss Natalie Barney: "At Home" on Tuesday night, she informed me, at 20 rue Jacob, from eight o'clock. The postscript was less than subtle: "Please bring your friend. I don't want to write her at the Armus's apartment because I don't like Vincent Armus."

"Good news," said Bill Shirer in his intense, diffident way. He handed me a thick envelope. "I sold a piece to the *Mercury*—just got the galleys."

We were both on our way down the stairs since, because of the labor action, there was going to be no paper today. I slipped the envelope into a folder.

"I will," I promised, "read it first thing tonight."

"Ah." His face fell a little. Shirer was a born newspaperman. He couldn't imagine somebody not gobbling down every printed word he saw, as soon as he saw it. "Well, sure," he said. "Tonight is fine."

We reached the rue Lamartine and stopped awkwardly in the middle of the sidewalk. I looked at Shirer's young, lanky features, his ever-present pipe and trench coat. He was twenty-one or twenty-two, I guessed, a decade younger than me, roughly the same height and coloring, but with a kind of freshness and enthusiasm I hadn't felt for years. You can see ghosts of people you've known. You can see ghosts of people you might have been.

"Come on with me," I said, buttoning the flap on his trench coat for him, "let's play hooky."

There is a fatalistic Gilbert and Sullivan song that cheerfully declares, with a jig and a nod, that there's nothing we can do to change our stories, "We're all born either Little Whigs or Little Tories!" If they had been singing about Parisians, they would have said we were all born either Little Left-Bankists or Right-Bankists.

Bill Shirer was from Iowa, by way of Chicago, and he had only been in Paris for seven months, but he was a Left-Bankist to his core. He lived in the Hôtel Lisbonne on the rue Vaugirard, halfway between the boulevard Saint-Michel and the green arm of the Luxembourg Gardens that curls around just opposite the Odéon Théâtre. He sat in on lectures at the Sorbonne to improve his French. He haunted the Shakespeare and Company Bookstore on the rue Odéon, in the hopes of catching a glimpse of James Joyce or Gertrude Stein. After dinner, he headed for the bohemian cafés along the boulevard Montparnasse—the Select or the Dome or the Closerie des Lilas—where all the expatriate writers and artists sat around till dawn, drinking absinthe and cognac and being geniuses together. (Needless to say, he already knew Hemingway.)

But he didn't know the Right Bank. He didn't know the working-class quarters of Belleville or Père-Lachaise or the bucolic Canal Saint-Martin, and he certainly had never made an excursion east of the Bastille and down into the swarming lanes and gritty backstreets of the Faubourg Saint-Antoine, where much of the immigrant population of Paris had collected like silt in a drain.

We stepped off a bus on the northwest end of the boulevard Voltaire and walked through a North African street market and into an alley lined with carpenters' workshops and ragpickers' stands. It looked as though a strip of Marrakesh had dropped out of the sky into gray, damp Paris.

"Well, what the hell," Shirer said, lighting his pipe and looking curiously around. Farther down the street a few poules struck a pose while their mecs guys stood nearby, waiting to sell whatever drugs were going that week.

"Not that way," I said. We squeezed eastward through the stalls and the litter and passed along a little black creek with Dutch footbridges over it. Sheets of dirty ice lay crumpled up along the water's edge. On the other side of the bridge were bare plane trees and vacant lots where, before the French Revolution, practically in the shadow of the Bastille, eighteenth-century Parisians had planted their crops and raised their sheep. We took a shortcut I knew down another alley and passed kebab carts manned by Algerian Mahgrebs, and two minutes later we emerged onto the cold and weathered cobblestones of the ancient rue de Charonne.

I had already looked up the house and the street in the *Paris Annuaire,* but there was really no substitute, as stubborn old Doctor Johnson said, for treading historic ground yourself.

"That's number 51," Shirer said, and we stopped and peered up, but not at the graceful eighteenth-century hôtel particulier that had once housed Jacques de Vaucanson and his legion of assistants and inventors. That was gone fifty years ago, replaced by a block of cheap apartments.

"I thought there might still be something to see," I muttered. "Some kind of building, some idea, some trace." I took a step or two down an alley and halted when a pair of black dogs came growling out of a door. "I thought there might be something at least to write about for Kospoth in the paper, one of my stories about odd Paris."

Shirer had out his map. "About half a mile from here," he said, "would be where the German line was laid out during the siege of Paris, up beyond those hills. You could write about that."

I was moving along the street and scarcely heard him. Vaucanson, if I remembered correctly, had bought the hôtel in 1746 and lived there till he died forty years later. His daughter, the flighty heiress of ducks, had been born here. According to the books the workshop had been in a big shed-like building behind the house, and it was there that he built the prototypes for the silk-weaving engines in the Conservatory Museum.

I tried to imagine the rumble and fanfare of the king riding up in his squadrons of carriages and marching in procession, all silks and ermine, through the hôtel residence and into the shed behind it, where he and the disagreeable Vaucanson could sit apart and cackle together and compare their illnesses, real and imagined. And when no one else was present, bend forward in conspiratorial whispers about certain thrilling but blasphemous projects. But there was not a sign of any of that now, not even a frisson, not even a tingle in the hairs on your neck. Normally in France the past is never really gone, never far away—

"I meant the siege of 1870," Shirer of the encyclopedic memory said, catching up to me. "The Franco-Prussian War, not your war."

"Well, I'm old, Father William," I said, "but not that old. Actually, the German line in my war was two or three miles farther east. But they were using Herr Krupp's new cannons then, and a great many shells ended up right here in the east of Paris."

Shirer sucked on his pipe and looked around suspiciously at the grimy face of the apartment building, as if the past were a giant cannonball that might come smashing back through the walls, into the fretful present.

Back at our bus stop I bought him a glass of wine in a bar opposite a cemetery gate. The bar was called "Mieux Ici Q'en Face," which means "Better Here Than Across the Street." It had a good view of one of the odder traffic lights in Paris, a strange contraption that had only one color—red—and rose up out of the pavement when a policeman blew a horn. Nearby sat a man whose sign said he would watch your dog for a franc while you went inside the cemetery.

I can never get enough of things like that, but for a reporter Shirer was sometimes not very curious. He reached in his trench coat and produced another copy of his article for the *American Mercury*.

"Just read one thing." He pointed the stem of his pipe at a paragraph about halfway down the first column. "Just read one thing. This is about Winston Churchill and his scientific advisor, a guy named Lindemann. You know about Winston Churchill?"

"I saw him once in the trenches, Bill. He was strolling along on the top of the sandbags smoking a cigar and pointing a swagger stick at the Germans, and they were firing like madmen, but nobody could hit him. He didn't even duck."

"You really saw him?"

"I saw Madame Curie, too, with her portable X-ray machine. You should have been there."

He gave me a look and waited his customary two-beat pause to see if that was a joke, then decided it wasn't. "In 1924 Lindemann told Churchill about new kinds of explosives, very compact, very powerful, but still only possible in theory. Now this year Churchill is wondering if these explosives could be carried in rockets. Look at this quote: 'Could not explosives of this new type be guided automatically in flying machines by wireless or other rays, without a human pilot, in ceaseless procession upon a hostile city, arsenal, camp or dockyard?' Remember what I was telling Eric Hawkins?"

I leaned against the bar and watched a bus go around the corner of the cemetery, leaning hard on its right wheels but keeping its balance.

"Or this one," Shirer read. "'It is very hard to transport oneself into the past,' Churchill says, 'when the jaws of the future are upon us.' Isn't that good?"

My mind swung back like the needle of a compass. "What

do you know, Bill, about codes and ciphers and such in the eighteenth century?"

Anybody else would have put down his glass and stared at me as if I were crazy, but Shirer simply frowned and relit his pipe. "Not the Morse Code?"

"The Morse Code came later."

"I know. Morse thought it up so he could communicate with his deaf wife. He used to tap out signals on her hand with his finger."

I finished my wine and waited. There was no point whatsoever in telling him that in the tunnels we had done the same thing, tapped each other's hands in the dark in a rudimentary code, flesh to flesh, except when we put on our special breathing gear.

Shirer shook his head and stood up straight. "Well, nothing then, I guess. Sorry, Toby."

I patted his shoulder and, like a good gray-haired uncle, paid for his drink. I was already out on the sidewalk, pulling my collar up against the wind, when I heard his voice behind me, small and tentative. "Unless maybe," he said, "you were thinking of Solresol?"

Thirty-Three

"No," said Major Cross. "What in the world is Solresol?"

I hung my hat and coat on a rack and squinted at the window of his office. It was twenty minutes till six, dark, and a strong east wind was fluttering and flapping its black wings against the glass as if it wanted to come in. This was a different room in the same suite of offices on the rue Taitbout, and it had fewer books and more cabinets and furniture than the other one. A little metal heater glowed by one wall, an old-fashioned coal-burning stove that the French for some reason called a "salamander." There was a metal desk in the center, piled high with papers, two spindly wooden chairs and a coffee table, and oddly enough, dangling from another rack by the far wall, a standard-issue British army gas mask, no cylinder.

"Solresol," I said as we each sat down on opposite sides of the coffee table, "was an artificial language based on music."

"Never heard of it." Cross placed a brown cardboard folder on the table and began to shuffle through it.

"Early nineteenth-century. Invented around 1825 by a Frenchman named François Soudre."

"No, sorry."

"Soudre thought you could make a universal language using only the seven basic notes of the musical scale." When Cross looked up at me curiously from his folder, I shrugged. "Somebody told me about it last night. There wasn't much in the big Larousse, but I thought maybe, as a learned archivist—"

"I've been reading about canaries, if that helps. Songbirds." From a shelf under the table he produced a decanter of honey-colored brandy and two thumb-sized snifters. "You kept them down in the tunnels, evidently. Somehow I never pictured that."

"It's a coal miner's trick, to warn about gas, or lack of oxygen—if your canary stops breathing and falls off his perch you're in trouble."

"And when you're in trouble you run for your kit," Cross said, and we both turned to look at the gas mask hanging in the corner. "Somebody's souvenir," he said by way of explanation. "This isn't my regular office. But you had other animals too, down below, not just canaries, yes?"

I had come to Major Cross's office because Colonel McCormick's note had ordered me, more or less, to cooperate. Kospoth knew that and had given me three hours off. This was to be the second and last interview, I had told myself. My firm intention was to keep my answers terse, brisk, unhelpful, and be out of there and on my way in twenty minutes.

But the mention of the canaries set off a funny train of associations. In Flanders there had been an enormous hairy kilt-wearing Scotsman named Auchinleck who spent his spare time trimming the delicate little claws of our canaries—not an easy sight to forget. Which made me remember the red London double-decker bus that arrived one rainy afternoon, loaded to the roof with wicker cages of sparrows and canaries donated by a girls' school in Kent.

"Mice, for example," said Major Cross.

"Mice," I agreed. "We used mice too." There had never been any shortage of mice in the tunnels, or rats or fleas.

"According to another interview," Cross said, tapping his folder, "Norton-Griffiths had an aviary constructed at Calais, where he actually bred canaries by the thousands."

"My friend Root at the paper has a file he calls 'Facts Too Good to Check.'"

"This person seemed to be sure."

"Nothing Norton-Griffiths did would surprise me. I don't know about the aviary. I do know we weren't the only ones who used canaries. The infantry used them in the dugouts, too, under the trenches—because every explosion produces gas, and the gas could linger in the trenches and kill you. What you probably won't find in your file is the fact that some of the tunnelers kept bigger animals than canaries, for mascots. I was once down at the end of a tunnel by myself and when I turned around to go back I bumped into a spotless white rabbit cleaning its paws. If he'd had a vest and a gold watch, I could have been in *Alice in Wonderland*."

Cross stared at me for a count of two, like an older, grayer version of Bill Shirer, then shook his head and started to laugh, a big, surprisingly deep laugh that came from his belly and shook his thin flat face like a leaf.

"I like your literary allusions," he said, still laughing, rubbing his nose with the back of his wrist, "very eclectic and refreshing." He leaned forward and refilled my snifter. "So what happened," he said as he leaned back and kept on smiling, "the last time you went down?"

I looked at the window behind his right shoulder and said nothing, nothing at all.

Cross waited. He felt in his coat and produced a dimpled brass cigarette case. Then he stretched one arm over to the desk and found an ashtray for the coffee table. "They say you were a 'Proto' Man, but I couldn't find that term in the manuals—what was a Proto Man, Toby?"

The human instinct to answer a direct question, put to you by name, is strong. I took a cigarette from the case he had left open on the table. "A Proto Man was somebody in special breathing gear, a 'Proto Suit.' You used it on rescue missions or when you were very deep in a tunnel where there was probably gas."

"Something you wore, then?"

I lit the cigarette with a match he handed me, drank about a thumb's worth of brandy, and watched the gray smoke begin to rise and coil on a draft of air from the window, like a snake charmer's trick.

"There were special oversized goggles for your eyes," I said. "You had a hood, a big double-folded white canvas bellows on your chest, two or three gauges, a nose clamp, a couple of oxygen cylinders strapped to your back. There were two very fat rubber hoses that came up from the bellows and into a mouthpiece. The idea was you breathed oxygen from the cylinders while the carbon dioxide you exhaled got scrubbed clean through a second pouch that was filled with caustic soda granules."

"Something like that?" Cross pointed his cigarette toward the gas mask.

"Not really. The Proto was much bigger, clumsier. It weighed a ton. You looked like a machine. You looked like a deep-sea diver who's popped up in a coal mine."

"And everybody had a Proto suit?"

"No. Only a couple of men in each unit. There was a smaller version called a 'Salvus,' but it just worked for about twenty minutes."

"And the Germans had these suits too."

"The Germans had something called the Draeger Suit. Instead of gauges it had a transparent window in the pouch, so you could see the granules. You could watch them moving up and down with every breath and changing color. Otherwise it was the same."

Cross pulled a stapled sheaf of papers out of his folder and flipped to a page in the center. "June 11, 1918," he said, not quite reading. "A little bit after the Battle of Cantigny. You were in the lines east of Reims, near the Marne, and the Germans blew a camouflet deep in your tunnels. This was a British tunnels unit attached to General Pershing."

I studied our cigarette smoke, which was flattening out against the ceiling now like the top of a bluish-gray mushroom.

"It says they sent you down in your Proto Man suit, with three other enlisted men, to rescue your people, and you had got five of them out when the Germans blew another charge."

They liked to do that, I said. The Germans liked to delay their second charge till a rescue party was down. Actually, so did we. Or maybe I didn't say anything at all to Cross. I wasn't sure. I couldn't hear myself over the tintement of my ears. I watched the smoke creep across the ceiling and vanish into the shadowy molding. When I was a boy my grandfather the lawyer had rather cruelly made me learn to swim in the ice-cold waters of a place north of Boston called, deceptively, "Singing Beach." I was not a good swimmer, but he made me learn, so I wouldn't drown. Because, he said—and I remember his words exactly—because "the Ocean Doesn't Care."

"According to the reports," Cross said, "when your team couldn't function anymore because of gas poisoning, you still went back one more time, to rescue your last three men, and the Germans blew a final charge while you were down, and you and the three men and a German soldier in a Draeger suit were all trapped in some kind of narrow hollowed-out space about eight feet wide and three feet high."

When I didn't say anything to that either, he turned to the end of his papers. "'Sergeant Keats,'" he read, and deliberately or not his voice took on a faintly British accent, "'had been seriously wounded in hand-to-hand combat in the tunnels. He was bleeding profusely from his scalp and his shoulder where he had been shot twice. When rescuers finally reached him, at thirty meters depth from the surface, he was unconscious and covered with dried blood and rats. At our best estimate he was trapped in the darkness with four corpses, pinned under a fallen timber, for upwards of forty-eight hours.'"

I stood up and worked my shoulder back and forth and started for the door. The ocean doesn't care. The tunnels didn't care.

"Apparently," Cross said, "the German in the Draeger suit didn't die in the explosions."

I shrugged on my coat and reached for my hat.

"Apparently," Cross said, "at some point during those forty-eight hours the German revived. He sat up in that strange mechanical suit and started crawling toward you with his gun. And you shot him."

I couldn't hear a thing over the drumbeat of blood in my ears. I watched my hand reach mechanically, like a machine, for the lever on the door.

MAJOR CROSS: It must have been absolutely terrifying, to turn on your flashlight down in that black coffin of a space and see his goggles start to move, his chest begin to breathe, the blood from his wound start to flow again—

SERGEANT KEATS: *[no reply]*

MAJOR CROSS: As if he had somehow come back to life.

Thirty-Four

"No," Root said. "What the hell is Solresol?"

It was about six-thirty in the evening then, one day after my brandy and chat with Major Cross. It was dark and bitterly cold. I was sitting on a three-legged stool next to Root, who was himself reclining more than sitting on an elaborate chromium-plated, leather-padded barber's chair, with a black and white striped sheet tucked around his collar. For the moment all you could see of him was his red face and the tips of his shoes. These he now wriggled with childish satisfaction, pretending, he said, they were mice.

I leaned back so the barber could step around me to the gas burner on the counter where he kept his cups and razors. The only other people in the room were two old men in wool vests and black berets who had arranged themselves like bookends on either side of the window. They were watching shopgirls come and go on the rue Monsieur-le-Prince.

"Solresol," I told him, "was a musical language. A kind of code,

I guess. It was invented in the nineteenth century by a Frenchman. You could write it down in notes, like music—do, re, mi—and speak it or sing it, whichever you liked. Evidently as you shifted the stress you changed a note from a noun to a verb or an adjective."

"Ask Shirer about it. He probably speaks it."

"They used to teach Solresol all over Europe and America, up until about 1880. Victor Hugo could speak it, James Audubon, Napoleon III. They taught a course in Solresol at Oxford."

Behind him the barber had gotten his burner lit and was heating a tiny cup of water over it, paying us no attention at all.

"One of its charms, apparently, was that you could also hum it or whistle it or play it on a French horn."

"Ask the man Shirer."

By now the cup was frothy with a stiff yellowish-white meringue, which the barber stirred with a brush. Then he turned and lathered Root's face till he looked like a cake. Then he dove forward and began to shave with quick, short, artistic strokes.

The man Shirer, of course, had told me about it in the first place, and from our little excursion to the Faubourg Saint Antoine I had gone straight to the Reference Room of the Bibliothèque Nationale.

It was amazing, as my father used to say, how much had gone on in the world before a person was born. There were still Solresol textbooks in the Bibliothèque Nationale, dozens of them, school grammars, three different editions of an official dictionary. Like Esperanto, Solresol had been a commonplace fact of life through much of the nineteenth century, and now it was as obscure and forgotten as Ozymandias.

I had copied the basic rules from one of the grammars, and Elsie Short had spent the better part of the last two days in Madame Serboff's storage room on the rue du Dragon, twisting the tines in our duck's throat, tapping, stretching, adjusting the eight extra cams to make it quack or honk like Victor Hugo. Result: an ungodly series of pinging metallic noises, but nothing remotely resembling a code or a message. The problem, Elsie said, was either in the cams or in the whole loony idea.

In a neighborhood Parisian barbershop it was the customer's job to remove the sheet, wash the lather off in a sink, and then dry his face with a communal towel. I watched while Root went through the ritual, muttering something in his crumbly French that made the barber laugh. At the door he patted his cheeks happily and took his hat from the rack.

"Remind me what a cam is."

"I showed you one, in the Ritz. They're disks, about the size of a dime. Or in this case even smaller. They turn gears."

"Does a typewriter have them?"

I thought for a moment. "No."

Root opened the door and scowled at the blast of cold February air. "Then I don't give a damn," he said.

The rue Monsieur-le-Prince runs northwest from the Luxembourg Gardens toward the Seine. Since it was the night of Natalie Barney's Open House, that happened to be precisely the direction I was going.

It was seven o'clock by then, and there was a light drizzle and the wind was harder and colder than ever. I left Root at the corner of his building and made my way over to the nearly deserted place Saint-Michel, ordinarily the busiest spot on the Left Bank. From there I walked along the river to the pont des Arts. Then I pulled my collar up and my hat down and pushed my way out to the humpbacked center of the bridge, where I leaned against a railing and listened to the passing barges slapping against the current—do, re, mi—sol, re, mi.

Parisians call them the Right Bank and the Left Bank because the earliest maps all showed Paris as you looked downriver from east to west. And the right bank, of course, was the Right Bank. I loved the neat and orderly French mind, deluded by logic.

The place to really see Paris, all the guidebooks agree, is from a bridge, any bridge, preferably at sunset or dawn, but probably not on a dark February night when the wind is blowing little silver bullets of ice. I held onto my hat and watched the traffic.

A clock on the quai Voltaire struck the quarter hour. Something was coming with the wind, I thought, something was coming to a head. I felt my nostrils flare against the stinging cold, the way they used to do in the war, before the artillery fire began. My left hand fumbled in my pocket and traced the edges of Natalie Barney's invitation and I lowered my head and started to walk. Proto Man goes to a Party.

At the rue Mazarine I cut through a maze of narrow streets and cobblestoned passageways that, apart from a scattering of electric lights here and there, must have looked pretty much the same when Thomas Jefferson and his private secretary William Short walked up and down them at the end of the eighteenth century. Then I emerged onto the better-lit rue Saint-Benoit and tapped on the window of the Café Camargue and William Short's bright, blonde, twentieth-century descendant turned and gave me a dazzling smile.

"You drink too much," Elsie said as I slipped into the chair beside her. "So I ordered coffee."

"I like to drink."

She reached over and patted my hand and the cat Byron leapt up on the table next to me and purred a warning. "My chaperon tonight," she said, "needs to be sober and alert. I've been reading about Natalie Barney. I really shouldn't go at all."

"You'll be the belle of the ball."

"That's what I'm afraid of."

There was no good answer to that, so I took off my overcoat and kissed her quite long and hard on the rouge à baiser and then took off my hat.

Elsie blinked and gave a slow, very different kind of smile. "Some chaperon."

"Madame Serboff says you didn't come by this afternoon."

"Ah. Well." Elsie sat back so that the Greek owner could deposit two strong black coffees on the table, served as it often was in those days in sherbet glasses. She ladled sugar into hers and frowned so hard that the cat backed away. "Well," she said, "about that. I've been giving it a lot of thought, all yesterday and today, and I just don't see how your theory's going to work, Toby Keats. That's why I didn't come by. I've tried everything I can with the cams. I simply don't understand how the duck could make a sound on its own, not even a quack, that would turn into a musical code."

The disadvantage of the sherbet glasses, of course, was that they didn't have handles, so that you had to sit and stare at your coffee until it cooled down. "What about the tines in the throat?"

"Probably there just to break up the food when the silly thing swallowed."

"Like hens' teeth."

She didn't laugh. "Hens don't have teeth. Two of your cams are probably extras. Or maybe duplicates. I didn't look. I just put them back in your envelope."

"They look like they have different bevels."

"Well, I'm sorry, I just don't think it makes any sense, not the gyroscope theory, or the idea that Saulnay wants to give it to the German army. When you come right down to it, he just wanted the duck for himself. He's a toymaker."

She took a sip of her coffee, made a face, and spooned another mound of sugar into it. "You're a very persuasive person, you know, despite all your bad jokes and the way you live like a crab in that terrible room. When you get an idea, you're like my father, you'd have to be hit on the head to make you change direction."

"That could be arranged," I said. "I'd prefer a cam."

She laughed. "Anyway, in the clear light of day"—she looked at the window and the dark street outside and gave a wry shrug. "In the clear light of dark, I guess, even the Bleeding Man seems like a Jules Verne story. I'm not as stubborn as you are. I guess deep down I don't really believe Vaucanson ever did more than talk about it. I certainly don't believe I'm going to find it now and make my fortune."

She raised the sherbet glass of coffee with both hands until all I could see was her Delft-blue eyes. "But here's the good news, Toby Keats," she said. "Vincent wants to buy my duck."

Thirty-Five

NATALIE BARNEY LIVED IN A THREE HUNDRED-year-old house that she had bought in 1909.

Three hundred years is old, even in Paris, even to somebody from Boston. Her house was located ten minutes from the Café Camargue, a couple of blocks down the rue Jacob from the even older building where Benjamin Franklin and John Jay had signed the treaty with the British in 1783 that ended the American Revolution. A few years ago the Paris branch of the American Chamber of Commerce had put up a small plaque on the Franklin house, and on warm days you could often see an American or two standing on the sidewalk reading it. In 1916 some of the wild-boy aviators from the volunteer Lafayette Squadron had thrown a stupendously drunken party in what they thought was the very room where the treaty was signed. Then they had gone out to the Battle of Verdun and shot down German pilots till the sky ran red.

Elsie and I left the Camargue at exactly half past eight and walked five minutes north, heads bowed against the wind, arguing all the way.

What Vincent Armus proposed, she said for the third time, was to give her two thousand dollars for the partially reassembled automate. That was a very good price, she thought, for an antique toy in such terrible condition. Even before it was broken, establishing that it was truly Vaucanson's Duck was going to be hard. She could write to Mr. Edison, but he wasn't going to be interested in something that badly damaged. Besides, he wanted a doll who could talk, not a duck who couldn't even quack. In any case, legally the duck belonged to her. And two thousand dollars was a very good price, a terrific price, whether or not I agreed.

"Just 'whether,'" I said, stupidly pedantic. "Not 'whether or not.'"

"Whether or not," she said grimly, "it's the original Vaucanson's Duck, he wants to buy it. It would suit his collection of birds, he says."

"For cash?"

"For three hundred dollars now, the rest in six months."

"I say No."

"And I say Yes," she said, looking at me with Delft-blue daggers. "And you don't really have anything to do with it."

At which point we rounded a corner and found ourselves on the rue Jacob. Ahead of us, amid shrieks of laughter and gusts of wind, a line of grumbling black taxis was discharging fellow guests at the curbside of number 20. We joined them, slipped through a brightly painted blue wicket and crossed a cobblestoned courtyard to the front door. There one maid took our hats and coats and another led us down a hallway and pulled open a pair of French doors.

"I don't think he has two thousand dollars to pay you," I said. "I think he's going broke."

"Oh," said Elsie, and took one step forward. "Oh, my."

Root has a theory that because the great seventeenth-century architects were first trained as artists and spent years drawing the human body, when they began to design buildings and rooms, they instinctively found the right proportions to put around the human frame. But whatever Natalie Barney's living room had looked like in the seventeenth century, in 1926 it had clearly undergone a modern metamorphosis.

The room in front of us now had been carved out of three separate smaller rooms— you could see the old ceiling beams and supporting timbers—so that it was twice the size of the drawing room in Vincent Armus's apartment. But tonight there were at least sixty people, male and female, laughing and smoking, crowded into the single space, along with a grand piano and a buffet table in one corner, and all sense of proportion had clearly been blown to pieces. At the far end of the room, a row of tall windows exposed the famous garden. Beyond them I could make out two or three columns of the Sapphic Greek Temple.

"It was supposed to be a small, intimate literary gathering, you know, champagne and chocolate." To our right, from another hallway, our hostess herself materialized, splendid in a shimmering white cocktail dress and three great loops of colored beads that reached all the way to her hips. I thought they looked like bicycle chains.

She smiled at me, took Elsie's arm. "But as you see, it's gotten rather out of hand. You can find yourself a drink, Mr. Keats, I'm sure, while I show our friend around."

"Duck soup," I said, and gave a little bow.

"Sober and alert," Elsie muttered, and then I watched as Natalie led her away, toward a group of handsome young women dressed in tailored men's suits and bow ties, à la garçonne.

The drinks were dispensed by a stout Negro woman in a musketeer's cape and a cocked hat with a feather. I took a glass of vintage Veuve Cliquot that, Prohibition or not, you probably couldn't have bought in New York, and dog-paddled my way across to the other side of the room.

More than sixty people, I decided. Far too many people for

the modest old seventeenth-century spaces. They were more or less equally divided between men and women, and most of the men were in drab business suits or evening clothes. But the women—the women were wonderful, the women were like flocks of birds in a Parisian park, bright, glittering, in constant fluttering motion, breaking the gray smoky air of the room into noisy scoops of color. Some wore cocktail dresses like Natalie Barney's. Others were crowned with red or green turbans or fashionable "princess" tiaras. The red of the turbans, I knew from the *Trib*'s social page, was called, quite poetically, 'strident geranium red.'

Elsie had slipped out of the clutches of the garçonnes and was standing with Natalie Barney by the buffet. She motioned me toward her and I turned to put down my glass.

"The architects," said a husky French voice to my left, "have warned poor Natalie that the floors will collapse if she lets people dance."

"But I see a piano."

The voice belonged to a very tall, very elderly woman, who patted my shoulder kindly. "That's because she is going to subject us quite soon to the music of George Antheil. From the back your gray hair made me think you were going to be much older," she said in English. "I'm Annick Perret. Is that your petite amie?"

I looked back at Elsie.

"She's perfectly safe, you know," Annick Perret said. "Natalie never tries to seduce someone at her Tuesday events. These are for 'culture' only. But if your friend comes back for the Saturday salon—" She wagged her fingers in an inimitably French manner and grinned through a dense layer of powder and rouge. "Oh, la la!" she said, and quickly added, "Don't look at my face. I've had it redone so many times I look like one of those ceilings by Michelangelo. Come sit down over here and tell me your name and get me another drink."

I did all three in backwards order and as I sat down the Muse of Coincidence must have turned her ironic gaze on me, because

Annick Perret leaned very far forward, gripped my arm with a bejeweled claw, and said, "I heard Natalie say your name. I think you must be the Mr. Keats who wrote those very amusing articles about automates?"

"You read the *Tribune?*"

"I like the American slang. And you see, I have a small collection of automates myself, French and Swiss. They were made by my grandfather, whom you somehow very oddly neglected to mention."

Despite my bad ear and the noise of sixty chattering Frenchmen, I still imagined I could pick out Elsie's rising voice. I twisted my head and saw her and Vincent and Libby Armus, walking toward the piano.

The grip on my arm tightened. "His name was Hervé Foucault," Annick Perret said, and the Muse of Coincidence laughed out loud, "and he lived in Neuchâtel. He was, how would you put it in slang? He was the 'fancy man' of that terrible little pute, Jacques Vaucanson's daughter."

The piano burst into a Charleston. I took one astonished look at Libby Armus bent over the keyboard, fingers flying, and then lifted a startled Annick Perret out of her chair and guided her around a corner, into a book-lined study with paintings I ignored and a beautifully upholstered lady's chaise longue.

"If you shut the door, too," said Annick with another broad grin, "it will do wonders for my reputation, even at seventy-nine. Especially at seventy-nine."

"I know about Jacques Vaucanson," I said, pulling out the chaise for her. "But not much about his daughter."

"You were in the war, were you not, poor boy? The eyes always give it away." She rubbed the nubby fabric of the chair with her palm. "So much in a hurry, so single-minded, all of you after the war. You think the world could end at any moment. Sit right there. Do you see this ring?"

She held up a crooked finger that was bent by arthritis

and age, and also by the weight of a thick, beautifully worked band of silver with a teardrop ruby set in the center. "This ring belonged to Jacques Vaucanson's daughter," Annick said. She turned it under a lamp and it caught the reflections of old leather books, gold-stamped bindings, three hundred-year-old light. "Angélique was her name, Angélique-Victoire de Vaucanson. She married the son of the Comte de Salvert, but he was a fool and she was a flirt and my grandfather Hervé, of course"—a proud and rather salacious chuckle—"was adorably handsome. And a genius with his hands, which a woman always likes."

I was trying to do the math in my head. "You couldn't have known her?"

A snort this time, not a chuckle. "I'm not as old as all that, young man. I was born in 1848, if you want to know, in the Dordogne, in Les Eyzies-de-Tayac. Angélique was dead before that. But I come from a long-lived family, and my grandfather was younger than she was. He lived to be ninety-three. I remember him well."

"And the ring?"

She rotated it slowly, hypnotically, in the light. The distant piano stopped and applause rippled into the room.

"Well, it first belonged to the king," she said, with a little nod of satisfaction and pleasure. "Then it belonged to her, that was the story. Louis XV of disgraceful memory must have given it to Jacques in the middle of the eighteenth century. When Angélique ran away with my grandfather, her husband the comte cut off all her money. How she lived after that nobody knew, because my grandfather never made very much from his automates. But everybody thought Jacques had secretly left her all the jewels and gold that he earned from the king, for the silk machines in Lyon. He must have hidden it somewhere before he died, from the tax collectors. But he told Angélique where, and whenever she needed money evidently she just dipped her hands into a treasure chest, like a pirate queen."

"In Neuchâtel?"

Annick Perret's plaster-white face turned slowly toward me. Up close I could see what a work of art her maquillage was— eyebrows completely shaved and replaced by two thin curling lines; eyelashes tipped with purple mascara; her mouth a deep, sly scarlet bow of strident geranium red.

"That was the very odd thing," she said, almost in a whisper. "She always disappeared from Neuchâtel for six or seven days, and when she came back, my grandfather said her carriage smelled of limestone—he was from near the Dordogne, and he would know. The Dordogne is limestone country. To tell the truth, I always thought he was in on the secret."

I leaned back and took a deep breath and wondered if a cigarette would offend her. Out in the big room a new and very different kind of piano music had started, angry and percussive, nothing like a Charleston.

"George Anthiel," Annick said with disdain. "He once wrote a ballet for six player pianos and two airplane propellers."

"Did your grandfather," I said, choosing my words as carefully as I could, so that nothing could possibly go wrong, "ever talk about something called 'Solresol'?"

She frowned at me, at the open door and the music, and shook her head.

"When he worked for Vaucanson, did he ever make musical automates? Music boxes?"

"Like the Flute Player, you mean?" She shook her head again. "Those were very early in Vaucanson's life. My grandfather came to him almost as a boy, at the rue Charonne, and he worked on the weaving machines. In Neuchâtel he worked for the Jacquet-Droz family, and none of them was particularly interested in music. They rarely made music boxes."

"They made," said small, blonde, absolutely gorgeous Elsie Short from the doorway, "automatic Writing Machines. You should remember that, Toby. They made the first automates who could hold a pen and write out actual letters and words, and they could write all sorts of things, in French or English."

"There's still one of them that works perfectly well," said Annick Perret, smiling at Elsie and beckoning her forward. "'The Writing Boy'—it's in the museum in Neuchâtel."

"What they wrote," Elsie said, staying right where she was, looking straight at me, "depended on the cams."

Thirty-Six

IT WAS ALMOST ELEVEN O'CLOCK before we could make an exit from Natalie Barney's party. Twice we eased our way, like fugitives on the lam, through the big drawing room toward the hallway, and twice we were stopped, once by Libby Armus, who had someone Elsie positively needed to meet, once by Natalie Barney, who took us both over to shake the limp paw of the composer and pianist George Antheil.

Even then, we had scarcely reached the sidewalk of the rue Jacob when Vincent and Libby Armus came out of a clowd of furs and top hats and caught us at the curb. Libby led us all toward a waiting taxi (no Mercedes this time, I noticed with interest).

"I would very much," said Vincent Armus, bending close to me, murmuring, "very much like to conclude my business deal regarding the automate, Mr. Keats. Elsie is hesitating. I understand you are somehow a partner in it, or at least she wants your consent. Actually, I don't understand that at all. It's her property."

I pulled up my collar. The rain had died away, but the air was misty, and a fidgety, uneasy wind was still brushing off the wet rooftops, sending some gray clouds scudding east toward Switzerland. Through a gap overhead there was a pale white new moon with beveled edges like a cam.

I absolutely hated the high, tense whine in my ears that Johannes's fist and pistol had given me, an unearthly sensation like a piano wire stretched through my head. "I'm not sure," I heard myself say, "that it's a very good business deal for her."

"Mr. Keats—"

Libby Armus peered around his shoulder. Her beaked nose was red with cold, but her expression was cheerful, friendly.

"Mr. Keats, do you need a ride in our taxi? Did you like the music?"

"I liked your Charleston fine. Not so much the other guy."

"Is it more money?" Armus said. "I would be willing to pay—" He paused and squinted at the moon. "I would be willing to pay six hundred dollars down in cash, right now, three thousand in total."

"Sweetheart, cash? You know we shouldn't be buying more—" Libby turned toward Elsie. Elsie put her hand on Armus's sleeve.

"Toby and I still need to talk some things over first," she told him with an apologetic grimace. "It's my property, but we have a kind of arrangement. And besides, I don't want to sell you something if it's broken or, worse yet, not genuine."

"I'll take my chances on all of that," Armus said in the same impatient voice. "My offer is very generous. You won't do better. I would really like to settle the thing right now. As for being broken, I can repair the duck myself. Whether it's by Vaucanson or Houdin, I want it."

Libby Armus, cheerfulness replaced by a small, tight expression of worry, had moved over to the open taxi door. "Are you getting in back with me, Elsie dear?"

"I'm going to walk," Elsie said, taking my arm, "with Toby."

*   *   *

We were halfway down the block when a side gate opened in a wall alongside number 20 and Annick Perret hobbled out, talking over her shoulder to someone inside. As she saw us she waved and said in English, "Such a handsome couple!"

Both of us nodded and waved back, and then we turned the corner onto the dark and leafy rue de Furstemberg and Elsie dropped my arm like a sack. "I'm still mad at you," she said.

"It wasn't Solresol at all," I said, and took her arm back.

"Correcting my grammar." She stopped in the middle of the sidewalk, grinning, put a hand on each of my coat lapels, and studied my face. "Whether or not, Toby Keats. The Writing Boy!" she said, and kissed me so hard that, as Root would say, my socks rolled up and down.

She was wearing the same green raincoat she had worn the first time I saw her, and a darker green cloche that reached down to her forehead in the flapper fashion. The night mist sparkled on her face like jewels. I kissed her back, slowly, for perhaps a month and a half, and when we had both come up for air we started to walk again.

"There was probably never a code," I heard myself saying as we turned another corner. "Either Vaucanson or Foucault—or both of them—just set up a machine to write out in plain French where the money was—"

"And wherever the money was," Elsie said excitedly, "that would be where the Bleeding Man was, too. Because he kept it all hidden, everything was hidden from the tax collectors and the Church."

"Where it was, where it is now."

"Don't you dare correct my grammar."

We debouched on the rue de Buci, which had an open-air vegetable market three days a week.

"And the secret location," I said as we picked our way between the empty stalls, "was kept in the Duck."

"Which Angélique-Victoire inherited—"

Elsie stopped and frowned at the boulevard Saint-Germain just ahead. "This isn't the way to the Armus's apartment."

"No."

"It's the way to the rue du Dragon."

"Yes."

"Are you leading me astray, Toby Keats?"

"I certainly hope so," I said, taking her arm again.

We turned and walked west, leaning into the wind. We passed a Métro sign and the wolf-gray stone haunch of the Saint-Germain Church. The Flore was almost empty, the Deux Magots was closed, and most of the side streets looked deserted. We crossed over and turned south on the rue du Dragon.

"I don't even know," Elsie said, shivering as the wind began to nibble and bite, "where Neuchâtel is."

"It's in Switzerland, on the Lake of Neuchâtel. Population about four thousand. It's five hours away by train."

"It might not be," she used her warning voice again, "the right automate, you know. The cams might not fit, or they may be too old and damaged. And there still might be no Bleeding Man after all."

For an instant, for the single pulse of a thought, I wanted to say there was always a Bleeding Man. Poor maudlin Toby.

"Did you really tell that old lady," Elsie said, "that I was your petite amie?"

"I did. I told her you were one half of a handsome couple."

"Root says there were camp followers in the war, all of you soldiers had mistresses."

"Not me," I said, turning and holding her at arm's length so that I could see the red spots of cold the wind had rubbed on her cheeks. I was about to make a joke to avoid the subject of the war, as usual—camp followers were off-limits, Hors de Combat.

But I was fumbling at the same time in my pocket for a key and distracted, because something was not quite right. Ordinarily Madame Serboff locked the door to the building at eleven and went to bed. After that, to get in you had to ring her bell and wait on the sidewalk, stamping your feet and blowing on your fingers in the dark, until she had lit a cigarette and put on her pink flannel robe and floppy slippers and come shuffling and muttering out to the front. But given the strange hours of the newspaper business I had my own key.

"Toby?"

"Take your hand out of your pocket, Mr. Keats."

I turned around slowly, fingers curled and tingling, and saw the small piggish black eyes and white jowls of Henri Saulnay, long expected, long forgotten. I felt something round and hard jam into my back.

"My nephew Johannes is behind you," Saulnay said. "He's armed and unpredictable. Come this way, both of you."

Elsie started to pull me away. Saulnay reached over and slapped her once and then stepped back, and Johannes showed her the gun.

"I'll yell," she said, staring at the gun.

"And he'll shoot," Saulnay told her, "your friend."

I saw her face, white and frightened under the cloche, then Johannes pushed me hard toward the door.

There was a main entrance to the building, and a lower entrance under the steps, where the dustbins were kept. We went down the steps and into a narrow passageway, past the coal chute and the gently hissing boiler that in theory supplied the rooms with heat. It was only two feet below street level, with narrow windows at sidewalk level, and both Saulnay in the front and Johannes behind us had flashlights, so that we weren't really underground or in the dark, but even with all that I stumbled and my hands began to shake.

"Where's Madame Serboff?" I said.

Saulnay ignored me. We went down four wooden steps. I heard Saulnay turn a lock. Elsie said something, breathing hard. Johannes jabbed me in the ribs and I walked through the door. On the worktable in front of me I saw Elsie's toolbox, a tiny oil can, scattered wrenches. At one end were bits of springs and levers, some crumpled sheets of brown paper, and sitting in the middle of the paper, as if in a nest, its melancholy eyes fixed on me and its metal beak gaping in surprise, Vaucanson's goddam Duck.

It was Madame Serboff's storage room, of course, where Elsie had been coming each morning. Johannes shoved me to one side and closed the door. On the other side of the table Saulnay switched on the overhead bulb.

"Turn the lock," he said. Johannes stretched his arm over to his left and slid a bolt. Saulnay pulled Elsie's work stool out from the shadows and lowered his bulk onto it.

"This belongs to Johannes." Next to the brown paper, he picked up a banana peel, rather fastidiously, with his right hand. His left hand had slender wooden splints on the two middle fingers, held in place by a cloth bandage. "We were here for much of the night and of course became rather hungry. But that's no excuse. Germans are not usually so messy. Bonsoir encore, Mr. Keats. Tie him up in that chair, please, Johannes."

He cleared a little more space around the duck and leaned back so that his face hung by itself in the light. Johannes prodded me onto a wooden kitchen chair and lashed my hands behind me with a rope. Then he drew the rope under the chair bottom and tied my ankles to the lower rung and stepped back. Around the sides of the storage room there was nothing to see but a bicycle wheel suspended from a wall. To the left of the duck's feet, in the clutter of parts and tools, lay a small beige paper square, as inconspicuous to me as the Eiffel Tower. I took the cams off, she had said, and put them back in your envelope.

"Well, I have to give you credit, my dear Elsie Short." Saulnay beamed at her as if they were back on the lecture platform at the Théâtre des Automates. "From what I had understood, our mechanical friend here was hopelessly broken when Mr. Keats had his moment—what was it, Keats, at the Métro? Panic? Terror? Johannes described it quite vividly. Something to do with the trenches, perhaps? Never mind. The duck looks good."

The duck, I thought, looked very good. It looked as if it had come back to life, if you could say that about an inanimate object. I kept my eyes fixed on its back and tail, where Elsie had somehow found and inserted a few green and black authentic duck feathers. I kept my eyes far away from the beige envelope.

"When I saw the duck before," Saulnay said, "in my toy shop, I only had a moment, not nearly long enough to really inspect it. Even then I thought there was something wrong with the wings."

"The joints are rusted, that's all." Elsie rubbed her face where he had slapped her.

"Show me."

"Look for yourself."

He held up the splinted fingers. "A little domestic accident," he said, "when I was chasing our friend Mr. Keats in the Marais. It's not serious but awkward for working with tools. Show me."

Elsie looked at the bandage without expression for a moment. Then she leaned forward and twisted a rod I couldn't see and the right wing came off in her hand. At the same time, almost exactly as it said in Vaucanson's book, the flexible tube of the neck rose and straightened as if the duck were about to swallow.

Saulnay leaned forward as well, into the light. I strained against the rope on my wrists and let my eyes go to Johannes, but he was a good two feet away, staring back at me, and the pistol in his fist was almost touching Elsie's back.

"Again," Saulnay said. He concentrated intensely on something in the duck's motion. Then Elsie did the same thing with the left wing and placed the two wings side by side on the table, next to the envelope. I pressed my feet against the floor and made the chair legs scrape.

"Let Elsie go," I said.

"Nonsense." Saulnay picked up a tiny screwdriver with his good hand and began to probe the joint where the right wing joined the body and the rods from the now nonexistent pedestal would have turned the cams. He glanced up at Johannes. "Check your knots."

Johannes was broad-shouldered and angular, not heavy and flabby like his uncle. He had changed his quilted Alsatian jacket for a heavy wool blouson and a black roll-necked sweater and I could smell the sweat and oil on it as he came close. He knelt and stretched out his left hand to test the knots, but he kept the pistol in his right hand carefully back. After a second I recognized it as the same Webley revolver he had used before, at the Métro, a deadly efficient weapon, elegant and brutal in the best English tradition.

A car rattled by on the street above. Johannes yanked the knots once more and stood up. It was well past midnight, I thought, maybe even later. Madame Serboff would be fast asleep on the other side of the building, five or six doors and a corridor away. The other nine tenants were even farther away, upstairs, useless.

Meanwhile the duck was rapidly going backwards in time, so to speak, falling apart in pieces. The torso was wingless now. Methodically, a jeweler's loupe in one eye, using his good hand only, Saulnay opened the greenish-brass belly plate with a pair of pliers, detached one of the webbed feet, and laid it aside. He unscrewed the neck halfway. Under the single electric bulb his white face had tiny black veins and scratches like marble. I had once spent a rainy afternoon in the Louvre looking at the old Roman busts of senators and consuls, and Saulnay had that kind of face, I thought—stern, fleshy, confident, interested only in the things in front of him, not in the spiritual world his small, hard eyes couldn't see. The German toymaker had a Roman face. He picked up one of the wings and spun a cam.

"I know more than you think," I said, and he raised his head.

"About Vaucanson, his daughter, the code or the message in the duck that you want."

Saulnay held the wing steady. The little cam spun and spun and then wobbled to a stop.

"Except you don't care about the duck," I said, "you care about the Bleeding Man."

"So you said before."

"You care about the gyroscope. You want to sell the gyroscope to the army, the German army I assume. Maybe even give it to them."

He studied me for a long time. Johannes moved closer to Elsie. Saulnay's hand was on the table, inches from the beige envelope. I willed his eyes to stay on me.

"An interesting theory," he finally said. Then he walked around the corner of the worktable toward me and Johannes raised his Webley pistol level with my chest. "He's just talking to distract us. This has something to do with the wings and the cams," Saulnay said to Johannes. "I don't like Americans, but I don't underestimate them."

"He won't shoot," I said. "The noise would wake up half the building. There's a gendarmerie on Saint-Germain. You'd never get out."

Saulnay smiled and twisted his upper body so that his right hand moved in little circles over the table. "Such a clutter," he said. "Things out of place, paper, food." His hand hovered over the detached foot, the wings, the beige envelope, then dropped like a hawk into his overcoat pocket and came up with another pistol, a small square automatic. "If we had enough time," he said in the same conversational tone, "I would take you out to the Métro entrance or a sewer and see what exactly makes you fall apart in the dark, underground."

"Let Elsie go."

He came around to the corner of the table. "There was something about the cams," he said. "I could tell from your eyes."

"What's a cam?"

"You must have seen men get shot in the war, Sergeant Keats. It's an astonishingly painful wound. It can take a man many hours to die from a single small bullet through the navel. I want to know about the cams."

"I don't know anything about cams."

"I can count in French or English or German," Saulnay said. "One of them will be the last language you ever hear. Un, deux—"

"Stop!" Elsie said. "I'll tell you!"

And I lunged at the table, driving up with my feet, twisting forward with the chair on my back. My ankles came free but not my hands. Somebody's gun fired once, twice, and I fell under the table on my back like a turtle, kicking. For a moment all I could see was the underside of the table. Then the lightbulb clicked off, on. Saulnay's white face sailed by and the door slammed.

When I finally righted myself and worked my hands loose, it could have been thirty seconds or two minutes later—I had no idea. Distant voices were echoing, receding. The table was on its side. The floor was covered with tools and paper and bits of metal. The lightbulb was drifting gently back and forth on its cord like a pendulum, illuminating the storage room section by section as it passed.

In the cold, swaying light there was a strange absence of sound and life—there was no duck, no envelope, no Elsie.

PART FIVE
The Bleeding Man

Thirty-Seven

AT ELEVEN O'CLOCK THE NEXT NIGHT, not quite twenty-four hours after Elsie Short had disappeared, I found myself sitting in a stalled railway car somewhere east of the French mountain town of Besançon, halfway to Switzerland.

"The conductor doesn't know why it's stopped," Root said, lowering his long frame onto the seat in front of me. "And he doesn't know how long it's going to be stopped. And he doesn't really seem to give a damn."

"Probably," said an Englishman working his way down the aisle, "you've had a flood or a mudslide around Champagnole or Belfort. Some of the bridges up there aren't so stable, you know. Good deal of fighting over them toward the end, Mulhouse, Thann, Besançon. Bloody geography lesson, that's all the War was." He was about the right age and had a stiff left leg that he dragged along like a log and he looked at my gray hair and paused with his hand on the seat back, waiting to see if I wanted to reminisce.

I didn't. I looked across to the other row of seats, where Vincent Armus was sitting by a window, staring at the motionless black landscape.

The three of us and the Englishman were on Wagon 118 of SNCF train 3246, which left Dijon five days a week at 3:25 P.M., after you connected from the Gare d'Austerlitz in Paris. Train 3246 had six commuter-style cars with American-style aisles instead of compartments, and it was pulled by one underpowered diesel locomotive. From Dijon, when it wasn't stalled on a siding, it rolled through thirty miles of stumpy gray winter vineyards in northern Burgundy, turned east, and ambled over to Besançon and then to Belfort, and finally took a deep breath and climbed up the rugged foothills of the Val de Travers, leaving France at last for the little watchmaking border town of Neuchâtel.

Neuchâtel was the only place in the world I could think of where Saulnay would have taken Elsie.

If, Inspector Soupel had said, Saulnay had really taken her.

Maybe, he had said, maybe she went on her own accord. Maybe she changed sides, maybe, Monsieur Keats, you're imagining things.

Armus made a kind of sneering noise through his nose and stood up. Root and I watched him go down the aisle and around the bulkhead where the toilets were.

Why bring him along? Root had said. Why bring Armus along at all? Armus was a snob and a prick, and he was fifty years old if he was a day—why did we need him?

There was one good reason.

Nobody else in Paris—nobody else I knew—understood how to fix an eighteenth-century automate or make one start if the mechanism didn't have an On-Off switch.

I worked my dry tongue across my teeth and then stood up.

"Now what?" Root said. "Getting out to push?"

I ignored him and walked to the end of the car, opened the door, and jumped down to the track. It was cold outside but not raining. Some days in Switzerland it failed to rain. The glow of the train lights obscured the sky, though I thought I could make out the dimmest possible halo of white far ahead, higher in the foothills, possibly the city of Neuchâtel, unless, of course, it was La Chaux-de-Fonds or Fleurier or Thann or God-Damn-Your-Eyes or any of the other dozen or so milk run stops the train was scheduled to make before it quit for the night. There were all kinds of geography lessons.

Up ahead the locomotive was throbbing quietly like a cat on a rug. Steam was leaking out of the hotboxes on the wheels, and I could see the tip of somebody's cigarette near the folding steps of the carriage in front.

Trains, I thought with disgust. My Boston grandfather had been a train buff. His father had helped design one of the earliest steam locomotives on the East Coast, around 1840, for the Baltimore and Ohio. In those quaint days, my grandfather said, some of the locomotives were so crude that they didn't even have brakes. When they rolled into a station a gang of roustabouts rushed out to the track and pulled them to a stop with ropes hooked on to the locomotive.

Trains. After the Franco-Prussian War of 1871, because of a number of costly miscalculations concerning rolling stock and empty troop cars, the Germans had started teaching their staff officers how to draw up railroad timetables. Ultimately the Germans learned to do it with such precision that they could shuffle men and equipment around a battlefield ten times faster than ever before in military history. Train scheduling became a required subject at the Berlin War Academy. Then the French and the English military academies had followed suit, so that you could argue, as Norton-Griffiths liked to do, that the whole astonishing continent-wide scale of destruction and horror in the 1914 War was the direct, logical consequence of Europe's super-modern railway network.

With the exception, evidently, of the Dijon-Neuchâtel Line.

But I didn't care about the history of trains. Or Vaucanson's Duck. Or even the goddam Bleeding Man. I had brought Armus along because there was nothing in the world I wanted to do except find Elsie.

I walked around the last carriage and peered down into a ravine of restless shadows. We should have hired an automobile in Paris, I thought, the way Armus had wanted.

No, Inspector Soupel had instructed. Don't hire a car. Don't leave Paris on your own. Don't go anywhere. Bulletins and descriptions of the alleged kidnappers would be sent to gendarmeries all over eastern France. Soon enough, he assured us, the great apparatus of the French national police system would be in motion. To do anything ourselves would be both stupid and illegal. And if, for good measure, we tried to drive in those mountains in the winter, he said, the Swiss police would soon be pulling our frozen corpses out of a lake or a river bottom. Trust the authorities. Sit still and wait.

Say no to bullshit was what Norton-Griffiths used to tell us.

I suddenly hammered the flat of my hand against an iron panel and comically, improbably, as if I had jammed a spur in its flank, the little train shuddered and bucked and sixty yards up the track the locomotive snorted.

Thirty seconds later we were moving.

Inside our car Armus was eating a cold cheese sandwich that he had bought in Dijon. Root hung onto a strap, talking to the Englishman. As the train started to pick up speed, I lost my balance and sat down heavily beside Armus.

"Eleven forty-five." He held out his watch for me to see.

"Two more hours." I started to get up again, and he gripped my arm.

"You understand that I don't know anybody in Neuchâtel," he told me for maybe the twentieth time. "I did business there before the War, but the men I dealt with are all gone by now." He wiped cheese from his mouth with a handkerchief and looked at Root, then shifted on the hard bench to face me directly. "You're responsible for this, Keats. She should have come back to the apartment with us. She should have sold me the duck. You're a stupid, stupid man."

There wasn't a lot to say to that. It seemed to be the Parisian consensus. I braced my hands on the seat back in front of me to get up, and he put his hand on my arm.

"The Swiss police," he said, "will never agree to what you want. I said that before. If it weren't for Elsie I wouldn't even be here. But if we're going to do this thing, you cannot tell the Swiss police."

"No Swiss police," I said. Outside, far below us, a single light in a window hung for a moment in the black landscape, then flew away like a bird.

"No Swiss police," he repeated. "If they've gone to the Jacquet-Droz exhibit, that will be clear. We can find that out. If not, we turn right around and go back to Paris and leave it to the French police." He shivered and pulled up the collar of his coat and both of us winced as the train wheels squealed on a trestle and began to slow down again. I looked at my watch and then, for the second time in our acquaintance, Armus surprised me with a complete reversal of tone.

"Let me tell you something ironic, Keats," he said. "Not many people know this. In August of 1817 two very strange people arrived at Neuchâtel from Paris. They weren't in a train, of course, in 1817. They came in one of those big lumbering Alpine stagecoaches that nineteenth-century travelers took to cross over Switzerland and down into Italy. Astonishing what they endured in those days, just to travel. The two people I mean were Percy Bysshe Shelley and his wife Mary. She'd married him just a year or so earlier, though not in a church."

"We arrive in an hour, the British Army up there says." Root slipped into a seat in front of us.

Armus sniffed. "Percy Bysshe Shelley," he said, "was a poet and a morbid hypochondriac. No one could mention a disease without his taking it on."

"Like Vaucanson," Root said.

"Like Vaucanson, like Louis XV, like the surgeon Le Cat, like any number of monomaniacs back then, materialists who imagined that an artificial body would be better, stronger, healthier than their God-given flesh and blood bodies. Percy Shelley and Mary Shelley came to Neuchâtel specifically to look at the automates that the Jaquet-Droz family had on display. He was a poet, but he had a sense of humor. He wanted to see the Writing Boy, he told Mary, so that he could study a perfect android version of himself."

"A Mechanical Mirror," Root said.

"But evidently he was disappointed. Certainly he wasn't inspired to poetry by the Writing Boy. And after two days he hurried his party off to Geneva. But Mary Shelley was far more imaginative than her husband. She had already lost one baby. According to her diary, while they were still in Neuchâtel she went six more times to see the automates by herself and afterwards the image, particularly of the heaving chest and moving eyes of one of them, in some real sense haunted her. A year later she started a book."

"Frankenstein," Root said, spoiling his story.

And the train shivered and shuddered and came to a halt again.

Thirty-Eight

IT WAS ALMOST SEVEN-THIRTY IN THE MORNING by the time we finally rolled, creaking and groaning, into Neuchâtel, pushed from behind by another locomotive that had to be sent out from Dijon when our own used up the last of its nine lives.

The sleepy customs agent stamped our passports without looking at them, and we walked out through the deserted little station and onto the windswept, charmless town square that fronted it. Empty. No taxi, not even a dogsled.

While Root and Armus rescued our grips from the baggage compartment, I found a public telephone. I wanted to call Soupel or Mrs. Armus, but the telephone only took Swiss jetons, not French coins. I hung up and shaded my eyes against the rising sun, as if Elsie or Saulnay or Dr. Frankenstein's artificial man himself might come staggering out of the light.

It was still bitter cold but clear. We were at an altitude of about two thousand feet, yet Neuchâtel, what I could see of it in the breaking dawn, had the feel and look of an Alpine village much higher up. Above the rooftops and shuttered facades, pink-topped mountains rose in the east, jagged and forlorn.

These were the Jura Mountains, I knew, the source of the archaeologists' word "Jurassic." They had probably looked pretty much the same when prehistoric Jurassic hunters loped across them in animal skins and bare feet, or when eighteenth-century Angélique-Victoire Vaucanson had hurried past them on her way to the mysterious spot where her father had hidden away his gold and his gyroscope and his own version of an artificial, walking, talking, breathing Frankenstein Man.

"The lake is over there." Armus pointed one gloved hand toward the east. "The main church up there."

"Where's the museum?"

"This way."

Neuchâtel was not a market town. It was a watchmaking town and Swiss cuckoo-clock-making town. It had an old church and a turreted château and a squared-off medieval prison tower and one hundred and forty-three public fountains, if you believed a sign by City Hall. But without a farmers' market, none of its cafés opened at five in the morning the way they did around les Halles in Paris. We followed the street Armus had pointed out and went down a steep embankment toward the lake. From the top of our hill it looked long and flat, like a giant silver thumb pressed into a valley.

At what passed for a lakeside marina, shabby by Swiss standards, one café owner was just pulling his shutters back. We tramped inside, puffing steam like three little trains, and saw two fishermen at the zinc bar being served coffee and cognac by a teenaged girl with Mary Pickford bangs. Root ordered the same for us, and six croissants, while Armus and I took a table by the window.

"That's it. Musée d'Art et d'Histoire." Armus inclined his profile toward a tree-lined esplanade two or three hundred yards away, overlooking the lake. At the far end was a brown and white gabled building, big enough and plain enough to be anything from a hôpital to the local lycée. Three black sedans were parked at its front door, but there was nobody in them.

"Today is officially Friday, eight hours old," Root deposited a tray on the table and the girl from the bar began passing out cups. "Thursday, yesterday, according to our lovely Lady of the Coffee Bean here, the museum over there was closed all day, and it doesn't open again till noon."

"Somebody's there now," I said, and looked at the cars.

The bar girl murmured something in Root's ear and he turned his head slowly toward the museum and the cars and then back to me. "Those are the police, she says. People broke in last night and beat up the guard."

It took us almost ten minutes to walk the three hundred yards to the Musée d'Art et d'Histoire because we had first to cut back into the town, then climb a deceptively steep set of stairs to the esplanade. By the time we reached the front entrance the three black sedans had been joined by a blue and white squad car. A line of flimsy yellow sawhorses blocked the door.

In Paris, if a major museum had been broken into, the police would be swarming over the grounds like wasps and no mere civilian, certainly not a bedraggled trio of foreigners, could expect to wander casually into the crime scene. In the village of Neuchâtel the only police in sight were two yawning, uniformed gendarmes leaning against the sawhorses.

We stopped a few yards short. "Wait here," Armus said and strode briskly ahead.

Root and I looked at each other. A few months ago Root had written a piece on the novelist Tolstoy for the Book Page of the Sunday *Trib,* and he had devoted a whole column to what the great Russian writer called "shading"—his theory that human personalities were little more than perpetual bundles of contradiction. If you waited long enough, the passionate man turned cold, the coward turned brave, the hero could smile and smile and become a villain.

Twenty feet ahead of us Armus stopped and gestured abruptly to the gendarmes, and then before our eyes the pompous literary historian of the train last night metamorphosed into a kind of Prussian Commandant, staring down his nose at a pair of worms. He stood stiff as a flagpole in his fur-collared overcoat and spoke quickly, in icy-cold French. After a moment he reached in the coat and presented them a business card, and without bothering to look at us snapped his fingers in our direction.

"We're from the Chase Bank," he muttered as one of the gendarmes pulled open the front door, "and unlikely as it may seem, you're both my assistants."

Inside the front door there was a corridor lined with exhibition cases and then a set of ticket booths and turnstiles. At the turnstiles a middle-aged woman, still in her hooded parka and heavy boots, held up her hand and stopped us again.

She was warier than the gendarmes, but Armus was irresistibly patrician and condescending. He repeated his cool, bald-faced lie that he had come on behalf of the Chase Guaranty Bank of New York, Geneva branch, which underwrote most of the city's theft insurance. It was necessary at once, he insisted loudly, that he inspect for damage to the museum's collections, in case there was a monetary claim. The Swiss attitude to money has no shading about it. They don't like to annoy banks. The ticket taker held Armus's business card up to the light as if it were a counterfeit bill, then told us to wait while she went for her supervisor.

The instant she stepped out of sight I shoved a turnstile open and started trotting rapidly down the hall.

Nobody saw me.

I ignored the signs for all the other galleries and followed the red arrows for the exhibit of "Les Androids des Jacquet-Droz." Behind me I could hear somebody protesting, then Root's calming voice. As I turned right at the extreme rear of the ground floor, I saw an ornately framed portrait of Jean-Baptiste Bertin and his dog by a river. It took two more steps for my memory to jog and remind me that Bertin had been the Comptroller General of France under Louis XV. He had also been an enthusiast of automates and he was the secret funneler of money and instructions from the king to Vaucanson. It was Bertin's encoded memoranda to the Treasury, Elsie had told me, that first showed that the king's gold was being used for something wilder and more dangerous than silk weaving looms.

Elsie. Why would Saulnay take Miss Elsie Short with him? The skeptical Inspector Soupel had wanted to know that— there had been no ransom note, no message. He only had my word for the alleged abduction. What use could she possibly be to the toymaker?

Four men in business suits were standing by a broken display cabinet. Shards of wood and glass had already been swept in a pile, in the neat Swiss manner. They had the look of real insurance men. They turned toward me with puzzled expressions. Then I heard Root behind me telling them good morning in loud English, and I pushed by them and around one more corner and entered the Salle des Jacquet-Droz, where the three last surviving automates of Pierre and Henri-Louis Jacquet-Droz and their French assistant Hervé Foucault were housed.

In a sense, from Elsie's descriptions, I already knew what to expect, what the Jacquet-Droz automatons would look like. Even so, I wasn't prepared for the luxurious charm, the obsessive Swiss perfectionism of the setting that had been built for them—the space in front of me was a three-sided recreation of an eighteenth-century drawing room, with false windows and brilliant red velvet wall coverings, more antique paintings, mirrored gold girandoles, and silver sconces. Along the left and right walls were two handsome Louis XVI sofas. Four or five chairs stood around a chess table. A painting of an Alpine landscape had been propped on a tripod in a corner. Everything was here, everything was in its neat and ordered place.

Except that there were only two, not three clockwork figures.

The one on the left, I knew, was the Draughtsman—a pint-sized boy in a green velvet jacket sitting at a little mahogany desk. He held a piece of paper with his left hand, a pencil with his right. When he was set in motion, Elsie said, he could trace a butterfly, a dog, or the king's profile. The one on the right was larger and dressed as if she were going to a ball. This was the Musician that Saulnay had described in his workshop in Paris, a girl in a bright yellow gown who sat with her fingers poised over the keyboard of a small polished wooden organ, ready at the touch of a switch to begin to breathe and play.

The space in the center was empty.

"You are—?"

The one other human being in the room was a man with straw-yellow hair and an air of mild surprise. He was holding a notebook in one hand and a pen in the other. He had on ski boots and gray trousers and a blue blazer with a red and yellow medallion and the words "Départment de Conservation" stitched above it. I muttered "Police, wrong room," turned on my heel, and went out again just as Root and Armus entered the corridor.

"Toby—?"

There had been a plan of the building on the wall by the turnstiles. I headed left out of the automates' room, toward an outside door. On the right, exactly as on the plan, was an open door also marked "Départment de Conservation" and I went through it quickly, smiling, like a man who knew what he was doing.

"The Writing Boy is safe, yes?" I said in my best Parisian French. "Unharmed or damaged?"

Two technicians, with notebooks this time, one of them in a white laboratory coat, looked up frowning.

"Somebody broke in last night, n'est-ce pas? They tampered with the Writing Boy, yes?" I said.

Because that was what they had to do. Because a night and a half ago, in the police car between the rue du Dragon and Inspector Soupel's damp basement office, I had suddenly understood exactly why Saulnay had taken Elsie with him, and it was for the same reason I had brought Vincent Armus with us—to operate the automate. With his hand in bandages, Saulnay couldn't do it himself. Johannes was a thug, Johannes couldn't do it for him. But with a gun at her head Elsie Short could.

The two Swiss technicians transferred their frowns to Root and Armus behind me. I stepped between them and pushed them aside, and found myself face to face with Mary Shelley's mechanical inspiration, Hervé Foucault's secret pal, the ultimate Jacquet-Droz automate, which I would live long enough to hear called the world's first programmed computer.

The Writing Boy had been built in 1772, four years before Thomas Jefferson wrote the Declaration of Independence. He was twenty-eight inches tall, made of carved and painted wood. He had blonde hair, fair skin, pink cheeks. He was barefoot. He was dressed in a kind of flowing eighteenth-century blue silk shirt and cloak and he was seated, like the Draughtsman in the other room, behind a mahogany table or desk to which he was attached at the base. He had a quill pen in his right hand, a real inkwell beside it.

"I don't know who you are, sir." The man in the white coat was swiveling from Armus to Root to me.

"It's all right," Root said, grinning, shaking their hands with both of his. "He's from Paris, we're all from Paris. Mr. Armus is an expert on automates. The police called us in."

The Writing Boy, desk and all, was resting on a worktable surrounded by stacks of paper and miniature tools like the ones Elsie used. He had been partly turned around to his right and the cloak and shirt pinned up to reveal the lower part of his torso. And from that bare space somebody had removed a wooden plate about the size of my outspread hand, so that, thanks to the pale Swiss morning light streaming in through the window behind us, I could see his thick metal spine and golden clockwork.

All of them—Vaucanson, Jacquet-Droz, Foucault—all of them had concealed the mechanism of their automates inside the carefully sculpted bodies of human beings or animals. Elsie had told me that with some wonder. They did it because they wanted to show, not a mechanism, not a gadget or a truc, but something that looked like life itself. The Prometheus Complex, she called it. When my hand gripped the Writing Boy's shoulder, his head turned an inch or two and his eyes rolled toward me, questioning. But by that time I was peering into the occult mechanism of the cylindrical spine and the rings of levered disks and impossibly tiny cams going up and down it.

Forty cams, each one controlling a single character or letter, more than enough for what the Writing Boy always composed for public exhibition: Je pense, donc je suis. I think, therefore I am.

Most of the cams were made of a grayish-black metal—old, worn, lusterless. But toward the top of the spine, on each side, somebody had removed the old ones and in their places inserted, bright as lighthouses if you were looking for them, four slightly thicker, copper-colored, cams.

If you change the right cams, Elsie had said, you change what he writes.

"Don't touch those!" The man in the white coat grabbed my arm. I shoved him away. The other man started for the door, but Root blocked his way.

"You have to leave right now—I insist." White Coat was back, clawing at my arm again, trying to pull the Writing Boy and the little desk out of my reach. Papers and tools went flying, the automate tilted. I pushed him aside and righted the Boy.

"You—!" he said, and I hit him hard twice in the neck, just

below the ear, where Norton-Griffiths had trained us to hit in the tunnels, where the nerves and the cams all bunch together under the bone, and he dropped to the floor like a hammer.

By the door Root and the other Swiss technician went stiff and silent. Armus took a deep breath and said nothing.

I swung back to the worktable and began to paw through the tools and papers and boxes scattered across it.

"They put those cams in," Armus said, "last night. The shiny ones." He bent beside me, shoulder to shoulder, and squinted into the gears.

"Elsie put them in. That's why they brought her. With Saulnay's hand in splints they had to have somebody who could make it work. Johnannes wouldn't know." There was absolutely nothing I wanted on the table, no scrap of paper, no message, no trail of bread crumbs, nothing.

"Toby," Root said from the door. "The floor."

"Make it write," I said to Armus, because that was why I had brought him, the only reason in the world. "The new cams changed his text. I don't know how to make him work, but you do. Wind him up, plug him in, do what it takes."

On the floor the man in the white coat was stirring, coming groggily to his knees. Hardheaded Swiss. Armus didn't bother to raise his head. He was still dressed in his fur-collared topcoat and pearl-gray wool suit, and he looked as if he should be strolling down the avenue Montaigne with an ivory cane and a poodle. But he had been collecting automatons since before the War, he had a house full of tools, and he had made his Bird Bush spring into action with a flick of his thumb.

"Hit him again." Armus glanced at the man on the floor.

"There's ink, the pen is ready." I turned the Writing Boy slightly on the tabletop and Armus moved around to the side. By the door Root was making a pair of gags with handkerchiefs. I tossed him a roll of cord from the table.

"I don't know," Armus said. "They always hid the starting

mechanism. You have to wind them up, sometimes with a key, sometimes a handle. This one maybe. Or—no. Here. This."

He stretched one arm around the little desk and slowly rotated something I couldn't see.

It was half-past eight according to the undoubtedly accurate Swiss clock on the wall. Outside, the Lac de Neuchâtel was stirring in its bed, the pale winter sun was riding a strong east wind higher in the sky, aiming its beams at our windows. As always with artificial life, nothing happened for a space of five, six seconds. Fiat lux. The Writing Boy's doll-like face gazed straight ahead at a spot on the wall. His bare feet stayed where they were, crossed at the ankles. Then the familiar whirring, clicking sound of creation began and a moment later his right arm, slowly, smoothly rose in the air.

He turned his face to the right and dipped his quill pen into the inkwell on the desk. He shook the pen twice. I write, therefore I am. His face lowered toward the square of paper in front of him, and with an almost imperceptible nod, methodically, confidently, as his eyes moved back and forth following his pen, the Writing Boy's hand began to trace whatever message it was that Jacques de Vaucanson's daughter and her lover had secretly taught him to write, the place, if Elsie and Saulnay and I were right, where the Bleeding Man was hidden.

What did it take? Thirty seconds? Fifty? Nobody in the room was counting. By the door Root and the other technician had stopped their scuffling. The man on the floor was blinking madly.

Armus and I hovered by the square of paper, watching each careful, deliberate scratch of the quill. When it stopped, Armus snatched the paper free and spread it on the table.

"What?" Root said from the door.

Armus shook his head in disgust. "Gibberish."

"Code," I said, thinking of Vaucanson and the universal grammar machine and Solresol. My ears were buzzing in pain. "A goddam eighteenth-century code."

"We need to leave," Armus said. "I hear people coming."

"He's supposed to write 'Je pense, donc je suis,'" I said and banged the table with my fist.

"Now," Armus said. "We need to leave now."

"Let me see it." Root bent over the table where the paper lay. On the paper the automate had traced in inch-high blue-black letters this message:

f t d Pre ggdg onc je suis

"I'm opening the door," Armus said. "We're going."

"That's not gibberish." Root looked up at me. "Toby."

"We have to go!" Armus was in the hall. There was an outside door to the right, leading straight to the esplanade. Far down the corridor voices were booming.

"That's not gibberish," Root said. Root of the quick, capacious, analytic mind. "That's shorthand like McCormick's cabalese at the paper. Those are directions. Font de Pré—left, left, right, left. Gauche, gauche, droite, gauche."

"Font de Pré?"

"It's by Le Puy," Root said as we started to run. "Southwest of Lyon. It's a cave, Toby."

Thirty-Nine

LYON IS THE SECOND LARGEST CITY IN FRANCE. It was already ancient and important when Jacques de Vaucanson lived there in the middle of the eighteenth century, building his silk-weaving machines and slipping away into the Dordogne Valley on his blasphemous secret projects.

The Romans founded Lyon as a colony in 43 BC and called it "Lugdunum," which sounds like something out of *Gulliver's Travels*. And almost the first thing the new colonists of Lugdunum did was construct an enormous amphitheatre on a hillside overlooking the convergence of the Saône and Rhone rivers, for gladiators and chariot racing. It still existed in 1927. From the train station platform I could crane my neck and see the funicular railway up to it and, under a black ceiling of clouds, the monotonous ruined arches of the amphitheatre wall. But compared to the cave dwellers of the Dordogne Valley, sixty or seventy miles to the west, the Romans had practically come yesterday.

"Over there," Root murmured.

Armus and I both looked up. On the opposite platform, two sets of tracks away, a pair of gendarmes, fat as teddy bears in their heavy blue overcoats, were strolling with their batons clasped behind their backs, studying the crowd of waiting passengers.

The big station clock above the tracks read 1:38 p.m.

"They will not," Armus said, "have the slightest interest in us."

He was right. I knew he was right. We had left the museum by the esplanade door, at a dead run, and nobody had seen us, nobody had followed. At the little Neuchâtel station we had scrambled aboard a local Swiss train for La Chaux that was already starting to roll. From there to Besançon. Besançon to Lyon. We had taken nothing from the museum but a scrap of paper. A mild case of assault, with no property damage, was not going to provoke the Swiss police into an international manhunt.

"Not the slightest interest," Armus repeated, and all three of us stood up as a grimy black locomotive came hissing and clanking along the platform, pulling a line of battered pre-war carriages. An engineer with a beret on his head and a pipe between his teeth watched complacently as the wheels braked and gave one last ankle-scalding burst of steam and the carriage doors popped open. It didn't look like a Time Machine, but it was about to carry us back 20,000 years.

Time, of course, was everything now. As best we could figure, Saulnay and Johannes would have reached Neuchâtel about ten hours before us, dragging Elsie with them. They would have broken into the museum after midnight. Then, if Saulnay had understood what the Writing Boy was telling them . . . No question that he had. Saulnay was used to automatons, how they worked, how they could be tinkered with.

"Some men are born to hangovers," Root said. He sat down

and offered me a paper cup and then held up a bottle of red wine he had bought at the station in Lyon. "And some have hangovers thrust upon them. Bread and sausage in my pocket." He flapped his coat with one arm. "You need to eat, Toby. Even Armus took some sausage."

I glanced over at Armus, who was sitting directly in front of Root in our tiny, cramped compartment, head lolling slightly from side to side in weariness. His eyes were shut, his chin was buried in his scarf. After two days of French trains his clothes were rumpled and filthy. The elegant fur collar on his overcoat was smeared with a sticky unidentifiable film.

Shadings, I thought, Tolstoyan contradictions. He looked nothing at all like the Prussian Commandant who had frozen the brains of the two gendarmes in Neuchâtel with his glare, not a bit like the Patrician Prick of the Champ-de-Mars. He looked like a railway tramp, a down-on-his-luck vagabond.

I had my own theory of character, which was not Tolstoyan. It was a theory that had been drummed into me long ago by an editor at the *Boston Globe,* who used to grab my lapels on my way out to a story. People are simple, he would say, stories are simple. All you ever need to know about somebody is this one simple thing: What does he want?

Deep, deep down, where obsessions start, what does he really want?

I watched Armus's head jerk with the rhythm of the tracks, and I had no idea what he wanted, I had no idea at all. Then I rubbed my own unshaven chin with the side of my hand and turned back to the window to study the rain. I wanted Elsie.

They wouldn't have harmed her. That was my constant inner refrain. They wouldn't hurt her. But they wouldn't let her go either, because they would need Elsie's good hands one more time, for one more task. So they would hire a car somewhere and take to the roads. That's all they could do. Saulnay would assume that the trains and the buses were watched. But whether he hired a car or stole a car, he still wouldn't get to the Dordogne Valley before the train.

The window was streaked with wriggling white worms of water. The road alongside the track looked icy slick. Out in the passing forest the trees and bushes were bent low, bowing to the cold, hard, driving rain that had begun to fall just west of Lyon.

Root couldn't sit still. He got up and opened the compartment door to the train corridor, stuck his head out, closed the door again.

"Saint-Bonnet," he said, repeating the plan we had already worked out on the train down from Neuchâtel. "Saint-Bonnet is six miles north of the cave where they're going, more or less. What we do, in Saint-Bonnet, we find the gendarmerie, Toby makes them call Soupel in Paris, they send out the troops. We don't have to go anywhere near Font-de-Pré."

"Bravo, Root," Armus said sarcastically, without opening his eyes. "I will make you my general."

I wiped condensation from the window with a handkerchief and jammed my hand back in my pocket.

Above the evergreen forest rose a line of bare, gray cliffs, wet and jagged boundaries as tall as a five-story building, like walls. They paralleled the track on either side of the river for as far as I could see. But not regular, geometric Roman walls, made of uniform blocks and arches. These were limestone cliffs. They weren't as big or famous as the cliffs much farther west, in the Dordogne Valley, where the Cro-Magnon Man had been found. But by some geological twist, these cliffs had been dug out over the eons by the cold, fast rivers that crisscrossed the Massif Central. They were limestone, they were highly porous to water, soft to the touch of the wind. From the train, they looked wrinkled like an elephant's hide, grayish-white, and wildly irregular.

Along with the Dordogne Valley, these were some of the oldest settled parts of Europe. Men and women had been hunting along the streams here and living in the cliffs since before the Egyptians erected their first pyramid, or the Mesopotamians settled into villages along the Tigris. Living in the cliffs, in the caves in the limestone cliffs.

Mary Shelley, I thought, had picked the wrong landscape for horror. Snow-capped mountains weren't terrifying. High, bright summits, close to the sun and sky, weren't frightening. Caves were what you wanted for sheer terror, sheer claustrophobic terror. Caves deep in the earth. Tunnels with no light at all. You climb up for light. You dig down for darkness.

"Ten minutes," Root said. "Ten minutes to go."

On the opposite bench Armus, fully awake, stared at me without speaking. Root poured me a paper cup full of wine and tore me off a part of a stale baguette and I sat and gnawed and stared right back at him.

By now, I thought, there was really nothing left to say. We had talked ourselves out, from Neuchâtel to Dijon to Lyon—whatever Armus the collector and student of automatons hadn't already known, I had finally told him: the Bleeding Man and Elsie's theories, Angélique-Victoire, Saulnay and his nephew and the gyroscopes and the war. At that point in the story Armus had sneered. Saulnay might believe that he could sell the automaton to the German army. Saulnay might believe that because he was an uneducated thug. But not even Jacques de Vaucanson, in Armus's learned opinion, could have built a gyroscope small enough to fit in a mannequin's head.

Yet the Bleeding Man, even without a gyroscope . . . Jacques de Vaucanson's lost masterpiece of Art and Science was incredibly valuable.

A certain kind of person, Armus had said, might kill to find the Bleeding Man.

Once, and once only, had Armus flared into anger: if the cave had a name, people must have explored it—what could possibly be left for anybody to see?

But Root had written a story once, for the *Trib*'s Sunday Travel Section, about the tourist attractions of the Massif Central. And Root never forgot a word he had typed.

Font-de-Pré was only the name of a nearby farm, he said. The cave had been officially discovered four years ago, in 1922, the same year as the better known cave in the Dordogne called Pêch-Merle, where tourists and archaeologists came in droves to look at the prehistoric paintings, and nobody had paid much attention to the smaller, much less accessible cave.

But Font-de-Pré was certainly known to somebody long before 1922. The two small boys (and their dog) who discovered it had turned up, just inside its mouth, old eighteenth-century bottles and plates and half a wooden wheel that belonged to an eighteenth-century carriage. Cro-Magnon bones and wall paintings were undoubtedly somewhere deeper inside. But nobody knew for sure, because two days after the boys discovered the cave, the Massif Central suffered one of its occasional deep earth tremors and several tons of splintering limestone had fallen across the entrance.

"My legs hurt," Armus said.

"Five minutes," Root said.

At Saint-Anthème we entered a tunnel and I closed my eyes. At Saint-Bonnet the train rattled and swayed to a halt. Root tapped my arm and opened the compartment door, and we stepped out into the rain.

Forty

No plan, they used to say in the Army, survives first contact with the enemy.

Saint-Bonnet was tiny, barely big enough to call a hamlet. It seemed to consist of no more than the squat, square, one-story wooden train station, which was empty except for us; a bakery, closed at this time of day; a dozen houses strung along each side of a narrow, muddy road. There was a garage opposite the station, with a Michelin Tire sign over the door illuminated by the single Edisonian electric light I could see in the whole village, probably run off a generator. Everything else was kerosene lamps or cold, wet, gathering darkness, folding down from the limestone cliffs like a great black prehistoric wing.

Inside the garage there were five more lightbulbs strung over two repair bays. One bay was filled with wooden crates. On the other sat a battered green two-seater Citroën A 8CV. A pair of boots and trousers stuck comically out from under a running board. And behind the office counter, next to a charcoal heater, a cheerful teenage girl was eating a sandwich made out of a sliced baguette and a chocolate bar.

"No gendarmerie in Saint-Bonnet," she said. She looked placidly from one face to another and settled on Root, the youngest. "We're much too small. You have to go all the way to Le Puy."

"Can we telephone from here?"

The girl shrugged and inclined her head toward the front window, where the rain was flying past, almost horizontal to the muddy street. There was a telephone in the Post Office at Craponne, she told us, but it closed at two in the afternoon in winter. In emergencies, the train station could probably telegraph.

"There was," Armus said with barely concealed fury, "nobody in the damned train station."

The girl was unperturbed. She took a bite of her chocolate sandwich and turned around to peer through an open door at the Citroën. "You can drive that car to Craponne," she said, "for four hundred francs."

"Ridiculous." Armus pulled up his fur collar, already soaking wet from the short run over from the station. "That's much too much."

He doesn't have it, I suddenly thought. I remembered his overdraft, his overdue loan, Libby Armus's pinched face when he offered Elsie cash. The unemployed banker from the rue Jean Carriès doesn't have four hundred francs. Fifteen dollars.

Rain blew against the front window, scratching frantically at the glass. The wind shook the Michelin sign like a flag. I pulled out my wallet.

"You are," Root told the girl, "the cutest little highway robber I've ever seen." He counted out two hundred and fifty francs from his own wallet, slid a hundred of mine down the counter, and then from somewhere in his heavy coat produced two flat squares of chocolate wrapped in brown paper and tissue. "Mad money," he said to me in English. "Ça suffit?" to the girl.

She took the money and the chocolate and left us at the counter while she crossed over and down to the garage proper and said something we couldn't hear to the legs under the running board. When she came back she said, "You can have it in thirty minutes, maybe less," and brought out the inevitable French quadruplicate forms and quintuplicate forms. Cro-Magnon Man probably had to fill them out with a chisel.

"I'll drive the car," Armus said. "I'll drive to Craponne and call Soupel. You two wait here in case Elsie shows up."

I looked at the girl's office clock, which said it was only four-fifteen, though the sky and the rain outside made it seem like midnight. Police would still be hours away. Who really knew where Elsie was? It was no bad idea to get Armus out of our hair. If I found her first, we wouldn't need him at all.

"Our lucky day," the girl said to Root as she gave him the first set of papers and a pen and ink. "We go weeks without anybody hiring a car, and now, there you are, two in one day."

Root looked up from his forms. I put my hands on the counter.

"Today just after lunch," she said cheerfully. "Before the rain started, three more customers came in to rent. They took our big four-door Monasix Renault." She spread some more forms on the counter. "For two men and a girl."

Memory is the iceberg, thought is the iceberg's tip.

The electric flashlight, Norton-Griffiths had told me once, was a French invention, but the zinc-encased chemical batteries were perfected by an American firm called "EverReady" and that was the only kind of battery-powered flashlight he allowed us to have in the tunnels.

"Mademoiselle." As calmly as I could, I pointed to a set of banged-up metal flashlights beside the cash register and asked if they were for sale, with fresh "EverReady" batteries. The girl behind the counter wiped chocolate from her fingertips. That would be twenty-five francs more, she said, and held out her hand.

The other people were strangers, too, she thought, maybe Parisians because they had funny accents, like us. The older man had a limp. She slid two flashlights over the counter and looked at us curiously, then she went down to the car again.

It was ten minutes to five by the clock on the garage wall when Armus finally squeezed himself behind the wheel of the Citroën and banged the door closed.

"You should wait over there in the station," he told us in his peremptory manner. "In case somebody comes by train." Then he pulled his head back and pressed the starter button, and the unseen motor jumped to life, like an automaton. The girl raised the garage door with a chain crank, Armus eased the car's snout out onto the muddy main street. He gunned the engine, the two red reflectors on the rear fenders bounced, flickered, and disappeared around a curve.

The garage had no maps, but the girl drew us a rough outline on the back of our bill. Craponne was no more than twenty kilometers to the southwest, on what passed for the main road. But, she warned, it would be slow traveling today on that road. When it rained like this the streams flooded the pavement in all the low spots, everything flooded around Saint-Bonnet because the limestone was so porous. The cliffs turned into waterfalls, the roads turned into lakes. Font-de-Pré, she added, was barely two kilometers in the opposite direction from Craponne, but the entrance to the old cave was blocked off and dangerous because of falling rocks and water. Nobody from Saint-Bonnet ever went there.

Root and I stood in the open door and looked down the road where she had pointed. The rain was stronger than ever, lashing the sky. Armus would have been better off, I thought, renting a boat. Root was wearing a beat-up fedora and a heavy black canvas coat that he had grabbed on the way out the door in Paris, and it seemed to drink the water instead of shed it. Shivering and muttering, he buttoned his collar and started to trudge toward the train station across the street.

I stayed where I was, in front of the garage, under the light. "Root."

He peered back over his shoulder like an owl.

"You wait there," I said, nodding at the station and trying hard not to sound like Armus. "I can't."

He stood in the rain and nodded, then he turned and kept on going toward the station.

I was sixty yards past the last house in Saint-Bonnet when he caught up to me. Neither of us spoke. We hunched our necks against the wind, buried our chins, marched.

On the wet road, against the flying rain, it took us fifteen minutes to walk a kilometer. I found a road marker along the shoulder, shaped as they always are in France like a New England gravestone, and I used my flashlight to study the garage girl's map and then look at my watch. Root stamped his feet and blew his nose and we started off again.

To walk is to think. To think, remember. Most men, Elsie Short had said sardonically in the café, confuse autobiography with conversation. I swung my legs rhythmically, steadily along the side of the road, into the falling rain. The road was unpaved, like so many rural roads in France in 1927. The rain had turned the surface to mud, a dense, gritty mud that sucked at our shoes and froze our feet. I really was in a Time Machine now, I thought, I was marching in the mud in France again, I was going backwards with every step.

Going backwards in more ways than one. Craponne, I had somehow remembered half a kilometer back, was the town where Jean-Baptiste Bertin had established his country home, where scholars, Elsie said, had found his account book with the records of secret payments to Vaucanson, his fellow enthusiast of artificial life. If you wanted a place to hide your work, your money from Parisian eyes, Bertin's obscure country house beneath the limestone cliffs was hard to beat.

Root stopped ahead of me. His black coat, I thought, fit him like a shadow. He pointed his flashlight beam at a wooden post and called my name, and I had a sudden vision of Jacques de Vaucanson deep in the bowels of the earth, in a limestone cave, his torches dancing in the darkness like Root's flashlight, but giving off a sulfurous, blasphemous smell. The king approached him, weaving and stumbling. They stood together grinning like a pair of alligators. I saw a gigantic figure of glass and metal—

"Toby."

I wrenched my mind back from the eighteenth century.

"This is it," Root said. "Font-de-Pré."

I bent down to touch a whitewashed wooden post. There had been a chain looped around it, going to another post a few yards off, but this post was leaning badly and the chain was in the mud as if wheels had gone over it. I could barely read the official metal plaque attached to it with a piece of wire: "Fermé." Buried in mud was another plaque: "Chasse Interdite. Pierres Tombantes." No hunting allowed. Falling rocks.

"Tire ruts," Root said, and played his flashlight beam up and down a churned-up gully just beyond the posts. "Two or three sets of them. One goes over in that direction." He pointed the flashlight beam toward a black mass of vegetation where two swampy, half-frozen ruts disappeared into the darkness. His beam snagged for an instant on something that might have been metallic, then the wind bunched the branches and leaves into a shaggy wet ball and whatever it was disappeared.

"The main ones follow some kind of old trail up to the cliffs." Root brought the flashlight back around to the right.

"If you stay close here by the road," I said, "you can signal Armus when he comes."

"While you do what?"

I didn't answer because I didn't know. I clicked my flashlight off and started to move up the gully, into the knee-high bushes and muddy weeds that once upon a time would have been part of a pré, a meadow. Close by on my left, I could hear, over the snap and flutter of the wind, the hiss of a stream curling off through the weeds like a snake. And beyond that, I could hear the deeper, angrier rush of a waterfall cascading down the cliffs.

Floods everywhere, she had said.

Where was the car that had made the ruts?

No big, heavy steel-bodied Renault, I thought, could drive very far through the mud and tangle of the field, let alone get through the dense line of forest that began just yards ahead.

I felt my way between the tire ruts. Each time I stopped I could see the cliffs hovering over the trees, an unbreaking wave of high, gray stone, Frozen Time, Calcified Time.

I had been wrong in Paris about Solresol, I thought, and wrong about how long it would take somebody to drive from Neuchâtel to Saint-Bonnet, and now I was probably wrong about the car too. I had almost reached the trees at the bottom of the waterfall before my flashlight picked it up, a brief glimmering of blue paint on a fender, almost as dark as Root's coat.

There was nobody in it, nothing. The back tires had sunk six inches down into the mud. I risked one quick burst of light on the empty front seat and crept around the front of the car toward the sound of falling water.

Saulnay's limp, I guessed. They would have driven as close as they could to the entrance of the cave because of Saulnay's limp. Could Elsie have jumped free in the darkness and run for help? I remembered Johannes's Webley pistol and jammed the flashlight in my coat pocket and followed a muddy track uphill.

Sixty feet from the car, the ground began trembling under my feet from the waterfall, and I could see why nobody came to Font-de-Pré.

In front of me was a jagged pile of boulders and splintered rocks at least twice my height. This had to be where the deep earth tremor had shaken the cliffs. The rocks were long, flat, stacked, and angled in all directions. The waterfall burst like a rocket out of a break in them far up the side of the cliff. The rocks and boulders beneath it groaned and creaked in the violent rush of the water, as if they were about to tumble and fall again, and against the silver gray clouds of the western sky they made a black silhouette like the knuckles of a fist.

Closer to me, not twenty feet away, a maze of tall crevices and cracks led inward and down, under the wet, slippery rocks, toward a thin black fissure.

I crouched and started to move forward again on bent knees, then stopped completely. Duckwalking, I thought, and told myself that if I bit my tongue I wouldn't laugh and I wouldn't cry and I wouldn't have to go down in the dark.

There were old boards by my feet, another chain, another warning plaque upside down in the mud—"Danger de Mort. Pierres Tombantes." My pulse was beating like a tom-tom. My hands were gritty and wet. I took a deep breath and braced myself on a ledge.

A light came on in the rocks.

For a long moment I stayed precisely where I was, motionless, not even breathing. Voices drifted out of the cave, over the roar of the water.

I could go in as long as there was light, I thought. I could go into a cave or a tunnel as long as I could stand up and see. Anybody could do that much.

I reached the edge of the last boulder and started to squeeze myself into the crevice. It was not much wider than a man's shoulders, not much wider than a coat hanger. The waterfall was just above my head to the left, whipping the air back and forth with spray. The rock surface here was rubbed slick by time and water, smooth to the touch like skin. I could still hear the voices moving away in the cave. The light inside made a wavering white crescent across the stone. I turned to one side and forced myself five steps deeper. It was like crawling into a bone.

I took three more steps and the light went out.

Forty-One

ELSIE'S VOICE CAME LOUD AND CLEAR, not a hundred feet away.

She was around a corner, well inside the cave, and she was telling somebody not to be a fool, but I couldn't hear more than that. I couldn't think about that. Even in the darkness, my eyes were closed as hard I could close them. I was as rigid as a stone. I was an automaton, immobile, without a key to turn and make me move. My face was drenched with sweat and with spray from the waterfall. My wrists were crossed against my face, a sign of weeping.

There were stages in panic, I knew. Paralysis, stupor, then the letting go. I had scratched my cheek against something sharp in the crevice and a trickle of blood was running down my jaw. Slowly, slowly, I wiped it away and lowered my wrists. A thousand French soldiers a day had died in the war, a thousand a day for four years, many of them buried or drowned in the mud when their shelters and dugouts collapsed on their heads. I thought about my name, Keats, which had always haunted me, the English poet in love with easeful death. When he was dying in Rome, I had read, he spat arterial blood into his hands, wet rags of tissue like Eric the Minor's lungs. A Bleeding Man. I bleed, therefore I am.

"You are," said Henri Saulnay, next to my ear, "just in time, Mr. Keats." And I sighed like a dead man and opened my eyes.

He had a gun, of course, probably the same little automatic he had threatened me with on the rue du Dragon. I felt it prodding my ribs, but my eyes were fixed on the flashlight he carried in his other hand, the bandaged one. It made a brilliant cone of light at my feet, yellow at the edges. The light twitched softly from side to side like a cat's tail.

"That way," he said in French. "You first."

The cave sloped downward at almost thirty degrees. As best I could tell in the darkness we were in an antechamber directly below the waterfall. As I shuffled forward I could hear the rocks grinding and scraping just above us, but the roof in the antechamber was high, ten feet high at least, and I didn't have to stoop. Step by step I started to breathe again. My shoes kicked bits of junk and detritus on the floor, loose pebbles.

Elsie must have been much farther away than I had imagined, because we kept on descending, turning through narrow passages whose ceilings dropped lower and lower. The passages were incredibly confusing. Once a strong downward draft of cold air passed across my face, and I tried to steady my head and remember elementary science—cold air sank, cold air sank as the night came on. Cold air sinks, warm air rises. To pull the air down into the cave with that much force, I thought, there had to be another opening somewhere, a back entrance, or a hollow under the waterfall.

"Stop right there," Saulnay said.

Behind me the flashlight beam played on my shoes and the chalky white floor. Saulnay adjusted an unseen piece of equipment.

I closed my eyes and tried to remember what Root had written in the *Trib* about the geology of the caves. The cliffs were limestone, of course, grayish-white and black, an extremely porous sedimentary rock. On top of the cliffs, two or three hundred feet above us, would be a layer of soil, but under that soil it would be limestone, limestone all the way down. The groundwater on top would leach down through the soil over the ages, and its acid would eat away the calcite in limestone, dissolving it and washing it away in waterfalls and boring out innumerable caves and tunnels. The result was a great plateau of rock riddled with holes.

In cold, wet weather, Root had written, it is as unstable as a house of cards.

Saulnay prodded me with the pistol again and we turned left at a corner that was marked by a grid of pink stalagmites rising out of the floor.

"That was the third left, Mr. Keats, if you were counting. Gauche, gauche, droit, gauche, as our little wooden friend in Neuchâtel wrote. There were two passages off to the right that I don't think you even saw. I notice your hands are shaking. It's a pity about your tremor. You're going to turn right precisely where my light is pointing and then stand as still as you can."

He touched my sleeve and I turned where he said and Elsie Short sprang up in the light like a jack-in-the-box and started toward me.

"Toby!"

I didn't stand still. I jumped forward and somebody knocked me sideways into the hard wall of the cave, and I went down on my knees and rolled through water. When I straightened again, I could see Johannes's big shoulders behind a flashlight beam and Elsie's green waterproof coat, and next to her, as the cone of light rose, Vincent Armus's white face.

"Keats," he said softly and extended his hands slightly like a martyr to show that they were bound at the wrists by a cord.

We were in a chamber next to a rushing underground stream. I felt the cold air moving across my face again, even colder now because I was soaking wet. I could hear the stream hissing, banging rhythmically against a loose rock. The floor was damp.

The chamber itself I thought was concave, like the bottom of an upside-down bowl, but that was hard to know for sure, since the only light came from the flashlights Saulnay and Johannes carried, and from a single kerosene lantern resting ten feet away on the ground.

"Keats," Armus said again.

When the flashlight moved away, the lantern on the ground gave him the effect of nightmarish deformity. Its light reached just to his chin, so that his eyes and the top of his head disappeared as he shifted his weight. He looked bizarrely incomplete.

"I didn't go to Craponne," he murmured, "I wanted to get to the cave first. I didn't think you would come. I hid my car off in the bushes, by the road. What I wanted—"

And he said something else that I couldn't hear, but I had already lost interest in Vincent Armus, and so, apparently, had Saulnay. He pushed Armus roughly to one side and played his flashlight up and down the cave wall on my right.

"Get over there, Mr. Keats, next to the girl, but keep an arm's length distance from her."

"My friend is going to be here with the police," I said, "any minute."

He didn't bother to reply. I didn't blame him. It had sounded feeble enough, even to me. I heard scraping noises in the shadows, the clink of metal on metal, and one by one I began to sort out other images. Water running down the cave wall. Elsie's blonde hair, her feet in the same brown shoes she had been wearing the first day in Paris. Armus's hands, bound very tight with thin rope. And on the opposite wall, as if it were flying straight out of the black rock and into my face, the fierce white wings and big eyes of a cartoonish-like owl.

I jerked my head back. Saulnay must have been watching. I heard him chuckle and saw him move to the other side of the lantern.

"Very good, Mr. Keats, you recover a little underground, in

your natural habitat. Mole meets Owl. That's one of the drawings they find in these caves sometimes. There's another over here—"

He waved his beam up and down. "This." A man's handprint materialized on the wall as if it had just soaked through the stone. Its fingers were spread wide and outlined in red and white. They seemed to be gripping a stone protuberance on the wall, the way you would grip a ball.

"That would be the artist's own hand, no doubt," Saulnay said. "He was signing his painting." Saulnay moved somewhere else in the chamber, and I half turned to follow him. As my eyes adjusted more and more to the darkness, the old skills crept back. I caught flashes of color, spots of movement here and there. I could have been a fish in one of Armus's tanks, floating in the dark like a dot.

"Or perhaps," Saulnay said, "this is the hand of our own Jacques de Vaucanson, because we know for a fact that he was here, in this very cave, this very space. Perhaps he left his signature for us, the way ordinary tourists write their names on the walls at Peche Merle."

I felt Elsie's fingers touch my right hand, and I shifted an infinitesimal distance closer to her.

Even as I moved, I heard the waterfall shift a little too, above the sound of the stream, and I felt its vibrations grow stronger through the porous limestone. Out of nowhere Saulnay's hard Roman profile appeared on my left.

"You have a vivid imagination, Mr. Keats. You're a writer. I want you to picture this scene. Picture Jacques de Vaucanson, dressed in his quaint eighteenth-century garb, wearing his powdered wig, his ever-present gentleman's sword. His servants grip their torches— real torches, not these metal 'EverReadys'—and one by one, in procession they slip and stumble and feel their way in. They go about two hundred meters, because that's all we've come, believe it or not, about two hundred meters from the entrance. There was no waterfall then as far as I can tell, or underground stream like the one over there. The cave was perfectly dry. Otherwise—"

He thumped his hand against hollow wood, a bulky shape, taller than I was. I had all along sensed its presence, I realized, but not seen it.

"Otherwise," he said, "this cabinet and what is in it would not have been preserved."

"He couldn't have worked in here." Armus had found his voice again. "Not with metal and automates."

In the darkness Saulnay moved again. "No, not with the automates. His workshop was in Bertin's house back along the road to Craponne, long ago destroyed. But every time Vaucanson left the cliffs to go back to Paris, he deposited the Bleeding Man here in its special waterproof, airtight cabinet, out of sight. He deposited the Bleeding Man and the money."

"Money?" My tongue was thick and stupid.

"The gold and jewels, poor Mr. Keats, that the king paid Vaucanson year after year, out of his secret funds. Likewise waterproof, rust-proof, perfectly safe down here from all prying eyes."

The gold and jewels . . . I turned slowly toward Armus, and even in the suffocating darkness of the cave I felt something like a light dawning.

What does he want? Of course Armus had tried to come here first. What he wanted, what the bankrupt Armus wanted, was the money. Not any gyroscope or automate. The duck would tell him the way to the money.

There was a loud crash somewhere in front of us, in the darkness, and I could feel the limestone shiver dangerously against my back. As far as I could tell, somewhere behind the cabinet, the cave wall had split open at the base and left a gap, a cleft. That was where the stream surged out of its interior channel deep in the limestone and came into the open. I could see the running water now, a yard wide at least, spreading across the chamber floor. As it curved around the wall, it made long phosphorescent ripples and kicked and chewed at the stone before it hit another cleft under the owl painting and drained out of sight again. Saulnay splashed sideways across the floor. He said something in German, got a muttered reply. The snout of his automatic moved back into the light. "Johannes is worried. He thinks the cave is not safe."

There is no darkness like the darkness of a tunnel, no emptiness. The cave was not safe, Johannes was right, the rain outside was swelling the stream inside to the breaking point, the cave was filling up with phantoms, faces slowly spinning, wet petals on a stem.

I had been wrong again, I thought, wrong about everything, wrong from the start. Because what was true for the bankrupt Armus was also true for the bankrupt, embittered Saulnay.

"The money," I said hoarsely. "It was always about the money, wasn't it?" I took a step forward. "As soon as you saw the duck in Bassot's window, you thought of the money—Vaucanson's fortune, the king's gold that Vaucanson took and kept because he was a miser. It was never anything to do with a gyroscope, was it?"

"It may be yet. You give me ideas, Mr. Keats. Move back, please. Move away from the girl. We're in a hurry now."

I took one more step toward him. "I know caves and mines. I've spent my life in them. That wall isn't going to collapse. You have plenty of time."

The pistol pushed out of the darkness into the light like a hand coming out of stone.

"Show us," I said, almost in a whisper, "the Bleeding Man."

There was only the sound of sloshing water, the moan and scrape of the limestone, gathering its weight above us. Despite the chill, sweat was dripping from my eyes, my nose. The Toymaker, I thought, would not pull the trigger yet. The Toymaker wanted to make his effect, frighten the children. He wanted to wind up his dolls and turn them loose and see them run off the side of the table. Let him.

I took one step sideways.

Saulnay lowered his gun. He was a twisting shadow, gray

smoke. When he spoke again he was farther away, just inside the lantern's glow. To his left stood the tall piece of furniture, which gradually, knob by knob, panel by panel, came into focus.

It was a mahogany armoire, an antique eighteenth-century clothes cabinet. They would have gone wild about it in the shops on the rue Bonaparte. It was at least seven feet tall, four feet wide, and Saulnay must have been right about the dryness of the cave when Vaucanson stored it there, because, though the feet and legs looked battered and warped by the water of the stream, the upper sections were straight and clean and one or two of the brass hinges still winked and glistened like fireflies in the light.

"If either of you moves, I will shoot."

It was Saulnay who spoke, but Johannes who came into view. He shifted the lantern onto a ledge just a few inches over the muddy floor. I could only see him from the waist down, half a man, two legs walking like scissors. His left hand gripped the Webley revolver. His right hand held a crowbar.

I willed my feet a few inches forward.

"There's a lock on it." Johannes worked the crowbar between slits in the cabinet door. "The cabinet's incredibly heavy."

"He would have lined it with lead," Elsie said from somewhere behind me, "to keep out rats."

Johannes half knelt with his crowbar, one pants leg in the oily black water, and his broad shoulders went down and suddenly up like a pump, and over the constant drum of the stream and the waterfall there was a long, nerve-shredding sound of splintering wood and groaning metal.

It was like opening a tomb, I thought.

Even the cave seemed to hold its breath. The door of the cabinet swung slowly outward, from right to left, and for the first time in two hundred years, light spilled over the glassy form, the naked head and shoulders, the eyes, the perfectly formed hands, the transparent crystal torso of the Bleeding Man. Vaucanson's Adam. Proto Man.

He was standing upright, the crown of his bare head just touching the top of the cabinet. As the light and shadows from the lantern wavered back and forth across his chest, there was the briefest illusion of movement, of breath, and I thought of the doll at the piano, the clown that came to life and terrified the children.

Then the cold air, running in from the depths of the cave, made something in his mechanism contract and start, and for one unbearable second the Bleeding Man seemed to shudder and exhale and take a step forward—

"Johannes!"

Johannes straightened and caught it in his arms. Saulnay limped into the light. He played his flashlight up and down the length of the automate's cloudy glass legs. I heard Elsie beside me gasp—in the flashlight's beam you could see the inner gears and metal cams and clockwork wheels that would have made the creature rise, walk, turn and turn again. And coiling around them, like the lace of a spider's web, thin blue-black veins were pressed between layers of glass, an eighteenth-century filigree of cracked rubber and dried-out blood, artificial life.

"Put it back—look at the bottom of the cabinet."

Johannes shoved the Bleeding Man back into his upright position. Under his feet, the width of the cabinet, were two drawers with silver knobs in the center. Johannes pulled at the drawer on the left. In a silent gliding motion it came forward to reveal, not scattered and loose, but neatly arranged in columns, by the careful, calculating hand of Jacques de Vaucanson himself, row after row of small engraved coins that had the true, authentic dull yellow glow of gold.

Saulnay dropped to his knees in the water and Johannes stood up. He kept his pistol aimed at the three of us. Saulnay turned and grinned over his shoulder at Elsie. "Louis d'or," he said. "Coin of the realm." His flashlight ran up and down the columns. "How much would you say, Miss Short, the king ultimately paid our friend for his blasphemous project?"

Elsie took a deep breath. "Twenty thousand louis, about."

"And the profligate daughter spent at least half, but that still leaves—" Saulnay braced himself on the cabinet and pushed to his feet. The Bleeding Man's left arm seemed to jerk, like a reflex.

"That still leaves enough money." Saulnay's bandaged hand raised the flashlight to Armus's pale face. "About a million and a quarter of your dollars, I would think," he said and swung the light directly into my eyes. "Reparation," he said in German.

For the next five minutes, as the cave grew colder and colder and the water in the stream rose by another inch, Johannes went through the tedious process of carrying pocket loads of coins from the drawers out to the chamber entrance by the stalagmites. In his haste Saulnay had brought no bags or boxes. The drawers of the cabinet were far too heavy for one man to carry by himself, even if they could be lifted from the frame. Johannes would have to work in stages while his fat, lame uncle watched. There was no other way except to unload the drawers piecemeal, stack the coins on higher ground closer to the cave entrance, then come back and start over again.

Saulnay positioned himself on the opposite wall, beside the drawing of the owl, and kept the barrel of his automatic aimed at the three of us.

"Johannes," he said, "has more rope in the car. When he's finished transferring the coins he will tie each of you very securely to one of these stone bars that come out of the ground—stalagmite, stalactite, I don't know the right English word. And then we will have to leave."

"Without the gyroscope?" I said.

He let the question hang unanswered in the air. The water from the stream was pulsing in through crevices in the floor now, deeper than ever. Another rock shifted over our heads, making a grumbling sound like thunder. Water was running in sheets now down the walls of the chamber. I felt it over my shoe tops, I could feel it turning the floor of the cave into mud.

"Perhaps not," Saulnay finally said. "Perhaps I ought to look more closely at the mechanism." I touched two fingers to Elsie's cold, trembling hand, like Mr. Morse to his wife.

Saulnay walked or waded across the narrow chamber, kicking up more phosphorescent ripples from the water. The gun stayed steady, in his good left hand. When he reached the cabinet and the automate, he stopped.

"You need somebody's help," I said, "if you want to get the gyroscope out of it."

No response.

"Somebody who understands the machine."

I took one tentative step forward and heard the water slosh. Johannes came splashing back into the chamber, somewhere to my left.

"You could sell the gyroscope to the highest bidder," I said, "for a lot more money. But you need somebody else to help get it out."

"Not you." The gun rose in the darkness like a conjuror's trick and seemed to come to rest on top of the flashlight beam. I saw Saulnay by the open cabinet, in front of the rigid and lifeless body of the Bleeding Man.

"Elsie could take it out. She knows about these machines. Let her help, let her go."

"No."

The beam and the gun shifted two feet and stopped at Vincent Armus's thin, haggard profile. "You."

I took three running steps through the water and crashed like a bullet into him.

Johannes shouted, the cabinet rocked and started to topple forward. A gun went off above my head—one, two spurts of orange flame swallowed by the darkness and the mad crashing echoes of sound and water, and then rock splitting, water exploding into the cave.

On hands and knees I somehow found Elsie and dragged her sideways, toward the stalagmites on the higher ground. We clawed through the mud and noise, up the walls of the chamber, over its lip. Then, stumbling, hauling ourselves frantically out of the water, we turned to see.

Below us the flashlight beams flew back and forth in the black air like ghosts. We saw Johannes rise to his knees, shouting. As the waterfall broke in through the limestone walls, one by one, the hollowed out chamber began to crumple and collapse. In the beam of the kerosene lantern I saw the painted owl dissolving in streaks. Saulnay staggered to his feet. He aimed the pistol straight at Elsie. Armus came into view. Saulnay grabbed at his coat. Then Vincent Armus surprised me a third and last time. He pushed Saulnay around and reached up high with his two bound hands and pulled, and the huge wooden cabinet tilted and turned and fell sideways onto them, pinning them down like Welsh miners in a tunnel. Then the Bleeding Man spun out of the open door.

His head shattered, his legs buckled, but he somehow flung his glassy arms wide, making a sound like a man in pain, and sprawled across them both, dead weight.

As Elsie and I scrambled higher, I could just make out three faces, then two. Then the mud and water burst over their heads and they gulped it once and were gone.

When we crawled out some half an hour later, onto the level space by the waterfall, the force of the collapse had jammed some of the falling rocks off to one side of the cave entrance, leaving a narrow shelf just wide enough for the two of us. Elsie held my arm with both hands. I gripped the edge of the crevice and slowly, carefully, with the cave to my back, stood up straight. To Root, standing down below in the rain and watching us, it must have looked like magic.

Epilogue:
PARIS

IT WAS ALMOST THREE MONTHS LATER to the day, ten o'clock at night, May 21st, 1927, that Charles A. Lindbergh leaned out of the left side window of "The Spirit of Saint Louis" and guided the little single-engine airplane to a perfect landing on the grassy meadows of Le Bourget military airfield just north of Paris.

He had flown solo and nonstop across the Atlantic from New York City, in thirty-three and a half grueling hours, so heavily loaded with extra fuel that he barely cleared the telephone wires at Roosevelt Field when he took off. He was the first person in history ever to fly that far nonstop, and in doing so he not only won a $25,000 prize offered by the millionaire aviation enthusiast Raymond Orteig, he also transformed—on a gigantic Edisonian scale—the way people would live and travel for centuries. But that, like my reading of Freud, and Root's transformation into a food critic, was still to come.

On a smaller scale, the arrival of "Lucky Lindy" in Paris was, of course, the biggest news story of the year—maybe even the single biggest news event of the whole frenetic, celebrity-mad decade of the 1920s, "Les Années Folles."

And as the plump, jolly, red-nosed Muse of Journalism must have intended for a reason, I missed it all.

I missed it because Herol Egan was sick that day and Root was filling in for him on the Sports Desk and because, despite our knowledge that Lindbergh had taken off the night before, nobody in Europe thought he would make it. The biggest news story of the day, everybody in Paris was convinced, would be the outcome of the men's doubles match in the French International Tennis Championships, to which, in an expansive mood and with two of Herol's free extra tickets, Root had invited Elsie and me.

I remember well that it was a warm, sunny Saturday, perfect weather after a week of fog and drizzle. The chestnut trees along the Champs-Elysées were in full bloom, and the great avenue was green and leafy and dazzled with sunlight, like an Impressionist painting.

We took a cab from the *Trib* and drove out to the old stadium in Saint Cloud, not the one you know now in the Bois de Boulogne, where they play what has become the Roland Garros tournament. The press box then was at the south end of the stadium, elevated over the crowd by about fifty feet. From it we could look straight down on the famous red clay of the tennis court. If you turned your head slightly to the right, you could look out across the rolling brown Seine and the Isle of Swans toward the heart of Paris.

It was a wonderful Parisian crowd that day—the men were dressed in crisp white flannels and Panama straw hats, and the women, in their bright floppy bonnets and many-colored sun dresses, bobbed and swayed like so many blossoms in a garden, the acme of fashion in what would turn out to be the last great year of the Flapper Era. Duke Ellington would open soon at the Cotton Club in New York. Al Jolson would make the first "talkie" motion picture, "The Jazz Singer." Babe Ruth would hit sixty home runs before the season was over, an untouchable record. Even in tennis it seemed like an annus mirabilis. The day before, in the men's singles championship, the American Bill Tilden had definitively beaten little René Lacoste (the "Crocodile") in straight sets.

That day, of course, the French were out for revenge. And indeed, Tilden and his partner Frank Hunter looked tired, while according to the sports reporters around us, the two French players, Borotra and Brugnon, were at the peak of their game.

We sat in the box and admired the day and drank chilled Sancerre on the Colonel's expense account. Between sets Root asked about Elsie's progress on her book. She was halfway through the final revision, she reported, and Mr. Scribner in New York said he wanted to have a look. (She should call it, Root thought, *The Duck Also Rises.*) Scribner was also interested in expanding my articles on automates from the *Trib,* maybe for a companion book. From time to time we glanced over at the Diplomatic Box, where the American Ambassador Herrick Smith had gathered a large party to cheer Tilden and Hunter on. But then, a little after four o'clock, there was a stirring in the Ambassador's box, and shortly after that the Ambassador and two or three aides slipped quietly away.

When the match was over—Tilden and Hunter lost in three sets—Root stayed in the Press Box to type his story. Elsie and I skipped the Métro (some things don't change) and walked on ahead in the gathering twilight, toward the city. Afterwards, I would learn that Ambassador Smith had left the stadium because he was told that Lindbergh, contrary to all expectations, had just been spotted over Ireland. Assuming his fuel held out, he would arrive in Paris that night, in the dark.

If I had been paying closer attention, I might have noticed, as we made our way into the place de l'Alma, that there were almost no cars or buses on the streets, and the cafés and sidewalks were strangely empty for a Saturday night.

In fact, as the *Trib* would later report, as soon as the news about Lindbergh began to spread, something close to ten thousand cars, taxis, trucks, and bicycles—nearly all the available vehicles in Paris, it seemed—had rushed wildly toward Le Bourget, so many of them that the four-mile road between the Porte Villette and the airfield was brought to a hopeless standstill. It was probably the first great traffic jam in European history. The police would estimate that over half a million people that night had somehow crowded onto the grass field (there were no concrete runways on it in 1927). Many of the cars and trucks were hastily lined up with their headlights on to guide the airplane in.

Bill Shirer, always working, got there in time to see Lindbergh come out of the night sky like a shooting star and circle the field twice before he landed. When the American climbed out of his cockpit, he never touched the earth, because the cheering French instantly heaved him onto their shoulders and rushed him toward the hangar. As soon as that happened, Shirer knew he had his story and he turned around and literally ran three of the four miles back to Paris, outracing the competition, which was still caught in the traffic jam. At the Champ-de-Mars he somehow found a cab to take him the rest of the way to the rue Lamartine, where he commandeered a typewriter and Kospoth's own private sanctum. Subsequently, he would attend a two A.M. news conference with Lindbergh at the Ambassador's residence (the aviator wearing a pair of Smith's elephantine pajamas), in which, among other things, Lindbergh praised the American scientist Robert Goddard and his work on guided rockets and gyrocompasses.

But all that, as I say, I missed.

Elsie and I strolled back from the tennis court arm in arm, as couples do in Paris. Near the place de la Concorde we went across the pont Alexandre III to the Left Bank and onto the dark Esplanade of the Invalides, where the great golden dome still glowed softly in the night. We talked a little of this and that, nothing at all of Saint-Bonnet or the Bleeding Man or the fortune lost and buried for good with Saulnay and Johannes and Armus deep below the rumbling limestone cliffs. At some point I think I looked up into the darkening sky, but I took no notice of the future, in the form of a guided machine with wings, droning past us overhead.

And as for what became of Vaucanson's Duck? When we finally returned to Paris, its partially disassembled self was nowhere to be found, not in Madame Serboff's storeroom, not in my garret, not on the shelves of Inspector Soupel's evidence room. True to its nature, and as it had done so many times in the past, the duck had simply vanished again, though I was certain that it would turn up somewhere else one day, revived like a clockwork phoenix.

At the corner where the rue de Bac comes down to meet the quai Voltaire, one of my favorite crossroads in Paris, Elsie stopped and sighed and looked up the river toward the gorgeous spotlit buttresses and towers of Notre Dame. They were riding the gathering darkness like a ship.

"Would you like to go back to the rue du Dragon, Miss Short," I asked, quoting my namesake poet, "with a gray-haired gent for a spot of 'pipes and timbrels and wild ecstasy'?"

Elsie smiled and took my arm again and we walked slowly east, along the river. "Writing Boy," she murmured.

Note

INCREDIBLE AS THEY SEEM, VAUCANSON, the excreting duck, the Bleeding Man, the Writing Boy, the museums of automates—all real, all as historically accurate as I could make them (it is a mystery why anybody ever called the eighteenth century the Age of Reason). For biographical information I have relied on *Jacques de Vaucanson: Mécanicien de Genie* by Andre Doyon and Lucien Liaigre. Also *Le Monde des Automates* by Alfred Chapuis, *Automata* by Chapuis and Edmond Droz, and the delightful *Edison's Eve* by Gaby Wood. Vaucanson himself wrote the book that Toby and Root read in Mrs. McCormick's hôtel suite; it was published in an English translation in 1742.

I have drawn phrases, anecdotes, and descriptions from Waverley Root's wonderful memoir, *The Paris Edition,* and from William S. Shirer's memoir, *A Twentieth-Century Journey.* There are two very good books about the Tunnelers of World War I that I have also used for material and incidents: *Beneath Flanders Fields* by Peter Barton, Peter Doyle, and Johan Vandewalle; and Alexander Barrie's *Underground War.*

Finally, for their support and encouragement, my deepest thanks to my beautiful wife Brookes and to my friends John Lescroart and Bill Wood.

About the Author

Max Byrd is the award-winning author of fourteen other books, including four bestselling historical novels and *California Thriller,* for which he received the Shamus Award. He was educated at Harvard and King's College Cambridge, England, and has taught at Yale, Stanford, and the University of California. Byrd is a Contributing Editor of *The Wilson Quarterly* and writes regularly for the *New York Times Book Review.* He lives in California.

CPSIA information can be obtained at www.ICGtesting.com
Printed in the USA
LVOW11s1616231013

358274LV00008B/1243/P